THE DIARY OF A LITTLE SOLDIER

Guy Hunter

The characters and events portrayed in this book are fictitious. Any similarity to real persons, living or dead, is coincidental and not intended by the author.

ISBN-13: 9798835084289

Cover design by: Art Painter
Library of Congress Control Number: 2018675309
Printed in the United States of America

To my Lady... Julieann. Even though the clouds of time roll by and all around may crumble, your rock and fortress will be ever yours.

(though you might want to replace "rock" with pebble and "fortress" with tin can)

The first face; you show to the world.
The second face; you show to your close friends.
The third face; you never show anyone; the truest reflection of who you are.

JAPANESE PROVERB

CONTENTS

STAGEDOOR

The vertical late evening rain wasn't making any difference to how wet the bricks were already. The old alley way, with its steps and railings, rusted old, dim and broken streetlights had fared well, being tucked between tall buildings, from the bombs that had scarred the area.

The sign reading "STAGEDOOR" (once painted with solid white brushstrokes though now faded and chipped, belied the majestic and extravagant flourishes of the front entrance) was illuminated by a dim single bulb lantern which was always lit and never seemed to break.

It had seen many people through its entrance way over the years, great and new, young and old and had been witness to huge adoring crowds, lovers' trysts, devastating failures and even murder. If only it could talk. It probably would have told you...but that's another story.

And tonight, tonight is another story. Tonight, a young lady and young man shall leave together for the first time. They're stepping into the beginning of their lives. If they knew what lay ahead, would they listen, take heed and turnabout or carry on regardless knowing that this will be different for the path is not yet made.

The door swung open and an excited couple came out, arm looped in arm, smiling, happy and laughing, oblivious to anything the wet drops could offer. Calls of "Goodnight" echoed and splashed around as more exited to go in different ways.

"See you tomorrow"

"Don't forget your cue" was shouted back which caused a ripple of amusement.

The couple momentarily paused, turned and waved, then kissed and moved on, trying to huddle from the rain under some imaginary shelter, the umbrella of love.

Out onto the main road, which was glistening with the reflection of streetlights, a taxi was hailed. It pulled up alongside the kerb, spraying unoffended droplets behind itself, carefully not wanting to ruin this precious moment. The young gentleman opened the door open for Cassie (or Cassandra to her parents), which she gladly accepted and climbed in. He leant into the window breathing in the smell of warm leather and sandalwood and passing a pound note to the driver "Hyde Park Avenue, please cabbie".

"Thank you, Darling. I'll miss you, be good".

"I'll miss you too, until tomorrow" said Robert as he waved and kissed the air goodnight.

The cab pulled away to its destination, with Cassandra smiling and sitting back in the comfort of her carriage, whilst Robert turned and started walking his way through the puddles back to his digs in Thayer Street. He could've shared the journey though he preferred to keep "the ladies honour" and love was comfort enough.

The hackney turned right at the lights and was now out of view. Cas leaned forward and slid open the small glass hatch. "Driver, Frith Street please" she said and closed the divide before any enquiry could come. Sitting back, still smiling, her clutch bag was opened and a compact and lipstick removed. Checking in the small mirror and adjusting any imperfections, Cassie wondered whether all the boys would be there tonight.

As Robert walked in his thoughts, he didn't notice the time of his steps or the cessation of heavenly drops, his face was wet with tears of his own. He was thousands of miles away, walking through his KwaZulu homeland smelling the mimosa trees that lined the track to their farm, reminding him of warm and beautiful motherly love and the hard pain of loss, hurt and rejection of its male counterpart. He had never been good enough.

Before his anger had time to rise, a rumble rolled around the dark skies above, unnoticed from the city streets, causing him to turn his collar up more and fasten his step.

“Not far to go” the buildings said, as he walked past the abundance of shop windows, selling everything he didn’t need and nothing he wanted. The paths were quieter as Robert neared his digs, beckoning him in, into the land of confusion and loneliness, a place to run away from your answers and hide from the truths.

The key was already reaching out to the lock. His hand dropped away, his feet turned, a moment’s hesitation and then Robert walked back into the night.

The cab pulled up to the club, its old-time windscreen wipers failing to keep with the times of the cats listening to the blows of an axe. Change and tip exchanged, Cassie stepped out of one world straight into another. The unassuming street level basement door opened with an outpour of dizzying allusive melodies, pungent with green, wet with sweat and hot ‘til you drop.

Before Cas made her way to the bottom of the concrete stairs, she met Ronald and Jay heading up.

“Hey Cassie baby, what’s happening”? said J, his body soaking from jamming too long on his kit.

“Yeah Cas” interjected Ronald “we thought you were on stage tonight? Didn’t you meant to have that thing with Robert”?

“Oh, you know how it is. I’d much rather be here with you boys. Is Tommy around”? she hoped.

“Yeah baby, he’s on right now, can’t you hear him”?

Straight away Cassandra recognised the trumpet blowing hard, bouncing around, not knowing which way the wind will blow…that’s Tommy. His lips will be locked tight with his instrument, an eternal battle of expression, the sounds of his soul blasting out and filling her every corner.

“I said can’t you hear him”? Jay shouted a second time.

“Oh yes, I thought it was him”. She lied, speaking instinctively before her mind had chance to come out of its dream.

Ronald and Jay carried on up the stairs, goodness knows where their destination was, but she knew where they’d probably end up. The three of them were virtually inseparable, a bit like a coin having three sides, the edge keeping them together yet separated, that was Thomas.

Once through the darkened heavy smoke wall, the dim-stained lights announced an arrival to the small, wooden round tabled room. The obligatory ashtray on each surface, filled with an assortment of odds and ends, no coasters here, as no one would see the rings left by the glasses of statements or cups of warm coolness.

Cassie placed herself in position whilst casually waving at Thomas, not for his benefit, but rather to let others know that she was part of the in-crowd, the select group, someone special, someone they couldn't ever be.

Tina, "...bitch" the thought came quietly to Cassie, arrived at the table to offering the sale of cigarettes, "and everything else you have to offer" came the inward sneer followed by "you even know I don't smoke". She even had the audacity to ask "or perhaps you'd like something to drink"? With veins colder than ice "tea" came the response, sending Her away, little miss wiggle pants. Tina knew exactly what Cassandra always ordered and wanted, though treated her like any another guest.

Picking up her clutch, she pulled out a slightly crumpled Woodbine and waited for someone to notice that it needed lighting. A young, spotty attempt of a man lurched too eagerly forward, open mouth smiling, offered a ready lit match.

"Need a light doll? Barry".

Closing her eyes with a dismissive nature, cut Barry out of her life forever, after the naked flame had been accepted. One puff and it lit. The few loose sticks had been collected over time and only came out when on her own in company and was a handy tool for gaining attention. She didn't need them to hide behind, if anything they were an unwanted distraction of her desires, she didn't want anyone to ignore her, not ever, ever, ever... again.

Tommy was just finishing off his set, he'd soon be over, wanting to embrace with his lean, perspiration-soaked body. He lived for his music, "Trad. was so passe" mused Cassie over her cup tea which had materialised out of nowhere. "Robert, on the other hand, wasn't much into modern" drifted her thoughts "but he was tall, strong and good looking" she listed "...in a different kind of way. And he had a wounded vulnerableness about him" making Cassandra feel protective and motherly...

Her thoughts were cut short as Thomas gripped her shoulder with those strong fingers.

"Hi kid, great to see you made it. Where the boys"?

Cassie explained that she'd seen them on the stairs as she was coming in, though added some unnecessary, speculative ideas to pad out the interest.

Tommy explained that Jay and Ronald had probably decided not to wait for him, to go to a party. He omitted the part of them not wanting to cramp Tommo's style with Cassie, though they, in turn, didn't fully explain that heads could roll with too many queens around.

"I'll drop you off home on the way to the party if you like"? suggested Tommy, not allowing for an alternative option. He loved Cassie with as much as his aching heart would allow, yet lately... lately. "Things had been going well, pretty crazy in fact" travelled across his thoughts "Serious even, yet lately a sudden change".

Tom stood behind Cassie and took her chair as she stood, waved and called goodnight to all, which was responded to by a hail of replies and an impromptu chorus of applause. Cassie liked the attention and waved back.

They exited through the dark brown wooden door next to the stage and straight out, into the servant's entrance, the open basement area below street level and immediately and passionately kissed. Their embrace was mutual, their bodies fitting each other, meant for each other. The door shut behind them, closing off the rest of the world and, for a moment, they were the only two who existed.

AIR RAID

The air raid sirens fell silent. The slow whine down and for a moment, just a moment ... everything was silent, the air and time itself seemed to stand still, as if hesitating to return to this moment. A deep tobacco cough, a baby's cry and then noise of hundreds of souls, scattered and packed over the platform and rails, scared and unknowing, came back into being.

The smell was awful. Though latrines had been erected, they could never accommodate the amount of people who had descended into the tube station for shelter. "How we don't all suffocate"? thought the 42-year-old father, whilst his young, beloved daughter clung terrified to his arm. The facilities were problem enough. Cassandra was staring at the old toothless man grinning, lying next to her, his urine-stained trousers and tatty torn jacket doing nothing to ingratiate himself on the family.

Mother, was busy sitting, looking around, never wanting to be seen as out of place, trying to stay aloof, but desperate to be noticed and acknowledged for the person who she was.

“Just ignore him” she said to Cassandra, somehow aware of her child’s distress, perhaps it was hers too of this “vulgar little man”.

You would consider that being underground and having tunnels that it would be cooler and well ventilated, but the mass of bodies warmed the small areas and the tunnels passed the odours around from one set of platforms to the other. Violence would erupt as neighbours clashed over the confine of space, thefts of belongings,

not matter how trivial and then... a distant thud. Far and distant... a pause of breath... everyone thinking the same thing “did you hear it”?

All too suddenly another followed another. Deep underground the population were trying to gauge which way the bombs were dropping. They were coming closer. Somebody screamed, someone shouted in reply “It ain’t happened yet” but nobody laughed. The thuds and explosions were getting faster and closer together, dust and small bits of masonry shook from the ceiling.

“Daddy”? cried the now terrified young Cassie, tears wetting her face, but they weren’t hers. He held her close, the Howitzers thumping deep in his memory, the screams of fallen comrades, echoing all around, reaching out again from the shadows of falling debris, unable to call out, unable to help them, frozen in his fear.

For a moment Cas didn't recognise the man she clung to, but she shared his heart and terror. She too felt the stillness that calamity brings, stuck in an unmoving pose of a mannequin model, yet whose mind can see all so clearly. Every detail etched forever. The shout of command, the deafening crash, exploding with such wanton ferocity almost made her laugh, but was instantly muffled dark grey air and choked by the deep smell of tons of newly exposed soil and rubble.

There was an instance where silence returned. A fleeting instant. Between the bomb and from when the screaming started. It was as if people were too scared to breath, in case the monster heard them and struck again. But once the screaming started, it did not stop. Some silenced but were replaced by moans, shouts of help mixed with anger at the suffering, some screams stopped on their own, silenced forever, never to give a parting kiss again.

Noises that had never been heard by her ears before filled her head, gurgling howls, the clambering of bodies climbing over the buried soul, the popping of her leg as a lady's hand grabbed her shoulder and pulled her cleanly from her part buried state.

Stunned by the overload on her senses, she

stretched out to call for her parents but was already being hoisted away by the frantic activity of survivors. Cassandra could still hear this one scream, sounding closer yet further from the rest. She tried to struggle in a pair of strong, bare arms, but the pain of her leg burst through her entire body. The screaming was not fading as she was past from person to person, it joined her on her journey. It was still there when someone surrendered their dark green, tweed coat and was placed around her shaking shoulders. Now she was in the open air, the scream sounded lost and on its own. She didn't stop screaming until she finally slept, even then it would haunt her always.

ROOKS END

Tess stretched out on the flowered coloured towel, the warm summer grass a bed of innocence below her and the safety of warm clear blue skies above. The pigeon was gently cooing in the tall old pine tree in the centre of the front lawn, reassured, as she, was that this was home, this was where she should be, comfortable, relaxed and secure.

Tess reflected that they had arrived at Great Aunt Janes the day before with the 40 mile drive up from London being the usual routine, though this time Dicky hadn't come, he was off somewhere, doing something, which tended to be the norm now. Anywhere was better than here. Mum had not succumbed to the anxiety routine before leaving, but that hadn't stopped Dad from smoking in the car, all the way up, which, like clockwork, made Eric sick at least twice. Regardless of the beautiful day, windows were firmly wound up (once, when down, some burning ash was flicked from the drivers almost finished cigarette, only to return hastily into

Erics eye behind) and followed by a statement of "If we keep them shut, it'll put you off smoking forever". Unfortunately, that didn't work, to any of them.

They pulled off the small road and onto the well kempt gravel drive. On the left you could clearly see the ghosts of people in the once, often used, small timber pavilion and tennis court. Playing with gay abandon, full of smiles, white attire, Pimms and laughter drifting all the way up to the large house.

To the right, the distant ancient apple orchard that wasps attended to stood as if waiting for something never to happen. Leading to the large double garage, that attached to the rear of the house, was a long red brick wall that hid the once resplendent Victorian garden, complete with three brick and glass houses that leant lazily against the mightier walls, supplying the house with all its vegetable needs.

The car drove up the stony road which opened into its circular loop by the black front doors with half pillars either side. The brass letterbox and lion headed knocker was as old as the house and had seen many carriages pull up for an evening of formal family entertainment. The lawns had hosted yearly cricket matches, laid on by the house for the villagers, which was held in high regard and, in more than one way, with good spirits.

Falling out of the car with his usual flare for showmanship, Eric asked his parents whether he and Tess could go and see Ruby.

"Go and say hello to Aunt Jane first" came the reply and with no moment to lose, disappeared, engulfed by the embrace of the welcoming house. The walls and floors creaked with gladness.

"Hi Aunt Jane" they shouted in unison, not waiting for a reply already thundering up the polite, red carpeted double staircase with the Laughing Cavalier hanging on the small landing, watching their every step. He smiled back at Eric knowing all the secrets the world had to offer.

Tess and Eric stopped briefly at the top on the stairs, pausing for an eternity to gaze into the small, glass fronted wooden cabinet filled with miniature furniture which had been used by salesmen of days gone by to show the select how fine the craftmanship was.

Amongst the array of tables and chairs were figures poised in work or transfixed still by human eyes, ready to start again when left

alone. There were tins of biscuits, loaves of bread, everything a house could need.

Without saying a word, except for maybe "They've moved since last time" in a magical hush, they leapt up and sped around the corner. A brief run around the floor, visiting all the rooms in one go. The warmth of the heavily wooden materials room, drawer upon drawer with fine brass handles all built in against one wall of the Sewing Room. The small front bedroom, peaceful and quiet, softly spoken, waiting on some long-forgotten sadness. Eric always needed to touch the window of this room, to say hello or feel the comfort of the lead lined panes.

On they went. "Hello bathroom" a cold, tiled yet cheerful place.

The large bedroom with three single beds, with a huge window overlooking the croquet lawn at the end, which Ruby would pull open the curtains in the morning whilst exclaiming "Rise and shine, Breakfasts almost ready".

Then came the door to the attic. If opened, the narrow wooden stairs would lead straight up. At the top to the right Great Uncle Crispin's room. The door was always open, though put too at night, if occupying the opposite room, so as not to catch glimpse of the candle that moved in its journey across time itself, none ventured in, unless in great need. To the left, was a little room with two small single beds and "the window". If the house was particularly full, and you arrived last, this would be your room...looking into Uncle Crispin's chamber. "But it had "the window" so "never mind" thought Eric.

Rather than go further and look in Aunt Janes room, they came to the corridor.

Standing in the main corridor of the first floor, almost opposite the children's room, was a gap in the wall where a door should be. It seemed as if, someone, a long time ago, had conjured a spell to create a passage way from this world to another. The first step would be over an old oak step, and a drop down of two inches, onto a soft dark fitted carpet. As you looked ahead the walls and floor twisted and turned over a short distance, ending with an ancient wooden door that was firmly locked shut. It seemed as if it never opened, but to the left wound a tight miniature staircase that beckoned you on.

Apprehension grew in the children's stomachs, not through fear, but excitement and expectation. Tess, being the eldest raised her hand of command and knocked. The slightest pause could be heard and then "Come in" in sweet softly tones.

The door was reverently opened and the prize was given. The little self-contained room for was a feast to the senses. Mrs Tiggy Winkle in the flesh. There sat Ruby. Great Aunt Janes housemaid. She was sitting in her neat armchair in front of a peaceful, glowing fire. Red coals glowing in each-others company, listening to the clack-clack of knitting needles, whilst the gentle voice on the wireless drifted through the warmth of freshly made scones. Ornaments, too many to count, of the year's untold stories, from places long since changed lay in their places only to be moved to wipe away the dust or clean the lace they sat upon.

Ruby smiled over her low rimmed glasses. And before words could exit from her visitors' lips…

"Now" she said "you should have gone and seen your Aunt first", with nothing but warmth and care in her voice. "Get along and I'll see thee later".

With no response but satisfied smiles of affection, the two young souls turned away, happy at last.

THE NIGHT

He stood in the rain. Night had fallen all around hours past and another day approached, yet could not be comprehended until he understood what had happened. For the first time since those early maternal blows had moved him from his path, he was truly in the now. Standing in all too familiar surroundings, he was and had lost. Everything in his life had grown until this point, it had followed a hazardous path made up of extreme risks and pleasures, foolhardy escapades, many ignorant decisions, all disguised as the arrogance of maturing, yet now, now his future had ceased to exist, all love, warmth and family gone. By his own hand.

He stood in the rain. Moments passed as he waited for the door to open. He could not even bear to think of when it would. He could only feel the total emptiness he felt. Everything was gone. Stripped of all things he had worked for his entire life. All the experiences, all the places, all the people, all gone, just the clothes he wore and the rain on his face washing away the stains of tears that had flowed a short time ago. He had already purged his self, already shocked as to how quick life can change, not just through the actions of your own or others, but also by the transition of his own soul. It was if something lived, deep down inside, always hiding, in the darkest shadows, waiting. The small dark claws gripping firmly onto existence, whilst the black sightless eyes shine malice and hate. The teeth, sharp with fear, bear themselves, not wanting to b seen for the dread of being discovered. This too had been suddenly ripped out, at last, as if some cruel irony in the playground of life, leaving an unrealised gaping chasm in the heart of a man. What had lurked and had dominion in the deep recesses was also gone. He stood in the rain. He could not move. He had nowhere he wanted to move to. Despair and sadness for all things were all he had, all he deserved and all he wanted. He had lost everything.

He stood in the rain. He had surrounded himself with silence. Even the rain felt intrusive yet important to the night. A light suddenly opened behind him, with a voice calling him in. He turned and followed, like an obedient dog, yet in stunned awe, climbed the stairs to a waiting alien bed.

He stood in the rain…

…and someone invited him in.

The grateful but undeserved shelter was given as a last resort, to who could not go further down except for that final step, and that was soon to be taken. Left alone in the large, spacious room, he empathised with the emptiness and cried once again. He shed his tears for all wrongs, his soul was torn and bruised, his heart felt the weight of guilt would crush his being. Weakness enveloped him and crippled him to the floor. Watching from above, he had surely been judged, yet love still held on, a single thread, lost and, at this moment, invisible. Prostrated on the wooden planks, his pleads for forgiveness poured out of his eyes. The rain spat at the windows with contempt, happy to see him suffer, knowing of the rites he must take to truly make amends.

He stood in the rain to fall asleep in a stranger's bed, for the first time, absolutely alone, in body and spirit. Lost in a nightmare of uncertainty and guilt. Horrifying demons had been visited and vanquished. The highest mountain had been toppled and possibly destroyed and all for what? He begged for compassion even as his dreams swirled about him, pulling and throwing his memories into a pile of confusion. The one person he ached to kneel down before and plead clemency to, was the one that he had pushed the furthest away.

He stood in the rain.

CAFÉ

Cassandra sat in elegant poise at the clean, small cubicle table, with its upright pew style benches fixed to the clean tiled floor. The glass pyrex sugar pourer sat at command on the red and white checked plastic table cloth, waiting to attend to the next customer's needs.

The shush of hot foaming milk being created behind the counter filled the senses, as the light chatter of a cup meeting the saucer was ended by the arrival of Mr Spoon.

From her position of facing the window, afforded a panoramic view through the large glass frontage of the intimate Italian café, of the life outside on the common walkways, whilst allowing to be noticed by passers unknown.

This, "type of place", was not one she frequented regularly, much preferring the comfort of Lyons or on a special occasion, being taken to the Savoy or Fortnums, where one could enjoy the acknowledgement of discretion and the anonymity of grandeur.

"Roberts running late. We had agreed to meet at 12" she thought "I only turned up 5 minutes late so I didn't have to sit alone, this is so embarrassing. He should've been early" she continued to muse " He's such a square...not like To..."Cassies thought was interrupted by the door bell ringing open and in stepped Robert. His cream overcoat slung casually over his arm, he wiped his forehead with the back of his spare hand and smiled broadly. With rushing breath spoke "I'm so sorry I'm late" he gasped "the meeting at the solicitors went on longer than expected. I had to run most of the way".

This impressed Cassandra more than if he had arrived early. The importance of having a solicitor had already improved Robert's status in her Mothers eyes, and a longer meeting meant more prestige. "I doubt Tommy could spell "solisitor"" she considered.

Robert waved at Giuseppe, who sprang into gleeful action in his well-rehearsed dance of the coffee bean.

Rob leant over and pressed his lips against her cheek in a greeting kiss, yet both hoped and knew how more important that glancing gesture meant. Sitting opposite, blocking some of the public's view, Robert took hold of Cassies hand, the coolness disagreeing with the small beads of sweat that lay on his forehead, and pulled her gently forward.

"I'm sorry if I've kept you waiting" came from his handsome mouth, thought Cassandra, "just been trying to sort through the Trust" he continued. She knew what Trusts were.

"I also bumped into Veronica this morning. She's off to France in a bit, for a holiday" he said casually, whilst thanking the waitress for the drink.

Cassie had frozen to the hardest block of ice as soon as she had heard the first syllable of "that" name. Veronica was someone who distracted the advances of her conquests. Cassandra wondered why he had mentioned "this so-called accidental meeting" with such nonchalance, even when she was sure, she knew how little she regarded this "woman". "Perhaps" she pondered lightly to herself "he thinks to make me jealous. Or perhaps there was more to be concerned about". Cassie was certain that Veronica had not seen her leaving Tommie's flat the other day, "Dear Tommy," passed through her mind "what an in love fool he was" she concluded.

Cassandra sipped at her tea with casual indifference, not wanting to rise any suspicion or reveal the true nature of the complex game she wished to conceal.

"When are you going to take me out again"? she enquired "You know how madly in love with you I am, I just hate being apart from you darling".

Robert was momentarily taken aback by the fullness and casual manner of the sentence that fell on his ears. He had waited his lifetime for someone to love him as he was. Not pretending to be another character or trying to be the best a sporting hero can be, nor competing against his jealous and abusive brother for the recognition of his confident, popular yet aloof father or for the tender love of his patient, compassionate mother. He had travelled over waters of pain, endured the passage of brutalised rape and the journey of thousands of miles for this simple collection of words.

They echoed through his being, as if, at once, emptied of all pasts, to be filled now by new meaning and new beginnings.

Startled by the clear beauty he felt inside he heard himself say “Marry me”.

The world stood still; all was silent. The traffic outside the window ceased to move, as too the birds caught in mid-flight, trapped in the poignant moment, the clock behind the counter hung, poised to count the next second.

The gentlest cough came from Cassandra’s mouth, barely comprehending the quietest words of dedication she has ever heard. Her mind raced. She was looking at the now still lips of Roberts mouth and, as if in the slowest dream, now looked into his liquid, smiling blue eyes.

FOUR TO SIX

The young boy was playing quietly in the corner of his cool, square bedroom, content with his world of cars and Teddy Bears. He looked up out of his open window, with the built-in wardrobe door behind him, as the clear blue sky of the city let the happy Sun shine its beams for all to see and be comforted by the fresh brilliance of its heat.

He was wearing his favourite blue striped T-shirt, red and yellow lines edged each band of blue and seemed to match his little red shorts, which, he thought deeply but not longly about, might be getting a bit small for him, as the slight chubbiness of his puppy fat legs showed.

Big Ted, as usual, was overseeing the situation that lay before him. Little Ted had been run over by Speedy (another small bear, but sporting a sewn on red jumpsuit) whilst driving his large, plastic red sportscar. The smaller metal vehicles had gathered around to spectate and make helpful suggestions, though none helpful. The undersized fork lift truck made easy work of moving the gargantuan obstacle that was still keeping Little Ted pinned to the ground, and the miniature fire engine was hosing the leaping flames that might engulf the area.

A soft breeze drifted through the early afternoon, as too did the constant distant hum of the afternoon traffic, though didn't distract from the unfolding dramatic events that were taking place in front of him.

Little Ted was remarkably intact after such an experience, yet, Eric thought, was in need of urgent hospital treatment and before you know it, an ambulance (flat-bed truck) was on the scene. Little Ted was hoisted carefully onto the back by the amazing dexterity of the heroic fork lift, who would probably get a medal for all his efforts, "later" again thought Eric as he couldn't see anything that could be used for one.

With perfect timing, though unannounced, Cassandra appeared before him, smiling, with the aluminium pipe from the vacuum-cleaner clenched in her right hand.

All play suddenly suspended and Eric smiled in return and watched as his mother said "There you are. I've been looking for you everywhere you horrible child".

Confusion crossed his mind, as so many conflictions piled into one another. Where else would he be in a small, terraced 3-bedroom town house, no garden to play in and no back door to exit from? Horrible? Had Little Teds serious condition, now fatal, already been relayed for all to know? And the metal attachment of the hoover…how odd.

Still smiling Cassie advanced quickly, now hand and pipe raised, swung with fast and ferocious glee. Eric thought distantly that the "donk" he heard made a humourous sound as it resonated and glanced off his up turned head. His arms instinctively going up to protect his young fragile skull. Tears sprang immediately to his eyes as he retreated further back into the corner of his room and mind, like an injured animal fearful of its predator. He screamed out a second time, not hearing the first, imploring "What did I do Mummy, what have I done" pointlessly.

"You know what you've done, you nasty child" she sneered, still grinning with manic satisfaction as she swung the pipe a third and fourth time, each blow permeating more hurt than the last.

"I'm sorry Mummy, I'm sorry" came the screams of the terrified body of the child, though Eric had fled the scene after the first blow, not feeling the pain, but hearing the agony.

Exhausted by her possession, Cassandra knelt to the side of the child and cradled his heaving sobs in her loving arms. "There, there" she softly spoke "I didn't hurt you that much, I just didn't know where you were". She concluded, rocking the injured child.

Fear and survival retreating, the silence of the room cautiously crept in as the young boys heart started to slow its frenzied beating.

Offering a tissue, useless in size for the amount of damage done, Eric noticed his mother too was crying, though seemed to be oddly satisfied at the same time of her accomplishments.

ROOKS END '43

Bentley, the chauffeur, was already waiting on the platform, cap under arm, resplendent in his olive-green tweed uniform garnished with sparkling gold buttons, and infantry polished black boots. He had proudly served the family for some forty years, beginning at the same time "His Lordship" had purchased his first. Standing, waiting with quietly concealed excitement, he wondered how long it had been since he had seen young master Guy. Though only about 30 years stood in difference between them, he had watched him grow into a gentleman, narrowly survive the battle field of death and struggle to recapture his humanity that had been torn from him.

The last couple of years had been difficult for all, especially in his profession with fuel rationing now nationwide, though thankfully the aged Lord was still required for duties in London on a regular basis and spare allowances kept him, and the missus, topped up with the little extras.

Bentley heard the steam train whistle its

impending arrival before it came around the bend to the open platform. Its brakes squealed mightily against the metal wheels as the pistons chuffed heavily for being forced to stop, hot dampness billowing the air. The whole train let out a sudden exhale of relief. With steam finishing its bellowing, the moustachioed station master stepped forward to assist the family alight from the first-class carriage.

The shock left him momentarily static. Though well attired, but not well kept, the three of them set foot onto the platform as if entering a forgotten land, grateful for its succour yet almost collapsing from the terror which they were leaving behind.

Wanting to race to them and gather them up safely in his arms and carry them forever under his protection, he slowly placed his drivers cap on his head and managed to wipe an ember from his eye.

Stepping forward, Bentley greeted the mentally lost family with a barely audible "Sr...ma'am" getting stuck between compassion and service.

"Thank you for coming to meet us. Our baggage should be getting delivered later". These were the only words passed or heard until they reached the family house of Rooks End at the top of the driveway after the ten-minute drive. The young girl disappearing behind her mother's garments was as quiet as a church mouse, as the door was opened for them to leave one entrance only to go into another.

Guy reached out and clasped Bentley's hand with unaccustomed gratitude, startling his nerves even more.

The simple sounding "Thank you" came forth, but it held with it a reserved silence as if whispering to God, the gratitude for all his blessings and hard lessons that had been delivered, whether recognised or not. All the answers that had been given in hushed tones, yet often fell on deaf ears, like the seeds of dandelion floating on the air, only to fall on rocky ground, unable to take root and blossom.

But this time his prayers had been answered.

The family were being made physically whole again, the trials of the previous weeks and months could be put behind them, like once before, and repairing would begin. For people in the security of open fields, where meadows still blossomed, lambs bleated want to their mothers and the birds sang their beautiful endless songs unaware of the buzzing of black fingers of death that tore through their sky, that made buildings fall and fires leap as tall as giants.

Bentley watched the family walk slowly to the greeting of the secure sanctuary, worried more for the lost youth of so many children, knowing that it could never be regained and fearful of what would become of all, as dark days lay ahead.

A WALK IN THE PARK (PART 1)

The black cab pulled up outside the unobscured old oak door that was tucked away in the corner of a small Bayswater building, wedged between the local tailor's cream frontage and an ancient looking cobbler, which displayed signage of thirty years before.

Fare paid, Cassandra took Erics hand through the door, into the smell of polish and floor soap. The dark brown wooden stairs angled upwards in sets of seven, broken with a small landing walkway, spiralling up to all four floors.

After passing the exit to a shared roof garden, clustered with pots and plants with an array of magnificent colours and hidden features hinted at by their tops peeking out from the back, they came to Gran and Grumpy's flat.

Knocking the door, the small head of Tippy appeared, peering out with well-coiffed white hair, understated lipstick and her soft, sincere and loving smile, an honest greeting to anyone who, especially, maybe, to gentlemen who might have frequented certain establishments in her younger days.

Her quietness was as elegant as a feather drifting on a lake of air, a breath could easily sail her away to heaven above.

Closing the door behind them, Tippy was already gone. Already returned to her small bedroom of broken dreams and loves many pillows.

The panelled walled corridor led to the kitchen at the end where Grandmother was cooking sausages. The smells mingled with the eau de cat and tipped with a hint of gas, from the entertaining cooker which Eric loved to light with a match and see how big a flame would leap out at his fingers, sometimes it was magnificent.

A cursory "Hi" and kiss to his Gran, Eric bounced off with his exuberant energy into the sitting room to find his Grandfather, probably sitting in his chair, and go through his routine of things needed to been seen and done.

Firstly, there would be the big hug and play with Grumpys wobbly bit under his chin, always requesting a flamboyant Donald Duck impersonation that would send ripples around the old man's face.

Secondly would be the examination of the felt lined tea caddy that had survived the trenches of the Somme and now housed a cut glass stemmed art nouveau bowl, conjuring images of their hedonistic socialite lifestyle, only to be sold years later by a heroin addict for a quick meaningless fix…but that's another story…

Next on the list would be a visit to wind up Pinocchio who walked with a waddle and shook his oversized head, often falling over at each attempt. He lived in a basket of toys which lay in a small cupboard behind a hand painted, wooden fireguard. Residing with him was Sir Winston Churchill. A clay figure, of uncanny likeness, about the same height but not proportion. Arms clamped firmly to his side and hands cupped behind, had a small hole on the corner of his mouth which allowed a thin cigar replica to be placed and lit. After moments, small smoke rings would puff out which caused ecstatic happiness at such amazing ingenuity.

After the roll top desk had been stroked and puzzled over, a visit to the dining room to hear the clock being forced to chime early and see the delicate small, but detailed painting of a single sailboat out on lightly choppy waves.

As luck should be, sausages, peas and chips arrived as if served in the galley where Erics mind lingered. They had their usual coating of cat hairs, which was politely ignored and removed and eaten in no time whilst squirming around to look out of the window to the fascinating world below. Opposite in the small street was a restaurant that was always busy, day or night. Black tables and chairs, some with umbrellas, decked the path and a variety of people coming and going, seeming to get friendlier and louder through the evening.

"Seems like a lot of fun" Eric often considered.

Once lunch had been completed, a trip to the bedrooms would be needed. Grandpas, creams and browns, housed the gentlemen's quarters, smelling of shaving soap, leather and sandalwood with crisp hospital corners and newly starched collars.

Grans was smaller, dark and...smelly. "No bad smelly" thought Eric "a more sort of, familiar smelly." Her dressing table was draped with shawls and beads, the mirror and glass top reflecting Flapper girl days of sequins and loose morals despite that she preferred the company of ladies and questionable men.

A final visit was to be had with Tippy. Sitting on the edge of her bed, light conversation could be had, vague and distant as if memories would be too far away to put into words yet never forgotten and always treasured. Those little sparkling jewels dancing in her head and Eric thought sometimes, sometimes, if you looked hard enough, you could slip in amongst the dreams in her eyes and find yourself on the lone dancefloor, being twirled about the music and lights with muted sound of melody playing gently for none to hear.

Having being lost in his own fantasy world where he often went, where time was measured in adverts and cartoons ruled the roads, Eric noted that it would soon be time for tea and that meant a journey home. This was an adventure as well.

There would stand a combination of options to unfold themselves.

Depending on who was to take him home would decide which route to take, unfortunately however, this never led to the spectacular array of crocuses, resplendent in their cacophony of colours, planted years ago by the old pet cemetery, hidden in a corner of the park, that thrived year after year. Upon Grandfathers deathbed, his last wish would be to see these little flowers in all their glory, each one as special as the next, as new life waiting to be born.

One route would take them by Tube. A short walk through a wide street that had found itself protected from the devastation, passing grand trees and a busy road only to pass a Martial Arts shop with its windows blanked out so none could see in. "Very odd" quietly thought Eric, occasionally asking why they covered the windows, as he enjoyed the Kung Fu T.V series and didn't see anything wrong with it. "Its not a Martial Arts shop" was always the same reply.

"Very odd" he thought even more.

Just before the station, stood the tiny angular Flower Shop with its curved glass door and owned and run by a kindly spiv, who was a mixture of Flash Harry and Ratty from Wind in the Willows. Eric was always given a free button hole and not understood banter was had, especially when a notepad and lick pencil was produced and money furtively passed.

Then, down the depths to the platform, where you could feel history all around, and if luck was on his side, a casual stroke of the chocolate dispensing machine might yield a reward, to be enjoyed on the three-stop journey.

Once back into daylight a short walk to home, past the bakers and chemist with a contraption that, when one had figured out how to work it, would measure your weight, as well as a metal circular stand with an assortment of postcards. One postcard amused Eric a lot. A hairy creature, with thin arms and legs, eyes wide and crazed, fanged teeth smiling suggestively said "I FEEL SIXY". One day whilst passing with Tess and his mother, Eric asked what it meant "Sixy"?

"It's not Sixy, its sexy" said Cassandra.

"Oh" said Eric, "what's sexy"?

"Ask your sister" came the reply.

So, for the rest of that journey home Tess explained about 2 sexes, (male and female) and something to do with bees.

"Very odd" thought Eric, but sexy became his new favourite word.

Today though, they were walking and that meant through the park.

RETURN

The old black taxi pulled up in the late morning city air, to the broad pavement outside the theatre, just in time for rehearsals to commence of King Lear. The two lovers stepped out, fresh, happy and rejuvenated, ready to take on the world as a stage, falling over each other as if drunken clowns in love.

Robert had never new that emotions like this could be experienced, let alone shared, joyful in union, with no pain of separation, knowing of the exhilaration of coming together again would be mutual and acknowledged.

They had spent their time in a whirlwind of love. The sun shining on their every moment as the clouds tried to block out devotion, failing, yet glad of the outcome.

Once the proposal had been spoken, heaven seemed to pick them up on the wings of songbirds and migrate them to lands unexplored. Finding new beauties and jewels that could be hidden, but left, exposed for all to see and recognise, with winks of past loves and days less travelled.

As the pair silently joked in the midst of infatuation, Robert turned at the call of their names.

Cassandra was walking across the slabs towards them, feigning disinterest but with sarcastic gloryness of her own.

“Oh look what Tommys done” she said, brandishing her hand for Veronica and Robert to see. “He proposed, and wants me to marry him. Isn’t that marvellous”?

“Oh…lovely darling” said Veronica, unsure of her wording and unsure for poor Robert.

Just a few weeks ago, she remembered how Robert had told her of his impending proposal and how he felt about her and how she had made him feel. In turn Veronica explained the course of true love never did run smooth and we know what we are but know not what may be, omitting that she thought Cassies life revolved around herself and affection was not always reciprocated.

But still, Robert relented in following his dreams and naïve desires, wishing to pursue not yet learnt lessons and damaged perspectives. In his literal pursuit of his conquest, he had been steered, as easy as a baby taking its first steps, by J and Ronald to witness Cassie and Tommy entwined in craving.

He was struck by how silent his hurt and anger screamed inside. The years of torture and abandonment by ones so close had prepared him well for this ordeal, yet nothing had equipped him for wrongdoings in this undiscovered country. Clutching at his heart, he now understood Macbeth's agony that drove to madness for all the inflictions made and staggered, wounded and bleeding, away from the vision that, even if eyes were plucked, would still burn to the bone.

He had fled straight to Veronica, who consoled him as she could, with gentleness and care, though full of life itself, not wanting to wait for the 'morrow nor care for what has already been. Innocent to start, plans that had already been made were quickly and easily altered and soon both were enjoying the Parisian life and all that the romance of the Seine could entwine. The centuries of a culture where passion is all.

Drama and pain are as essential to actors, as a stage and mask are imperative to the art, so when all are involved in life's rich tapestry...news travels fast.

Unsure how to respond to this interruption from Cassandra, as a life time had just flooded through under the bridge in the last two weeks, Robert graciously smiled and turned his back, pulling all the wind from the inflated gesture, and walked hand in hand into the theatre with Veronica, leaving his heart bursting with pain and Cassandra crest fallen but ready for vengeance.

As with all first day rehearsals, everyone was permitted to enter via the foyer, allowing reminders of how their patrons would cross the threshold from reality to distraction and enjoy a few hours where all were equal yet privy to a voyeuristic peek into an emotional tour. It was also used for all to see who had been cast in which roles, by way of publicity photos exhibited with characters names, an unusual but easy method.

This day, however, something different lay in wait. Word had circulated about an attractive acting couple, and an invitation for a lucrative modelling deal for a widely commercial magazine was ceremoniously pinned to the wall for all to see. Above it was a hastily hand painted banner "CONGRATS ROBERT AND CASSIE". A small smile, hidden from view, spread inside Cassandra.

THE ROOM

He stood, timeless still, his unseeing eyes only looking at memories past and forgotten loves with the sound of remembered children running about the house. His beloved Mother would surely ring the gong for tea soon, a task she took on herself as lady of the house and Father, in his study, would place his papers so, pick up his pipe and join the family in the day room to partake in this latest fashion. No doubt, his brother, scuffed knees from his latest high seas adventure, would regale all with his exploits, all whilst little sister fed her doll cooks sandwiches and cakes.

Staring intently out of the window at his memories, confusion crossed his brow, as worrying thoughts, deep set, disturbed his flow of flight.

For now, stood he, amongst the fields, wondering and lost, searching for something he could not find, even on such a beautiful day as this, cloudless and blue, the warmth bathing troubles away, the mists of misperception fell about him. Stumbling on, he had tried to ask his wounded friends, but they were as lost as he, each having their own paths of decisions to make.

He recalled a time... "A time"? he thought and tried to utter. When had there ever been "A" time? Everything was the same now, drifting like a leaf on a silver and golden brook, flowing against the rocks in one direction but being spun in circles, to come to rest against the soft bank, either to stay and rot or be pulled back into the eddies of the never-ending journey.

Was that his Father calling him, or just the sound of his horses' hooves clattering on the cobbled streets of a small French village. He liked to practice his vaulting skills on hedges down the lanes. Samson always ready to oblige, was a magnificent steed, strong and courageous, at all times ready for battle and a challenge, charging head on to meet threat and glory.

He... no, gone, lost, it was already getting dark. It seemed only just a few hours ago that Nanny had been getting him up from his mid-morning nap, yet already the sky was darkening and he would be alone again. He didn't like to be alone, he turned. Always alone. Especially when he remembered the pain. He felt he was becoming sad again. Why was he always left alone? He remembered saying goodbye to everyone when he left at the train station, the flags and waving, the cheers of happiness to be leaving, feeling a sense of duty and exhilaration, but he also recollected saying goodbye to them again in his prayers, but with a distant, intangible numbness that was lost to him.

The night settled in around him, wrapping him up in a cold, dusky embrace, the staleness of the air uncommon to his childhood bedroom. A slight chill brushed his bones as his thoughts went to the autumn afternoon and the lavender field that lay behind garden hedge at the end of path. How they collected the green stalks with purple fragrant heads only to take them home, back to the summerhouse and lay them out on newspaper to dry in the warmth of the wooden shed that held the croquet box, where sometimes now he could see his sister with Great Nieces and Nephews tea.

How long had he stood here thinking of his dreamless thoughts? No voice to spill from his lips, no visitors to pass the time. Just the light of his candle to keep him company as Great Uncle Crispin lay down again for his eternal sleep.

A FEW DAYS LATER

The rain had stopped, at last, its ceaseless torrent endured for days as if the angels themselves had wept and the wind had shaken the thin windows in their mountings.

He had been warned some twenty years ago, while walking through a Somerset town and confronted by an elderly man. From a distance he was noticed, small flat cap, glasses and moustache adorned his face, grey hair neatly cut and a well-dressed figure, hobbling gait with no stick was before him. A genuine simple smile was fixed under the facial hair and reminded him of a character they called Grandad at a church hostel where he had used to work. A balmy summers day hung around, slowing people in their pace, causing them to smile that little bit more and less likely to frown.

Despite the warmth of the day, this aged man had his coat jacket fully buttoned and tie and cuffs fastened well. No soon as paths were met, the aged gentleman spoke stopped in Eric's path and, in a kindly manner spoke "I'm sorry. I can't be your guardian angel anymore" then walked on leaving a dumbfounded silence.

And so brought about the beginning of the next chapter, just as he was now entering his final chapter.

Each step that was now taken was to be in territory unknown and unwanted. He felt as if he had been reborn, washed clean, yet as helpless as an infant child having no guidance to lead him and no options to offer him. Existence was passing full of loss and pain, though he seeked forgiveness and was filled with remorse and guilt, it was all the sustenance he could bear.

The days of confusion and pontification merged with seeking solace in letters written but forbidden to be sent, until the quietness descended upon him. Despair had been circling, like a white tipped shark sizing up its prey, ever watchful, feigning disinterest, though with each pass, looking for the gap to strike.

For decades he had been battling the demons that had been sewn into his soul which had led to a destructive and hedonistic lifestyle, trying to cover his insecurities and hidden memories with the overabundance of a sex, drugs and rock and roll lifestyle, topped off

with an alcoholic haze.

But all the tools of distraction were ages past and he had been left with the raw emptiness of nowhere to hide from the screaming that lay inside of the small boy being assaulted, behind the locked bathroom door, by the ravenous frenzied monster who he loved as his mother.

Now all was gone. All was silent. All had been lost. Suddenly, peaceful and still, collected and calm, clarity came to him as if the first gentle snowflakes fell from the sky. Everything became clear and transparent, everything was going to be alright after all, the solution was accepted with open arms and peace was at last in his being. Contentment spread about him as he planned his suicide.

PIRATES

The family had arrived a few days earlier after the two-hour drive (of smoke, vomit and cat mewling) which took them across the undulous green belt of the South Downs, with echoes of ginger beer and picnics, to their seaside destination. It was a yearly two-week affair, which saw the whole family, cat included, load into the old Rover P4 (lined with glossy oak and dark brown leather), crank started, to escape the confines of city life and arrive for the adventures that lay in wait amongst the gravel pathed woods, where pigeons made their wooing nests for all to hear on the quiet private estate.

Each grabbing their own bags or holdalls, ran fast through the small iron gate located in the middle of the front garden, between low aged hedges and onto the small winding stone path, down the little steps to the front door. The large house had been internally split in two, to allow separate accommodations for guest and owner, but still had ample space for all.

Rushing upstairs went the children, each

desperate to claim a bed for themselves. From the bedroom window, looking out onto the front landscaped lawn, the sea could just be seen between the large trees that had enjoyed the view for years and the narrow pebble lined passage way. Arguing over the three beds, whilst performing acrobatics and smelling the fresh ozone, the two children noticed their mother walk past, with baby in arms, going to settle him down for a rest, at that, they noticed a picture had been moved since their last visit.

The pictures lined the corridor outside and in the children's bedroom, portraying bizarre alien beasts and birds with terrifying oddness but whimsical humour. Sometimes they watched you but they were always there, a legacy left from the owner's father who delighted in scaring children.

Once the routine of settling in had been completed the holiday commenced with a selection of stone throws walk to the shingled beach, lazy morning strolls to the shops to buy sweets and cycle rides exploring the area where none had been before, as well as one of the regular highlights, playing Pirates.

It was another glorious summer day. The clear, hot blue skies, the distant sound of waves folding on the beach, dragging small stones back in their wet grasp and the occasional bee, humming lazily to itself amongst the pungent buddleia bushes. The old rusty swing was waiting to be used as were the overhanging trees urging young feet to tread upon their grown branches like they used to.

The two children started pulling out all manner of furniture, from the back door of the garage that led into the back garden. There, among the few small cobwebs and spiders, were the two, dust covered, heavy rubber lilos, the white egg-shaped plastic seat with padded red cushion lining, that any young child could sit in and get rolled about with much hilarity and the two revered black sun chairs, decorated with golden flowers, that great grandparents had sat under.

The items were strategically positioned around the garden to act as a type of obstacle course. Rules were made, a bee suddenly ran away from, and directions of how each piece of equipment was to be used. The swing was holding its breath in anticipation. Whilst Mother and baby got comfortable on a sun lounger at the side of the arena, Father magically produced, with much delight from the crowd, a small brand-new paddling pool. It did not take long to blow up and fill with water, though an eternity of eagerness passed for some.

All was ready, nail polish and emery boards for Mother, an easy exit for Father and the two buccaneers who surveyed their efforts with exhausted exhilaration. Just before games could commence, it was suggested that the youngest of the three should enjoy a splash in the pool and was duly placed on the outside edge, so Mother could do her nails and not be disturbed in her worship to the sun.

Boarding of enemy galleons began. They swung on the old iron ropes and leapt through the air onto the rubber decks. Minding the hungry sharks that lay in the water below, splashing hungrily, they made their way around the ship, repelling borders and skewering them landlubbers.

Many laps were needed to kill all the invaders and throw them overboard to the sated sharks as the serene painted figurehead lay stretched and glistening under the yellow sun.

Father appeared, running towards them, they braced themselves for the incoming battle and were confused by the actions that followed. He swiped up their pale, blue lipped little brother, who was lifeless and still, after tilting like a seesaw face first into pool. Water poured out of his nose and mouth as he was pulled upside down by his ankles out of the pool. Calamity and activity erupted, shouts and running and the incredibly fortunate, though not needed, arrival of the property owner, who had been an ambulance driver in the Second World War. The quick and accidental action of being lifted by his ankles caused Eric to take a breath, thankfully, for him, the first of many.

(AUTHORS P.S: Pirates would always hold a special place in Erics heart. At the age of about 6 he would be given a fancy-dress costume, complete with eye patch, tricorn hat and paper parrot, for a party of one of Tess's friends. It would be such a treasure that it was worn for about a month, in bed and out, until the need arose that it had to be washed and subsequently, "accidentally", destroyed. This would not be the last time fancy dress or pirates would figure especially in his life. Apart from the game of the same name that occurred in P.E lessons in his last school (which Eric loved), Cassie took Eric to see a performance of Treasure Island, featuring Spike Milligan as the cheese fixated Ben Gunn, a regular fixture at London's Mermaid Theatre, so regular in fact, that Mr Milligan decided to ad lib his lines causing much confusion to the performance. As for fancy dress...many years later Eric was invited to another party where he would attend, wearing an almost perfect, Captain Scarlet costume. Walking back home at three in the morning he found himself having to walk through a notoriously dangerous part of town. Ray gun at the ready he was zapping shadows and Mysterons and being indestructible... well, almost, was ready for anything. With the end in sight of the area, relief was easing his tension, when out of the dark came a cyclist, slowly and erratically coming towards him. The gangly figure looked sallow and gaunt under the streetlights, the deep-set eyes of a scaghead staring toward him. Eric stopped shooting and got ready for the normal publicised attacks of the vicinity. Incredibly relieved, the cyclist peddled past and Eric berated himself for being so stupid and casually looked over his shoulder to see the rider turning his bike around and returning. Adrenaline kicked in, muscles built and breathing came focused as the man on the bike pulled up along-side.

“Are you Captain Scarlet”? asked the voice in an almost reverent tone.

“Yeah” after all, how else could he answer.

“Wow. Cool. Is that a real ray gun”?

“Yeah. I’ve been shooting Mysterons” Eric half lied.

“Wow. Awesome” said the young man and cycled off.

Eric couldn’t believe this exchange had just occurred.

“Man” he thought to himself “That bloke must’ve been buzzing” and couldn’t help thinking what the rider would say to his mates or how his brain would think back to “that” night in years to come.

UNLUCKY FOR SOME

Cassandra couldn't wait to tell Tommy the news about the magazine contract that had been offered. All afternoon, she had annoyed Robert with questions, interrupted rehearsals with flamboyant prospects and tired the cast with her missed cues and make-up checks. Veronica felt deep sympathy for Robert and his sensitive, yet unaware, nature but also understood how a too good of an opportunity this would be to miss and what it could lead too.

The theatre always fascinated Veronica. The different point of view that one has, backstage, auditorium, lobby, gantry, dressing rooms and the stage itself, each having their own character and smell. The symbiotic relationship twixt man and art, creating new worlds for all to explore, not knowing where it will take you even with a script. Yet today a great tragedy was unfolding in many ways, heartache was to be revealed and misery endured. She knew her days would be numbered.

The afternoon rolled on with everyone feeling more exhausted than ever. It had not been a good day backstage and front, thankfully, even the dedicated director manager elected to call it a day. Feet shuffled, boxes and chairs stacked, lights started to shut down by the Bakelite switches and a fresh breath of air breezed across the stage. It was then they realised that Cassandra had already left.

Though still early evening, she went straight to the club to meet up with Tommy and the boys, knowing it was their home from home, to share the fabulous news. The buses were still running frequently and it was only one change needed to be dropped off at the corner of the street. Staring out of the windows, dreaming of all the things to be, she was rudely interrupted by the bus conductor for fares, clicking his clippers with hat at a jaunty angle. Without even looking she lied "I'm so sorry, I left home in such a hurry. I have to get to the hospital. My mothers had an accident and I left home without any money". with tears in her eyes and a loving forgiving smile on her face.

"Well," the man replied scratching his forelock "I don't right know what to say"?

"I'll pay next time. I promise" she lied again.

"Alright then me dear," he said "just this

once" feeling certain that he had just been hoodwinked.

And with that her stop came into view and she rose to alight the bus.

"Bye, thank you" she waved, stepping off the bus deciding which route she should walk to the club, as Cassie didn't want to have to explain herself or her actions again.

"Honestly" musing in her mind "people can be so tiresome".

Walking through the streets her mind conjured up all exaggerated possibilities that might unfold and all the attention that might result from such a potentially important photo shoot. She might get selected to be the face of Lux, be asked to open a new department store or spotted by an impresario or talent scout and offered a leading role in a movie, she felt the opportunities were endlessly exciting.

As her mind wandered, she barely noticed time pass while automatically taking the turns and crossing the roads needed to get to the club. Soon enough, the familiar corner of the street that cherished the venue came into sight and Cassandra's focus shifted, as did her momentum and her thoughts of how to tackle the issue of Tommy.

It was at that moment a plan revealed itself. A plan where she would avoid any uncomfortable questions, any recriminations, finger pointing or blame for what might unfold.

Her walk slowed as the idea rolled on and evolved and stopped her, literally, in her tracks. Thinking carefully, trying to weigh all the little nuggets as they made themselves known; she was surprised as to why the plot hadn't been exposed earlier. Slowly turning, Cassandra realised what had to be done, and started to walk home, away from the club and away from Tommy…for good.

ROOKS END (PART 2)

The weekend had been wonderful, as always, escaping across the roof top trying not to get caught, exploring the Victorian walled garden with its Mr McGregor water barrels, inhaling the heady fumes of lavender dust from over a hundred seasons of collection in the summer house and losing a kite (now stuck, waving for all to see) in the giant pine. There had also been a visit to Great Aunt Janes office, with her homemade jam cupboard conveniently secreted in the wall in the corridor outside. Years' worth of preserves lined the shelves, all with different coloured lids, all with different names, rarely two the same apart from the latest batches.

Jams and jellies for meats or toasts, for breakfast or afternoon tea, spicy or sweet all available to eat...if you were lucky.

There had also been the forbidden visit to the pavilion by the tennis court. Tess and Eric had convinced the adults of an escapade to the far end of the orchard, one of the furthest points from the house, though the ulterior notion was exploration of the crumbling wooden building on the edge of the sealed off, dilapidated and weed infested court. They had never managed to actually get inside before, but once succeeded, clambering carefully over brambles and avoiding nettles, mostly, they felt a sense of sadness, loss and disappointment.

The interior was certainly falling apart, beams had dropped, cobwebs hung about with little purpose, damp was bubbling the painted walls and a hole, big enough for a suitcase lay on the floor, also discarded and forgotten. The sadness though, lay not with them but in the air, the knowing of its numbered days and times before, long ago, never to be reclaimed. No adventure was to be had here, a journey of discovery maybe, but for here the adventures were over and the wait for the final blows suspended itself for all to feel.

Eric and Tess made their way back to the house, occasionally rubbing the hot stings which had been pointless accomplishments, deciding to split up and see what else could be found for entertainment.

Tess took the downstairs and headed straight to the voices congregated in the kitchen which had the large dining room and breakfast bar attached to it. If luck was on her side, a possible visit into the larder (the small room down some steps at the end of kitchen) and all the goodies that might be on show or offered.

Eric, on the other hand, took the small staircase upstairs, not forgetting to give a congenial nod to The Laughing Cavalier as he passed, in search for something interesting. No sooner had he reached the top, he heard a drawer sliding shut in the sewing room.

"Strange" he thought "I'm sure I heard all the grownups downstairs"? he concluded.

Going softly, so as not to disturb the monsters, he peeped round the corner of the door only to see his Mother in a most peculiar situation.

Standing, with her back to the door, in her arms she clutched a set of heavy tapestry, neatly folded, flowered curtains, and was attempting to force them down the waist of her skirt and under her red jumper.

"Hello Mum. What you doing"? Eric enquired.

Startled she turned, with an angry yet surprised look on her face said "They're mine, so I'm taking them home with me".

"Oh" said Eric "Why are you trying to hide them then"? feeling a bit confused and out of place.

Before an answer was issued, Father appeared in the doorway, shortly followed by Great Aunt Jane, people had been notably missed and curiosity raised, probably not helped by Tess mentioning to everyone that Eric had gone "Exploring" when questioned and had signalled upstairs. To all assembled that could mean another "Escape from Colditz" story being re-enacted, scrabbling across the roof to avoid the guards and so to jump into the large rhododendron bushes.

Instead, this time, they stumbled across and act of theft taking place and silence fell instead of the foolhardy young boy.

This was a stunned, awkward silence which Father broke, understanding, as all did, what was occurring.

"Cassandras been under a lot of pressure. She hasn't been well for a while". the words came out staggered as he spoke.

"Well my dear," replied Aunt Jane "you only needed to ask".

The air felt heavy with embarrassment and Cassandra looked more childlike than ever. No apology came forth, but things were tidied away and people led to cups of tea, no one quite knowing how to end this episode that had not been encountered before. The polite conversation steered itself towards the better notion of time to go home and bags were conciliatory packed and loaded into the car.

Great Aunt Jane neatly placed the curtains on top

of the cases in the boot and gave a seldom show of affection to Cassie as another fare well gift. The car, with all occupants present pulled away, still inwardly reeling from another episode of Mother.

Cassandra looked out of the windows at the countryside hedges going by wondering what she was going to do with two sets of curtains.

A WALK IN THE PARK (PART 2)

The black iron railings had stood guard through many years and ran the length of the northern part of the park, from Marble Arch (where an incident would take place involving a store Manager, a selection of sweets and an embarrassed Eric...with the "innocent" culprit, Mother) down to Bayswater. If patrolled on Sundays, with the gentle hum of traffic behind you going nowhere in a hurry, one could expect to see a mile of artists, from beatniks to squares, and each exhibiting and expecting to sell, their array of pieces, from pin art to oils, abstract to pointillism, the abundance of colour and shape was yours to peruse.

But today was not Sunday, today was another sunny day of youth, full of excitement of the prospect of a walk in the park and all that would be seen on the journey.

Despite the need for the wooden walking stick, Grumpy enjoyed the strolls with his grandson through the historic gardens, bringing back memories of his daughters' childhood and a slower, genteel way of living and imaginings of the royal hunts from hundreds of years gone. The large trees, with arms outstretched, were spread throughout the park, where children ran around them, lovers lay under them, but all enjoyed them as they brought a hidden tranquillity and calm.

As they walked in, Eric was already eager to run around the understated, majestic Italian Gardens, resplendent with four formal, rectangular stone ponds centred with umbrella fountains, each separated by wide walkways for the ladies and gentlemen to promenade and the low balcony with the stretching view of the Serpentine lake below. This was not the highlight however, for surrounding on all sides, were the tall willow trees. Branches and leaves hanging to the ground calling out to children to hide under their green protective skirts so as to frighten their guardians by disappearing when backs were turned.

This was a somewhat regular occurrence for Eric, for some years earlier a Nanny had been hired, much to his dislike, and had taken the child for a constitutional. On the walk back home, Eric had lagged behind and ducked into an open gate of somebody's front garden and hid behind the low wall. Much internal sniggering ensued as Nanny couldn't find him anywhere and went home distraught at losing her ward. Not realising this severity, Eric decided to present himself, but was taken aback to find no one to reveal himself to.

With slight disappointment, the owner of the house presented themselves and questioned the young child on his circumstances. Once the story had been explained, the kindly gentleman decided to walk Eric back home himself and inform all of the hilarity that ran through the boys' veins. Eric was surprised, when arriving home, that he found a hysterical mother, a father on the telephone to the police and a weeping Nanny, who he didn't like anyway.

After burning off some energy, running rings around his grandfather, ponds and trees, it was elected that they would go via a visit to Peter Pan rather than the Round Pond (where Eric had slipped in many a time...sometimes accidentally) and the Band Stand (where great tragedy would one day unfold). This was also the shorter route and Grumpys leg was already beginning to hurt, returning with it visions he would rather lay as buried as "they" did, another lifetime away in green, bird song filled fields now unrecognisable to the black, smoke holes that they once occupied.

Peter stood, as always, atop of a hill of bronze, with faeries, rabbits and all types of creatures poking out, burrowing in or enjoying the view of humans going by in their odd ways of living. His horn, which Eric could not discern whether it had already been blown or not, was still held in his hand, though someday it would start to disappear, reflecting the loss of innocence and beauty in our world.

Many passes around the statue were taken. Hand trailing over the smooth and lumpy, warm metal surface, holding protruding ears and smiling to the hidden mouse. How many other eyes and hands had feasted on the work, how many seasons had gone and when would it be seen again echoed in his heart.

Moving on from eternity with a skip and a jump, he caught up with his grandfather and held his wrinkly firm, soft hand, as he thought of nothing but warmth and of each step he took. Questions asked, answers given, they walked in silence, one looking at life, the other looking not to fall over.

Before time had to fly, the mews arch came into view, signalling that the end of their journey was soon. Eric had enjoyed his walk, as always but was curious on how his grandad was going to get home, having only betting slips in his pocket. He knew if grandmother was to do the return journey, then father would oblige a lift rather than take the tube, but for some reason it wasn't the same for Grumpy. He had often heard funny talks between his parents but could never fully understand them. “Adults”!? thought Eric.

Skipping had resumed as the two neared home. Thoughts of milk and possibly a doughnut or marmite sandwich was spurring him on, when Grumpy interrupted his train of food with “I’m going to have to ask your father to lend me a couple of bob” he said.

“Oh, he won’t do that” said Eric somewhat emphatically “he said he would never lend you money if you were the last man on earth”. he concluded.

Eric had never seen his Grumpy angry, and was quite intrigued in the sudden change of mood. Unfortunately, they arrived home, greeted all and sat down to cartoons, milk and Jaffa Cakes. “Nevermind” he thought.

ROBERT

Robert lay on his bed, head propped by three pillows, asleep and unaware, even of his dreams that visited him with tenderness care. Eyes flickering gently as he walked back up the dirt track to visit his family who all had long passed, yet greeted him with waves and smiles which had not existed in life. It felt good to be home and to see them all, even his brother, who had spent their childhood in a jealous rage, beating and raping his younger sibling with vengeance and hatred running through his veins.

His father was there too, standing by his seated beloved mother, who sat for pleasure and not for need, no longer tied to her wheelchair. Even his father radiated a loving warmth, giving Robert the urge to run to them all and scoop them up in his arms yet, at the same time, scared that if he touched them, they would vanish in the mist.

He felt at last a peace in his soul, balanced out and complete, no longer tired or confused, no need to worry about the past or regrets, no need for anything.

A hand reached out and gently brushed the fine hair off his brow and stroked the top of his head, it felt good and loving and opening his eyes he saw familiar faces.

Their three children, all with children of their own, sat around, still dearly loved, though never fully understood. He knew he had failed them all, but had tried in his own way, trapped in his own prison, not seeing where the doors or windows lay nor how to escape its constraints.

For once they were all here together and that itself was gladdening, the exquisiteness spread through him and made Robert smile. He wanted to tell them all about his gladness and joke and make them feel how good he felt, but speech had departed, unable to make those connections, so instead he pulled funny faces and gesticulated exaggerated hand movements which produced the desired effect. Chatting and laughter entered the ward. The other elderly gentlemen being infected by the life rather than the dying joined in with the chuckles of mirth and then needed the toilet.

A nurse came in to check on the unusual activity, and aid the desperate, and left, eventually, when satisfied with the circumstances.

Now that Robert was awake, conversation sprang up between the divided, brought back together, soon to be divided again family filling in for their father where necessary, unsure of how much precious time there was left.

This had not been the first time of gathering around a death bed, several false alarms lay in the past, each harrowing in their own way. The alcoholic induced coma, the lung cancer, so many hospital visits to both parents, each taking it in turns as their ages grew. Now though would be the last. No more pacemakers, no more accidental falls or missed medications, now the book was being closed but never finished as chapters were still to be finalised, questions not yet realised answered and secrets unearthed.

Time had ceased to be important, as too their differences, suspended for a short while, some uncertain and more confused than ever in what they were meant to be feeling or what they had done in their lives and their own frailty.

Slumber had taken the once proud man into its domain again, giving respite to a troubled soul whose dementia had already rid him of the complexities and insecurities of the vast ocean of life. He had been a wounded prince, washed-up on the shores of a foreign land, kingdom lost, never healed no matter how he searched in all the wrong places, for the elusive cure that hung around his neck.

His lady, an Egyptian slave in another life, had already passed suddenly, without warning or reason years gone but the love and turmoil still twisted in his mind like a peaceful, white dove wrestling with a snake.

He awoke again, Eric still by his side, winked and patted his hand with an almost toothless smile then returned to his dreams.

Eric stood, for unknown reasons he had decided to leave, there didn't seem to be any need to stay, Tess and Dicky stood guard and the last rites had been administered, so that was protection enough he thought. He kissed and hugged his older brother and sister and told them he loved them. He bent over his dying father and kissed his temple and told him he loved him too. Standing upright he instinctively said "See you later Dad" paused, knowing that he would not, turned and left feeling empty and lost.

Silence fell again on the ward, Tess and Dicky talked gently to one another as Robert, only a short while later entered his deepest sleep, troubled no more by pain or sorrow as the traffic carried on outside.

TESS

Tess sat up to the square, wooden kitchen table waiting for the large sheet of taped down paper to dry, preparing it for a new masterpiece that would hopefully materialise. She checked over the table making sure she hadn't forgotten anything before painting started.

"Brushes, paints, obviously..." she pondered "water, gin, palette, cat". "Get down puss" she said waving her hand and Celia taking no notice whatsoever. "Wine," crossed her mind "can't do without wine". The last word came out as she stood and walked to her large canvas bag and produced two bottles of wine, Red and White, decisions, decisions. Returning to her table, Celia had got more contented, but there was still room enough for a glass and two bottles amongst the utensils of her trade. Seating herself once again, Tess poured a glass of gin and a glass of white, saving the red for later and stared at the blank space again, hoping for inspiration to call, or perhaps another sip was needed.

Taking a hefty swig of the juniper flavoured

alcohol, her eye was caught by the shade of red on a metal pencil tin and reminded her of the small blue and red cardboard handbag that once was a prized possession. Always on her arm, it had accompanied Tess through times of need. Whether to be used to slap away a gentleman's unwanted advances in a cartoon cinema (where she sat with her Mother and little brother) or to carry a butter knife, used for flower bed digging, which often disappeared and the blame was centred on Eric (unbeknownst, though would be resolved decades later). The little bag would also be a trusted companion in which she could hide in when being sexually abused by the black clad family doctor.

Another sip. Still no inspiration. Another sip.

The painful memories were never far away. Remembering being torn away from her friends of years and the sudden death of her closest, the two sisters who she often played with when younger and the tragic housefire that followed, the sexual discomfort she felt from her fathers' touches, but her earliest and most confusing was the almost murder of her brother.

He had been born at home, on a quiet winter's afternoon, snow falling softly in the quiet hush of the city, with the cleaning lady helping delivery as the snow hindered midwife battled on bicycle.

Erics cot had been placed in Tess's bedroom, by the window, so not as to take up valuable playing space, but Tess didn't mind, having a baby brother was fun in itself, she liked to play mother. As the two grew, Tess would always be the older one and Eric would have to be told what to do, marry her friends, be the baby, carry the bags, whatever game they were playing Eric would have to obey her friends as well. Secretly he didn't mind, but sometimes Tess's friends said as they were married, he had to kiss them. Yuck.

Months had passed from the snows and early spring had sprung, a gentle warmth in the air was trying to battle the cold and Mother had put him down for a rest in the crib. Tess was downstairs sorting through her handbag, organising her toy makeup, like ladies do, tutting at nothing in particular, like ladies do, when she thought she would go and fuss at baby Eric, like ladies do.

Once up the stairs, she noticed Mother was not resting on her bed, like she often did, and turned into her bedroom to check on the cot.

Cassandra was leaning over the crib in still silence as Tess drew up alongside. It was at that moment she saw the pillow being pressed over the baby's head and a soft muffling coming from underneath. Tess touched her mother's arm, which caused Cassie to leap backwards saying "He's fine, we were just playing" with a look of distance and craze in her eyes.

Tess reached out and took yet another sip of her gin glass only to find it empty, so swapped it for the wine. Still no inspiration.

TOMMY

Tommy had been working hard, harder than usual. He now had a fiancé to keep and a wedding to fund as Cassies parents had lost a lot in the Great Slump and had never fully recovered from the heavy burden that was felt the world over. The club had been doing better than expected, good turnouts most nights where people were hungry for colour and change and that was what they were offering. It was a happening scene, with many musicians wanting to explore new avenues and experience the sounds coming out of America. The likes of Miles Davis, John Coltrane, Monk and Mingus were some of his personal favourites, Miles Davis being the only trumpet player amongst them. But he figured if he worked hard, long enough, something would give, maybe one day a tour in the U.S would come out of it despite what Ron and J said. Tommy knew he could make it, he knew it wasn't far away, the boys just liked to drag him, probably jealousy he thought.

He was surprised not to see Cas in the crowd

tonight as she said she would be there, perhaps their rehearsals had run over and she went home tired crossed his mind. "I'll check in at the cloak room and see if she's rung when I'm done" he thought, whilst sweating under the lights, almost missing the beat.

It had been another good turn out tonight, some fresh faces in the audience, no trouble and plenty of good feedback. It was always satisfying to see tapping hands on the table and nodding heads, it helped really get into their rhythm.

He finished his set and wiped his forehead with a wet hanky from his trouser pocket and stepped off the small raised stage with his horn, smiling and a small salute wave headed to the bar. A scotch on the rocks sat waiting for him but didn't hang around long. It was joined by its brother who also exited rather quickly, the third would have to be paid for. Gus, the barman, kindly offered a smoke and Tommy accepted, striking a match off the counter for light he took a long puff and exhaled. Third whisky in hand, smoke in other, he strolled though the seated bodies, heading to the cloakroom where Mandy was on duty tonight. Mandy didn't like cloakroom duties, feeling it was always a cruel joke of the establishments.

Tommy approached with a smoky wave of acknowledgement and enquired whether Cassie had rung and left a message.

Mandy, busily, in the quietest period of the night, was doing (trying to do) a crossword. "Hi Thomas," came the husky voice "No. No message. 7 letters: Ball on the Door"?

Tommy stared incredulously. "Mandy, come on" he said "What do you like doing best"?

"Knocking people owt.... oh, bouncer".

They both laughed and a couple came round the corner to collect the lady's coat. Mandy stood up, his 6ft 6 frame could barely fit in the small cubicle, but it was policy for all staff to rotate job positions, it just seemed unfair that he was never allowed behind the bar or waiting on tables. He liked waiting on tables, though was a bit clumsy.

Tommy returned into the club and saw Ronald and J now propping each other up, where they had come from goodness only knows, but they were here now, so they might know something, they usually did.

A brief chat later and none the wiser, Tommy felt uncomfortable of the no news situation, but figured that no news was good news, and he was sure that something would appear before the end of night.

The end of night came and still no news. Nothing. He couldn't understand it. He said goodnight to Ronald and J, who could hardly stand now, waved again to Gus, and told Mandy he should wear a pinny if working. Mandy said something in return, loudly, but Tommy and the last customers were laughing too loudly to hear the reply as they left through the door.

He hopped into his black Ford Anglia and decided to call round to Cassies house. He knew it was late, but he wanted to make sure his fiancé was okay.

It wasn't a long drive and as he pulled up to Hyde Park Square he saw the lights were still on. Relieved and surprised, he bounced up the small steps and rung the bell for her parents flat. It was promptly answered by Cassies mother.

"Good evening Mrs Pope" desperately trying to sound very sober "I'm very sorry to disturb you so late, but could I speak to Cassie please"? he softly said.

"I'm sorry Thomas" recognising him instantly "Cassandra doesn't want to see you"

"Oh" he replied with confusion "Well, tell her I'll see her tomorrow then".

"No Thomas, you don't understand. She doesn't want to see you... again...ever". Came the firm reply.

And with that the voice was gone. Tommy tried buzzing again, and again and no one answered. He stood in the street and shouted up, the lights in the flat went out. He shouted a few more times and remembered some lines to a poem "Tell them I came, and no one answered..."

All was still in the night, but his beating heart. He didn't understand anything of what had just happened, none of it made sense. He just wanted answers, something. Reeling he climbed back into his car and headed back to the club. Tomorrow, he thought, tomorrow.

AFTERMATH

The more he planned his suicide and nearer the time came, the calmer he was. Hitching to the Dorset sea town seemed an easy path to take, no need for stops for food and water was somewhat liberating as was taking his future in his own hands, albeit a destructive one. He had always had a fear of open water, especially concerning sharks, even in a swimming pool, when younger, the irrational thinking made him swim faster, often leading him to win races with his secret intact. It wouldn't be until years later the fact would emerge that his Great Grandfather had died mid-Atlantic, torpedoed then all people lost at sea by the hungry denizens of the waters.

He decided that there was no point waiting another day, why put off the inevitable, he would wait until movement had rested for the afternoon break and then leave quietly and unnoticed, no need for drama to spoil what was looking like a lovely day outside.

A final check around the room before he left, making sure it was tidy, and there was a knock on the door. Startled as to why anyone should be knocking, he answered and pulled the thin wooden fire door open. There stood his sister. His sister. He could not take in the sudden appearance of his own sibling, especially on his imminent departure. Since he had left their family home, some thirty years previous, his sister had only visited him three times, for a wedding, a christening and a funeral, he had visited her many but not the other way round. And now! Now!

All that came out of his mouth, sounding alien and disjointed having not spoken to anyone for a couple of days "What are you doing here"? was all he could muster.

"I was worried about you" she replied. As simple as that. His world collapsed. Someone was showing him compassion and concern at the pivotal point of his destruction. He tried to talk but his legs felt weak and the part of him left that had been keeping him under control departed. He had previously been wrong before when thinking that he had lost everything, now even his very being fled screaming. That one simple gesture of care and compassion finished him completely. His mind crumpled as he managed to sit on the sofa and he wept. He had never wept like this in his life. He could not stop, he could not talk, he could not see or hear. Just blackness and the outpouring of the sea of sorrow. No longer was he able to carry a load.

A hand rested on his shoulder, firm, authoritative. He heard his voice being called but could not register, still possessed by the escaping monster of his past, draining him until exhaustion.

He heard his name again, asking him to talk, but he could not, how could he. They asked him to look up yet he could not open his eyes, he could only weep uncontrollably.

Another voice, his sister "They're paramedics come to help you".

Confusion entered his mind. Uncomprehending confusion. "I was leaving. Paramedics here"? he blundered in thought. "who, how could...,... know...".

It was then senses started returning. Darkness lay outside. He was no longer in the room he had started to call his, but on the ground floor, sitting on a hard chair. Coldness was about as night set in. Hours had disappeared.

It was now that shock overtook his malaise, trembles shook his body and his teeth started chattering. Water offered and a sip taken. He heard a voice. "I think he's going to be okay now. Can anyone keep an eye on him"? was questioned.

"He can't stay here" a voice said.

"I'll take him home with me" his sister declared as a reply, "he can stay with me for a while. Until he feels better".

The crying seemed to be going away, drifting off downstream leaving behind the aftershock and solitude.

"Feel better"? went through his mind, not fully comprehending words or meaning.

A taxi was called for whilst the paramedics organised their farewells and thanks given and the vessel stared blankly in his seat.

He was led out into the night to the waiting car, buckled in and stared out to the passing void. Time nor distance had no meaning. He was suspended to the world where only the clock expressed any movement. Nothing made sense, yet all had been laid bare. Death would have to wait another day.

CHRISTMAS AT ROOKS END (PART 1)

Rooks End, covered in a pristine covering of snow, was waiting, as always, at the end of its familiar drive, waiting to be filled and give its appreciative embrace to any soul that might cross its threshold. Its fire was lit in the second sitting room, with its water clock, Dansette sideboard and television which was only tuned to BBC 1 or 2. The cupboards were full with a plethora of festive treats, a freshly baked ham lay in the larder, a newly plucked turkey hung by the back door and Great Aunt Jane (and Ruby) were putting the finishing touches to the Christmas Chocolate Log.

The Christmas tree stood subtly decorated in the first sitting room, up on the small stage next to the dressing up chest (which had been used by a hundred years of children at least) looking out of the window expectantly. The air was heavy with anticipation and suppressed excitement.

The car pulled up and out poured the family. As always, the children made it through the door first, shouting hellos and heading for the stairs only to be stopped in their tracks when replied by the two voices in the kitchen. As if a switch flicking inside their attuned heads, each slowed and turned and wandered casually to say their greetings.

Calls came from outside for a hand with luggage as Robert was having to make a hasty dash to the train station to pick up Grandparents and Tippy so as not to leave them waiting.

Cassie looked at her husband curiously.

“They don’t get in until half past” she pointed out quietly.“Oh, don’t they” came the non-reply “well, I might nip to the pub for a quick one while I wait then” he said climbing back into the car with an air kiss goodbye.

She felt another one of her headaches coming on.

The children knew the drill and had taken all the unloaded luggage to their rooms, squabbled who was going to sleep where, who slept where last time, whose turn was it to sleep where this and next time and “Well, if you don’t like it, you can always sleep upstairs on your own”. Both parents’ bags had also been deposited and a little bit of sorrow shed that no visit to Rubys hideyhole would be included. Once done, all congregated in the dining room, that was one half of the semi open-planned kitchen (the dining room being separated by a breakfast bar) to await the arrival of the Great Aunt Janes brother and wife (and Tippy) so festivities, and tea, could commence.

An hour or so passed until they heard the car on gravel and snow and Dicky, Tess and Eric dashed out, smiling and waving, the cold making no difference to their warm hearts, to see the newly arrived and offer assistance, only to see unimpressed faces staring back, except for Tippy with her gentle little wave just reaching above the car door.

The car pulled to a gravelly halt and doors were grabbed and chatter commenced from the excited children, falling on tired and weary ears. Behind the activity, Cassandra and Aunt Jane appeared, waiting to greet the thirsty travellers and to sympathise on the hold-up that must have occurred.

A hefty waft of alcohol and a rosy faced, unhappy grandfather came into view, followed by grandmother and ever smiling Tippy.

Great Aunt Jane spoke first "I'm sorry you were delayed; it must have been awful for you".

"The train was on time. Robert had an unfinished drink at the bar" came the curt reply followed by stony silence.

"Hello everyone," broke in Tippy softly "lovely to see you all".

“Well,” said Robert “I only had a couple”.

And with that, the episode was closed. Everyone knew the well performed dance that would be performed by all and were either too tired or relieved not to play it out again. Out came the suitcases, handed subsequently to the carriers who stared at them curiously, only just starting to realise where they were to go. Dawning realisation that they, after all, were sleeping in the attic, opposite old Uncle Crispins. It was Christmas.

KINDERGARTEN

Both Tess and Dicky had attended Market Lodge Kindergarten and it seemed obvious that Eric should follow in their footsteps. Eric, on the other hand, had a different perspective. Eric was quite happy staying at home, plugged into the radio or television, whilst sitting on his most comfortable seat (his potty, though not needed) or playing with Teddy, or Ted...or Speedy or even Wolfie the Hamster, life was pretty good, why change it?

Being the youngest of the three, he had been spectator on the unfolding life of schooling and really didn't understand what all the excitement was about. After all, Bleep and Booster taught him a lot as did The Pogles, he didn't trust Andy Pandy, weird girl, but did enjoy Open University (and the funny clothes and hair) and listening to the variety of music that came out of the warm, fish smelling speaker of the fitted radio.

"What more did he need" he thought deeply to himself whilst picking his nose. Butty, the house cleaner, had taught him how to clean and he often helped with his little red bucket and cloth. Snacks were delivered daily at lunch and tea time, and if he was feeling sleepy, or not, Mum would always give him one of her special pills, which always seemed to give him really vivid dreams. Yup, why bother with school or kindergarten.

Unfortunately, the inevitable day came and explanations given.

To start it was going to be just the morning, just to see how things go and "For you to get to know everyone" his mother said.

Hand in hand they walked down streets and lanes, waved good morning to John the Milkman, passing tall houses, small gardens and Timmy, the squirrel monkey in his cage, arrived at the school which was tucked away at the end of a quiet mews, unassuming yet cosy and humming with activity.

Being left with a stranger, wearing a tight polo neck top, nice smelling, long, centre parted hair and attractive face Eric was settled down at a table surrounded with other prisoners who seemed happy in their play.

Words were said and the children looked and responded, obviously used to such instructions and knowing where to find pencils and paper. Sitting at the small square table, on the miniature wooden chair, Eric was given a large piece of paper and handed crayons, "...of all things" he thought and asked to draw something. Eric thought long and hard "...something..." he contemplated "...what is something..." he continued to ponder to himself. Time continued in this way as he looked around him seeing many hands at work, all creating feverishly their imaginations, sharpening their tools or sucking their thumbs looking blank and distant.

Not achieving the task, though quite happily watching and dreaming, it was suggested that maybe a jigsaw puzzle might be more fun instead. "Hmm," thought Eric "I'm good at jigsaws". He was, in fact, good at drawing and had demonstrated a number of times on his bedroom wall.

The boy sitting next to him was also offered a jigsaw, "Obviously a kindred spirit" Eric would have thought if he knew the words, though possibly being a little younger and not very nice. The two children settled into organising their pieces when Eric noticed that his jigsaw had smaller, and more, pieces than his neighbours, who's also had redder colour in the picture.

All started well, until the other child leant over and took one of Erics pieces and tried to insert it into his picture, where it certainly wouldn't fit. Eric reached over, recognising the mistake immediately, and retrieved the error and was faced with a wall of wails and pushes. The angry child's face got very wet, very quickly, tears were streaming, nose was running and the noise and pushing wasn't much fun either.

Another grab was made at Erics jigsaw puzzle and it was at this time that a change of action was required. Making a small fist, Eric passed it, in a wide-angle swipe, in the direction of the noise emitter. The result was spontaneous. The room was suddenly silent, (he had not noticed much noise before, apart for the annoying child) except a couple of adult gasps and he was lifted out of his chair and moved to the grown-up chairs.

Unhappy with life, Eric too burst into tears and attempts of consolation were made, but to no avail. Tried as they might nothing could placate this unhappy child, until someone mentioned Cherry Cake. A small glass of milk and a slice of cherry cake appeared and looked at. He had never tried cherry cake, but it looked inviting. Sitting on his strangers lap the world became right again and before he knew it, his mother appeared to take him home. "What a fun day that was" he thought to himself again. Funnily enough, he never went back there again.

BIRDSONG

Ronald and J sat at the front of the church with a seat beside them, reserved for Tommy, who was running late. Most of the regulars were there, as were the staff of the club. Cassandra, sitting on the other side of the aisle was looking very glamorous wearing a large corsage and standing out from all around.

They had known Tommy ever since they were kids, growing up on neighbouring streets yet moving in different circles but being united through their love of music. Many were envious or suspicious of their relationship, but only they knew how deep their friendship was.

Ron's mind drifted back to playing amongst the bombed out derelict streets, exploring the ruins and finding damaged treasures they would prize or share and one time making a grisly discovery of an undiscovered skeleton in a buried entrance to a cellar.

Life had sped them through the years of changes, the biggest in the last five years with the end of rationing and the Suez Crisis, where once again fuel disappeared for some, opening up the black market once again, though this time more organised.

It was strange that Tommy should be late, he never usually was, but being such a special occasion, he wasn't driving himself.

J turned round and caught the eye of a fresh, young gentleman who he didn't recognise, and connected on some level "Maybe later" thought Jay in silent conversation. He remembered how he once came on to Tommy, mistaking his friendliness as solicitation, but was gently let down with such kindness and understanding that he knew he would always have a true friend to rely on.

As if in some mutual psychic understanding, Ronald put his hand on J's leg and gave a gentle squeeze, as if signalling it was meant to be the brides prerogative to be late.

Lateness was never Tommy's thing. He didn't miss a beat, a payment or a meeting, only once had he been late and that was in their teen years.

All three of them were working at a local pottery factory, it was long and hard work but it was good, regular pay and Tommy was saving up to buy a trumpet rather than renting one all the time. It was early starts and late finishes, the foreman was a fair but strict man, a stickler for timekeeping.

One morning, Tommy didn't show, causing the other workers to get the short end of the stick and abrupt temper meted out to all. Eventually a drunken Tom showed up just before lunch with raw knuckles and bruised jaw. The swearing match between foreman and worker was a spectator sport of its own, fascinating everyone around, even passers-by peeped through the open windows. People laughed, cheered and gasped at the tirade, neither side backing down or showing any signs of contesting the fight.

At last, the management had to intervene the contest. Tommy was led away to his corner, the staff canteen, by Ronald and Jay, whereas the opposing team retired to the manager's office. Words were still being bandied about, but after some 10 minutes peace descended and an adjudicated meeting attended.

There was considerably more silence, then apologies heard when the truth was revealed. Tommy's mum had passed away in the early hours and both he and his father had drunk themselves into a stupor and come to blows in their joined grief. Hands were shaken and time off was given, with pats on backs and tears in eyes, life went back on course.

A gentle breeze wafted through the church and the sound of a car pulling up, at last, outside made the organist spring into action, finishing his non-descript tune for something more suitable. Ron turned to Jay and smiled, gently holding his hand by his side as Tommy's coffin came into sight.

LOST IN THE SUPERMARKET

Window shopping was one of Cassandras pastimes, a handy diversion and means for of the chore of childcare but at the same time an opportunity to get noticed or gain attention, be it department store, shoe shop or museum.

This day would be an extra special trip, to Harrods, rather than Fortnums (where she once worked for a short while in her acting days), a chance to see and be seen, the food hall and possibly a look around the music department or pet shop, quite enough for an afternoon's entertainment.

Making sure that Eric was clean and well presented, she applied her make-up with care and sprayed a little hairspray in place. Checking her purse, she noticed that she had a couple of shillings more than she thought but didn't think that it mattered, as there was little intention at buying anything.

The thirty-minute walk took them past the lower part of Gloucester Road with its tube station (where, one day, a Dalek would be spotted, trundling around, jokingly terrorising people), Lyons Restaurant (visited at times when there was the need of a free meal, where a matchbox and dead fly would come in handy) and the butchers (where tick was often given yet frequently forgotten to be paid). Then up the Cromwell Road and past the Natural History Museum with its grand flight of stairs, past the unassuming Victoria and Albert and up into Knightsbridge.

Harrods was spotted a long way off, its flags fluttering high on the imposing building giving it an air of expectation. On approaching, Eric gave his slight customary bow which he enjoyed doing and received one back with a subtle tip of the hat from the green and gold uniform clad doorman. His white gloved hands pulled open the large door with ease for the lady and child, who entered into an afternoon of otherworldliness.

The first and last visit was to be the coolness and tiles of the Food Hall. Epic displays of foods from around the world surrounded the drinks bar which served exotic coffees or freshly squeezed orange juice. A tower of shrimp and sea food, a mountain of cheeses all shapes and sizes and a wall of hanging meats, coloured and cured to satisfy any palate. It was a dizzying sight to a child who lived on sausage and chips and marmite sandwiches (not forgetting the doughnuts).

Cassandra led him through the sights by hand, towards the lifts to take them upstairs. It was at this point that Eric realised that he had never got lost in Harrods. Many other smaller departments store he had been "mislaid" and had often had to hand himself into the Lost Property section, which his mother had always explained to him how to find it. It had become a frequent occurrence that Cassie had resorted to tying a helium filled balloon to his belt, so as to track him more closely when wandering struck. It would eventually dawn on Eric, when he had children of his own, how odd these events were and perhaps it was never that he wandered off, more the other way round.

The lifts in Harrods were a treat in themselves. Hosted by an either an aged, well-informed gentleman who would professionally give details of the floors and their history, or a younger, uniformed man (complete with cap) very precise in his wordings.

The doors slid open revealing the young man in his empty domain with hand on well-polished handle beaming a welcoming smile.

Before his request of "Which floor Ma'am" could

be uttered, his face changed to a startled gasp. Cassandra was falling towards him; child being pulled along into his nice routine of his day. Eric was watching this in slow motion, hearing the howls of exclamations from shoppers behind and the thud as his mother's head hit the wall of the wooden interior whilst being manhandle by the poor surprised youth. The emergency bell was rung. The floor manager came running. Room was "made way". "Give us some air, please" came the calls. All the while Eric stood and watched, "it's a bit like Tom and Jerry" he thought.

Cassandra, dazed and confused was helped to her feet and flinched in pain of her ankle. With great concern, the Floor Manager berated the lift operator for not levelling out the base of the elevator and went to call for an ambulance. Before he achieved his departure, Cassie implored him not to go to such trouble, she was certain that she would be fine soon and it was nobody's fault, but her own and didn't want to make a fuss.

Somewhat relieved, he insisted that Cassandra and her son should rest for a bit, just to make sure, and have a drink of their choice in the Food Hall, with compliments. Leading the way, he instructed all staff to assist this young lady and give her anything she desired. Hobbling to the barstools, two tall glasses of freshly sieved orange juice was produced and the Section Manageress took over care.

Enquiring "Is there anything that I may get you Ma'am" the reply came instantly.

"I'd love some smoked salmon and maybe some prawns and maybe some of those..." pointing to the dessert section "choc ice polar bears, please". Slightly taken aback the order was completed, as directed by both parties and duly delivered, wrapped and bagged. Climbing down from the stool the pain shot through Cassies ankle again and she rubbed her sore head, flinching in pain.

The Manager came over again, quietly watching from the side-lines and insisted that a taxi be called for to take them home, all expenses paid for. Helped to the front exit, a cab was hailed and instructed and delivered the mother and son home. Cassie thought "Bother, I broke a nail. Next time I won't trip so hard".

BACK AGAIN

His father had died in a car crash, when he, Robert, was seeking a company to join and start his professional acting career in England. A well liked, confident and charismatic local sportsman, he had admirable reflexes and had avoided many accidents growing up and living in the South African countryside. Unfortunately, those abilities were also his undoing. Travelling in a car one evening with a group of friends, they were confronted with imminent destruction and swerved to miss the onslaught. The car veered off the road and started a high speed roll down an incline to rocks below. The quick-thinking man flung open his door and launched himself out to safety, only to be struck by another passing vehicle, ending his life immediately, whilst all the remaining passengers and driver came to a safe and abrupt halt before plunging into a ravine.

Robert had been obviously traumatised by the news, and the journey back to his home land and subsequent funeral and return had difficulties of their own. His brother was still arrogant and cruel, despite the sorrow, and taking lead of the household even furthered his malice, though his mother tried to alleviate the open pains they all felt.

There was no closure for Robert. He could find no place to reflect on his relationship with his demised parent, too much noise littered his head, even in the stillness of the night with the crickets chirping their gentle lullabies. Anger and resentment, confusion and rejection all tumbled around each other fuelling his solitude, with questions unknown and answers not given he felt lost in the place he knew so well, so had to flee back to his goals and aspirations.

It was upon his return, that he found a new member had joined the cast. An attractive young lady, always giving him a smile, touching his arm (three Mississippi) and showing interest in what he had to say with no judgement, no conflict and no denigration.

Their friendship grew more obvious, on stage and off, as he felt the electricity spark between them and course through his being. For the first time, for a long time, he felt alive again, washed clean with something new to cherish, something good and pure.

They had been standing in the wings, waiting for their cues, he slightly behind her as she faced stage front. She leant back, the smallest amount, the warmth of her body climbed his chest and filled his senses as her shoulder touched his chest. He leaned his head gently forward to take in the fragrance of her hair, only to see her face turn slightly to meet his and their lips touched.

This small act, this small token gesture, insignificant in the history of the expanding cosmos where worlds collide and stars are born was all that existed for that fleeting moment. No thing had gone before this moment and no thing would exist again. Somewhere all those treasures live on and grow the exquisite flowers of romance.

He had never felt wanted before, apart from his adoring mother and now he knew what he had been missing.

A call came out, for all to hear, loud and clear, waking the new lovers from their slumber. Cassandra had missed her cue. Gently flummoxed and clearing their throats, Cassie came on stage still under the spell, unsure of what just happened. She too had been a participant of a too short-lived touch of something wonderful, something she had sought through the years and never found and here it was, in a small unimportant theatre, surrounded by small unimportant people.

But all of those events had been and gone.

Robert's love had been lost, then found in another, another type of love and now Cassie wanted him back. Tommy was gone for good, she said, it had been foolish of her, she only wanted him, she said.

"Our modelling job is still on" Cassie said to Robert, admittedly, and "we will be working together for a couple of days" she continued softly, getting closer. "I have missed you" she sighed.

With that the fish was hooked, though the reeling in would be more arduous.

CHRISTMAS AT ROOKS END (PART 2)

Morning came around quickly despite the three children having to spend the night crammed into the small, spartan two-bedroom attic room and Eric complaining about the army surplus camp bed. There had been the suggestion that they could sleep in the more spacious room across the way, but all had emphatically declined.

Breakfast was always a plain affair at Rooks End, toast and tea were all that was provided, but enlivened with the ancient flip toaster which, when the side was lowered, allowed the uncooked side to be rotated, as if by the magic of physics. A lot of toast was made on those mornings.

Time was wasted around the house in awaiting the feast of luncheon, playing in the garden, though not being allowed to set foot on the pristine snow of the croquet lawn, hunting around the house, though being forbidden to play hide and seek, so, much time was spent staring out of the windows and dreaming of childhood things and what had gone before.

The gong went for lunch, resonating its call throughout the old house and all and sundry beckoned to its call. Grandparents had already been strategically placed around the large, curved oak table with matching high-backed chairs, interspersed with the remaining family attempting, but failing, to go boy girl...Once the unannounced game of non-musical chairs had been agreed upon, carving commenced. Robert stood proud and brandishing the sharpening knife decided another drop, or two, of whiskey was needed before plunging in. With ceremonies taking an unexpected halt, expressions were made of hunger and "food getting cold" amongst other whispered mutterings.

The anti-climax was soon over, as the meats, ham: hot, turkey: not so, was passed around for all to place their own helpings of assorted vegetables and potatoes on the antique china and silverware. Eating still had to wait until all plates were filled, bottoms seated and grace said, but once completed the chattering of utensils and appreciative talk commenced, along with the pop of a champagne cork and a "Mind where you're aiming that Robert".

Ruby was still beavering in the background around the kitchen, tidying and cleaning away and getting the mince pies warmed, cream whipped, brandy buttered and inserting charms and coins into the festive pudding.

Once completed, Ruby came to the table to start clearing away, only to be shooed away by Great Aunt Jane in mock surprise to see that she was still there and insisting that she was to take some food for herself. Disappearing, the children were put to good use, collecting the empty plates and finished with bowls of excess food, making way for the grand finale as Robert was already in the far end of the kitchen sampling and heating the brandy, ready to be poured on top of the pudding for some lucky person to set light to.

Ceremoniously carried to the table, it was elected that Eric, of all people, should be allowed the privilege of lighting, much to the annoyance of Dicky and judging on his track record of when it came to fires. Match in hand and smile in his eyes, the flame was struck and reached out to be greeted by an enormous WHOOF! The fire jumped for joy as chairs pushed away in unison from the table and the youngest person in the room chuckled with mischievous pleasure.

The flames died soon enough, leaving a slight smell of singed fringe in the hair but no harm done, just a few tuts from the older members present, while Cassandra seemed unbothered by the whole affair, perhaps it was her pills.

Great Aunt Jane took control again and dished out portions, regardless of like or dislike, of the sticky fruit substance to all, with no objections, due to the hidden, exciting possibilities that lay inside. Normally, a single silver sixpence would be placed for the lucky finder, but this year was the inclusion of silver charms: a wishbone for a wish, horseshoe for luck, a button for a bachelor, a thimble for a spinster and a bell for a bride-to-be.

Again, all bowls served and toppings selected, eating began. Disliking the food most, but eager for the prize, Eric found the silver coin to his triumphant delight. Yelping out his happiness, congratulations were made, apart from Dicky, and polite conversation resumed followed by an explosion of coughing from Grumpy. Red faced and spluttering he produced a small, shiny horseshoe from his mouth that had been unwittingly swallowed, much to the amusement of Eric, who felt he'd just won a hat-trick, and to Robert who thought "Serves you right".

FIRST DAYS

Eric never really liked school. From the early days, where he would cling to railings and scream to be allowed home or at dinner times, where unwanted food would either be thrown, secretly, under the tables or stuffed into his shorts pockets and disposed of later (normally, rhubarb crumble and custard). Unfortunately, these tactics didn't always work and resulted in being stood over by an ever-watchful teacher, forced to clear one's plate, often resulting in a torrent of tears and excessive nose juices mixing with the forkfuls going into the mouth, either to be swallowed, spat out or recycled out through the nostrils, always pretty amazing when all three happened at the same time. Sometimes, a distant part of Eric would marvel at this process..." wow, a whole pea".

Apart from dinner break, Eric enjoyed the walks, often in crocodile style, around the busy streets, and didn't mind walking next to James as he had very soft hands or Andrew, as he was quite chatty and friendly. One lovely, crisp Autumn day that would change. Hand in hand with Andrew, who also tended to be...individual, he pulled away from Erics, not breaking his grip and started kicking a huge pile of raked up leaves, which he promptly, rather flamboyantly, fell into.

The whole line came to an abrupt halt as the teacher, ever watchful, came to assist. As Andrew lay, somewhat dazed, the smell hit everyone's nose with a resounding "Eurgh"! Even the teacher faulted in her tracks. Andrew rose out of the leaves, only to exhibit an impressive coating of dog mess, legs, hands, arm, shorts and particularly well inground in his shoes. Needless to say, the walk back to school wasn't pleasant, for anyone.

Another issue that Eric didn't respond well to, was toilet time. Regardless of the need, pupils would have to queue, and perform on demand, all while a male teacher watched proceedings, twice a school day, and that, in itself, created its own future issues.

Following in family tradition, Eric was sent on to Prep. Skool, which he detested even more.

The work was easier enough, daydreaming was easier and the teachers were a mixed bunch, ranging from borderline psychotic to character filled personas. There was the monotone chemistry teacher who often crossed his arms in an exaggerated fashion; a tall, thin, dark haired pleasant lady in charge of Art, always encouraging pupils to find their voice; the round, Italian, very patient French lecturer; the diminutive, green tweed, skirt suit wearing Scottish Maths teacher, her red hair tied severely back giving a no-nonsense air, yet incredibly good at her skill. Then there were the three English teachers. The Good, though often exasperated; The Bad, chain-smoking sadist; The Ugly, explosive, violent and terrifying.

But to Eric, life was a playground, unable to take much seriously, so it understandably came as a bit of a shock when he was informed that he was being sent into boarding. His brother had done it, his father had done it, in fact it was regarded as a norm to all male children for many generations (though unbeknownst, Robert rejected the idea, but Cassandra was the instigator).

Originally, he had started as, what was colloquially known as, a Daybug, taking the 50-minute journey to school on a daily basis, predominantly on his own, consisting of a 7-minute walk to a tube, then a change to a main line and another 7-minute walk the other end through a housing estate, where the arriving and departing school kids were often shot at with air rifles and catapults.

The constant expenditure must have been a

calculating factor, so weekly-boarding came into effect. This however, led to more problems than resolved. The first night at the boarding house was traumatic for most. In a dormitory of about 15 rejected nine-year-olds, the crying was constant, gently dying away, as one by one, fell asleep, only to awaken the following morning to years of traumatising unhappiness.

And it certainly didn't increase Erics like of school. Often, when being returned he would either try and cause the car to crash, (if being taken back in the family vehicle) either by unlocking the clip that held the driver's seat in place and suddenly pushing Robert forward from behind or lunging for the steering wheel at some inopportune moment. After a while he was returned by train, a safer option, but as the train was pulling away from the platform, would fling open the door and throw himself out. "Quite impressive" he would think to himself. This option would never be the more comfortable option. Nothing to do with the landing, but the kicking he would receive from an angry father as he was booted down the platform.

It was this that caused him to be entered into full-time boarding.

THE CENTRE

The shop was meant to be a new start, signalling a new direction for the family and business alike.

Dicky was coming to the end of his education, which would free up some monies, and had won a scholarship for some travel or something or other, Robert did not understand the complexities and found it difficult to talk to his now estranged son. They had always had communication problems, Robert being resentful and quick to temper with Dickies frustrated anger, which grew when Tess was born, but went to a new level on the arrival of his little brother. Sometimes they came to blows, which only served to divide them more and reminded him of his own childhood.

They had managed to secure a rented property nearby in a backstreet of Kensington, that would suit their purposes, and had set up the company with an old advertising executive that he used to work with, each fronting equal equity, though Robert would do the sales side and Harry would be predominately in charge of production.

Accountant and a secretary (of a more mature age to avoid..." distractions") hired, the shop was fitted out with black and white cuboid displays, with clear glass panels to present their unique and prestigious replica metalware, and chesterfield sofas for wealthy clients to relax on and be served coffee.

Cassandra seldom assisted in the business, turning up occasionally to check no shenanigans were about or to happily (and outrageously) flirt with an American businessman (or two) who might need to be cajoled into an extra expenditure. Besides, she often had her own diary to keep: hairdressers, beautician, people to see, pills to take and plenty of rest booked in. The "hairdressers" seemed an important part of the agenda, more so now to when the children were younger, as to having to take them with her tended to cramp ones glampuss style. Eric recalled, on one such occasion, happily playing with a small wooden giraffe whilst his mother went into the back of the hairdresser's salon. Time passed and then did some more. He elected that giraffe had enough playing with and asked the nice-looking receptionist "Do you know whether my mummy is going to be much longer"? The kindly looking young lady said she would check and disappeared (not literally, you understand). A few minutes later she returned with the proprietor and head stylist. He knelt down in front of Eric and said "Your Mummy's not here at the moment, she'll be back later" and left. So, he sat...and waited, and after what seemed like a very long time, did come back, through the door they had entered from when they first arrived. "Very odd" thought Eric.

He, on the other hand, enjoyed helping behind the scenes in the shop. Whether it be gift wrapping sales, sniffing the ink of the photocopier, or pulling a wall cabinet over his head, by mistake.

It was on one of these days, the first of many, that confirmed that his parents perhaps weren't being totally faithful to one another.

The first time he remembered the penny dropping, it took a long time, was at home. He was engrossed, as always, playing with his truck and, as always, someone/s were getting seriously run over on the upstairs landing. Mum was out...who knows? Dad was downstairs with a very attractive Australian blonde (a cousin, apparently) with a tight blue polo neck on. "She has a lovely smile" Eric said to Action Person who was naked and getting tied to a Cindy (who was also naked) (by the way, the names have been changed to protect identities). The game was going well, but a glass of milk was needed, so down Eric went to garner his chances. As he came down the stairs, he noticed an intriguing sight. According to his father, the cousin was just showing him her new bra. “It looked pretty enough” thought Eric. “There wasn’t very much of it” he told his Mother later.

But, at the back of the shop, and many years later, his Father was on the phone, with his back to the door, when Eric arrived for duties and overheard a “Yes, of course I love you” and a “Don’t worry, I’ll see you later”. Assuming that it must be Cassandra on the other end of the line, no thought was given and Eric went through to the back to make a Coffeemate special.

No more than 5 minutes of his arrival, his Mother walked through the door. “Well,” mused Eric “I guess that proves that then”.

Dear Diary,

I died and drifted in limbo and pain, free of the being that had laid hidden in plain sight, seeking out answers yet hearing none because I still wasn’t listening. I earnestly prayed for forgiveness, sincerely sorry for all my wrongdoings, sorry for the path I had tread, sorry for blaming others, I accepted my life and all my mistakes as mine and mine alone. I no longer heard my inner child cry in pain, all my pasts came to me, just as Scrooge had been visited by his ghosts.

Yet still I prayed.

It was all I had left, all I could do, I offered myself into his arms, not deeming myself worthy or wanting acceptance, just mercy.

I tried to run and die a second time, more determined, but was found and stopped by the person who had faced his own demons, though had not defeated them all.

That night I went to the unfamiliar bed, with its unfamiliar smells and unfamiliar sounds and slept. I slept the deepest and most restful sleep. I had not felt this way for many years. And as I slept, the heavens cracked above my head. An almighty boom was heard and the snow fell hard, out of season, not stopping until the morning.

People awoke in the town with astonishment. Roads blocked by the snow quickly melting to flood water, impassable to traffic, only this small town had been affected.

I arose rested and peaceful, I felt afresh and ready, though walked around just as amazed at the spectacle as others.

I felt that, as all things were changed, I should change too. I know I said I had prayed, but I seldom visited church, but being Sunday...I asked a passing stranger what time it was and I realised that services would soon be over. The stranger looked at me and said "Goodness, I'm sorry, I didn't change my watch".

Glad, I attended a local service where the sermon

was about my wrongdoings and the pain of sufferers, I couldn't stop the tears or believe what I was hearing. A lady gave me a sympathetic look. As I left I vowed to listen more carefully and sat in the churchyard patchy white and green. I sat and listened in peace and silence. I have not felt like this in over 40 years. I could have been sitting at my birth home watching the raindrops roll down the window. It was then I heard the voice, soft and clear. Startled at first, I let it direct me, I followed its course, curious to see what would happen and where I was to go.

I eventually came to a bench, a normal, wooden roadside bench. The voice told me to wait. Three times I asked or questioned, each time the same answer "Wait".

So, I sat and waited, wondering what I would see. I looked around at the normal street, the snow almost gone and traffic resuming it day. Trees and buildings around, fire station, a red bricked bungalow with a large car park, I considered some type of social hall. I sat and waited and watched. A car eventually pulled into the little car park opposite, a person got out and went into the red building. A few minutes passed and then another car, then another. Soon, a considerable number of cars were arriving and people entering this small building. I stood up, intrigued and crossed the road to enquire what event was taking place. To my amazement it was a Catholic Church and I was invited to attend, despite my denomination.

Incredibly, this service too pinpointed my errors.

I do not forget this time in my life. I was offered a new beginning and intend to take it and make a difference. I am truly free at last and do not intend to go back on my destructive path which was being used to hide my hurt.

MRS JARROW

The_old Dorset hamstone cottage had been nestled in the middle of the quiet, rural village for over 400 years, at least 200 of which had been in ownership of the same family. Its tall walled garden at the front and side had small, gnarled fruit trees, pruned by generations and a magnificent horseradish, so deep in flavour, it was strong enough to "scare the devil 'imself". The wisteria was "roight 'eavy 'n bloom" and bees were bumlin', "twas garn b proper roight 'arvest dis un" said young Tim (who was probably about 95) admiring the distant apple trees and Old Mary chuckled behind him with her toothless grin.

Old Mary lived on the edge of the village, in an old brick and wooden shed, no water or electric, just tilly lamps for light, a small open fire for heat and cooking. There were daily visits to the spring with her buckets, where, if your paths crossed, she would entrance you with her tales as you stood there, spellbound, not knowing what she was saying, but loving her honest company. She always wore her heavy woollen pointed hat and thick tweed overcoat with bare legs and wellies, how long she had lived, no one knew, she had always been here, with her boyfriend and talked with the broadest accent that even some of the old folk didn't understand. Old Mary knew all the herbal cures of the land and grew fist sized strawberries with the taste of beauty and purity, so much so, that you would have to stop whilst eating and marvel at life.

Mrs Jarrow sat on her padded window seat looking out through the lead lined panes at Young Tim and Old Mary conversing, looking up into her apple orchard, while the small round oak table in front of her stood on the cool flagstone floor, and gladly held her cup and saucer and, as yet, un-cut seed cake. She sighed as she turned away and looked around the room with its large inglenook dominating the space and remembering her childhood stories and the flames that used to dance about. She would be sad to go. But the house was too big for her on her own and there was none to leave it too.

The house creaked in agreement, as the old footsteps walked the floors going nowhere, but retracing their well-trodden routes.

The 3 bedrooms and attic were crammed with the past occupants' clothes and trinkets, hundreds of years' worth of dresses and tabards, hats and fascinators, jerkins and jodhpurs, all stacked as high as the ceiling, as well as the sawn-off Elizabethan four poster, cut down to size to fit. And if the rooms were not filled satisfactorily, then the barns had their treasures also. The cider press, not used for 25 years, still hadn't been repaired since the day it was made stood wanting and covered in dust. The dipsomaniacs delight, the pile where bottles of all shapes, sizes and uses, lay discarded and had been covered over years of leaf fall and fire ash.

There was one bottle though, a special bottle, that lay hidden, even from Mrs Jarrow, a Witches bottle. A few feet from where she now sat, were her stairs for taking her to bed, behind a small wood panelled door. Under the stairs, boarded in some 300 years past, someone lay a glass bottle. The size of a flattened 1-pint milk bottle, though mottled, a rich black, blue and green, as if oil had been kept in it yet permeated the glass itself. And inside, inside clippings of hair and nails lay and a scrap of paper, now too faded to read, but would have revealed the true purpose of this hidden, cloth covered container. Used to protect or curse, none would know, but one day soon, it would become discovered.

RIFF-RAFF

The photoshoot contract had gone well and had immediately garnered possible fruits, in the guise of auditions and modelling contracts, more so for Robert than Cassandra.

They were driving back, in Roberts recently purchased banger, from the final day when Cassie suggested dropping in on the club to see the boys and let them know how it went and how wonderful it all was. Robert was a bit unsure and was tired, but after some persuasion relented, "As long as we don't stay too long" he suggested.

They pulled up outside the club, easily parking and went down the stairs, ignoring the hat check, and went straight to a table. No sign of the boys as Cassie scanned around, but she was certain they would be here soon, instead she signalled for service, keen for a bit of attention.

"So," a familiar voice said behind them "you're here. Bit late aren't you"? They turned in unison to see Tommy standing, with arms crossed, horn in hand.

"Oh, Tommy darling, how lovely to see you" cooed Cassie with ease.

"See you brought your fellow with you. Hard luck chap, look-out" came the reply.

"Yes, erm, Cas told me you broke it off" Robert replied.

Tommy laughed, throwing his head back "That's what she told you, ay? Other way round dear boy."

Cassies face faltered when her eyes met Roberts. She didn't understand why he looked so shocked and unsure where to put himself. He stood, knees weakened and walked away out of the club and passed his car and walked again into the night.

Back inside, Tommy sat down with Cassandra, who was feeling uneasy and cornered.

"You've been a bit of a minx Cassie, haven't you"? Tommy said, signalling for his usual. "How about we start again Cassie, you know I love you".

Cassie was stuck. On one hand, Robert financially secure, handsome and then there was the modelling and acting to think of. On the other, Tommy, was here and Robert had left, how else was she going to get home.

Robert was tired. Tired of it all. Tired of trying to keep it all together. He missed home. Missed his family, even his brother, perhaps not, but he missed what his brother could have been.

He missed his father too and the unresolved issues. He felt played, he felt used. Used and abused by so many people for their own benefit. Dumfounded, Robert walked. The years of upset grew with each footstep he took. It started to rain again. "English bloody weather" he thought to himself. He started to feel hemmed in with all the tall buildings reaching over him, crowding around and suffocating and the raindrops themselves were too heavy to bare, adding insult to injury, smothering him with their dampness. Robert needed open space, the all-encompassing veldt, wide open, glorious skies where you could breathe and fill your lungs, gallop for miles with simple life in your heart.

His hand reached and touched Inkosi, his trusted childhood steed. He reached up and stroked his mane, pulling their heads close together and whispered soothing clicks into its ear. Robert told Inkosi, not to worry, everything was fine, its just a distant storm, they'd be home soon. He swung up with ease onto the horses back, and steered it away from the dark foreboding clouds and galloped off in whatever direction they were heading. He called out and waved to a group of locals and servants working along a fence fixing the road and putting up new posts. The lights flashed as the storm clouds neared, but he was happy to be riding again, happy and free, though his head hurt and part of him felt cold.

The horn blare surprised him as he got up off the wet road and stumbled onto the pavement. Warmth trickled down his face with cold wetness and he staggered on, confused at his surroundings and trying to reach again for Inkosi who had bolted. A man leant in to face him, to close and scared Robert swung wildly at the figure, screaming at the nightmare and calling for the buildings to stop laughing at him. The swirl spun around him like a nauseating wave, flipping him inside and out, desperate to unsteady his connection, scratching at his eyes and dancing the black belief.

It went on forever. He was there and nowhere. With time and without. He felt nothing yet everything. Hot, cold. Heard, silence.

The light made him shake. His eyes flickered open and he was awake. Tired, confused, but awake, lying in a hospital bed with Cassandra by his side.

CHRISTMAS AT ROOKS END (PART 3)

Plates had been cleared away, the Queens Speech watched with reverence (including Grampa and Eric standing for the National Anthem), after lunch games played amongst the whisky fumes and Afternoon Tea consumed with Great Aunt Janes Chocolate Log.

All the grown-ups retired to their rooms, for a brief siesta and to reboot themselves ready for the evening's drinks party, leaving the three children alone. It was the only time this ever occurred and they were always lost at what to do. Knowing their strict guidelines, as dictated by Aunt Jane, they sat virtually motionless watching television, not daring to move in case something got damaged, it seemed different with all adults absent.

Time thankfully passed quickly and before long started to hear water going through the old pipes of the house, and doors opening and closing upstairs. This only made Eric get more fidgety and got told to sit down and behave by Dicky who was seriously and intently interested in motor racing. Things got the better of Eric however, when he heard movement in the kitchen, he slowly moved backwards away from the television engrossed Dicky and when he was out of view materialised smiling in front of a startled Ruby, who was preparing cocktail snacks for the imminent guests.

He was closely followed by Tess, enquiring if they could "help or taste anything"? Ruby directed them to some sandwiches she had already prepared, that needed crusts cutting off. "Hmm, crusts" thought Tess, she loved bread and she hadn't eaten much lunch, having been told once that she should always leave some food on her plate for Mrs Manners, it was polite. This would be the start of her life long struggle with bulimia.

As they were busy trimming, and nibbling, Robert came down to prepare the drinks and get a head start on everyone else as Cassie was still having a lie down after taking one of her pills.

Dicky appeared and automatically was given the task of carrying the bottles and lay out nuts as the first of the invited guests knocked at the door. They walked in, before the door had been answered and Eric was surprised to see them being escorted by Aunt Jane, not realising that she had actually gone to pick them up in her car.

Soon enough more familiar faces started to turn up and as Eric had been given the duty of Doorman, kept getting patted on the head with comments like "Oh you must be Derek" and "Haven't you grown". It was cold in the corridor by the front door and the party sounded like it was warming up, no other cars could be seen coming up the drive, so Eric decided he needed a drink as well…

Entering into the first sitting room the fumes hit. The heady mix of smoke and laughter, gin and music, port and lemon. Weaving around the head patting and perfume he searched for the drinks table to see what he could find. A bowl of salted peanuts and cheese balls looked at him, all alone, so Eric thought he'd take it for a walk into the kitchen for a quiet chat instead, just like he'd seen his parents do with the occasional guest at other parties.

Ruby was just finishing off tidying and getting ready to retire when Eric arrived with Tess, unknowingly behind.

"Look what Miss Jane bought a while back" she said, bringing out a blue metal tube fixed to a stand. "It's called a Sodastream". She explained its use and how it worked and made him and Tess a fizzy orange, which tasted disgusting but drank it anyway and asked for another. Ruby obliged and chivvied them away.

The Spirit of Christmas was definitely present and Poor Pussy was being suggested. Eric found this game hilarious but didn't really understand it. One person was chosen to be "The Cat". They would, on hands and knees, have to circulate and behave like a cat, rubbing themselves against other people's leg and get stroked on the head with the person saying "Poor Pussy". For some reason, which Eric could not understand, some adults found it more humourous than he, especially when people over acted. It was normally about this time when he would be sent to bed.

"Eric," called his mother "time for bed".

FULL-TIME

Being a full-time boarder had its perks, few admittedly, but some. There was being allowed up the main staircase, usually only permitted to Teachers and Prefects, no specific bed time on weekends, but the best was less competition with the television and cooks treats.

Most weekly bugs went home on Friday after school, so when the full-timers got back to the boarding house, the lucky first few would dash downstairs to see Cook, who, hopefully, had just finished baking some biscuits or scones. Piping hot from the oven she would allow a few to "disappear", they would be scurried away to a hiding place, behind hanging coats or part closed doors, sniggering and scoffing and "ho..., ho..., hop". Crumbs dispersed, a dash back up the concrete stairs so as not to be missed by a prowling teacher, meeting hopeful latecomers descending and hearing "Aw" in the background. This was counterbalanced, very unfairly, with a Saturday morning of triple Latin with an equally ancient Mr Oarman, who often fell asleep during class and would berate any pupil disturbing his slumber or failing to notify him of end of class.

Eric felt himself lucky among some other full timers. Others were sad all the time, not matter whether in play or work, a handful only seeing one or both of their parents maybe only twice a year, if they were fortunate. Children of international models, politicians, celebrities or the affluent, they all shared the same pain and tears, no matter where they came from. Unfortunately, in their future, they might put their own children through the process, forgetting how they were damaged only to pass it on from generation to generation.

Being a target for bullies didn't help with a healthy welfare. No matter which school attended, someone was looking for a way of spreading their problems, looking for an outlet. As he grew older, the imagination of the torturer grew as well. Starting with plain old kicking, punching, tweaking, headlocks (all favourites of teachers as well, not forgetting blackboard wiper and chalk throwing), things would progress to strangulation, filling a bath with water (by way of a milk bottle filled at a river, a 5-minute run away), whipping, but the most uncomfortable was hanging. No noose was needed, just a coat hanger. The unsuspecting victim would have a coat hanger placed inside their coat, which would then be fastened up and the victim would be hung up on a nearby coat hook. Seemingly humourous, rules applied. Left dangling, passers-by were expected to irritate the child further in any manner they felt fit, you decide, but on no account was help to be administered, unless you wanted the same treatment. Tears and pain came quickly for many, sometimes being left there for a long half hour.

After a prolonged period of unhappiness, Eric decided to make a change and runaway back home.

He thought carefully how to do it, having little access to money and a long walk that he could get busted on, he then remembered that one of his teachers, a friendly History teacher, lived an easy walking distance from home, with many well-known routes. The end of the school day, midweek, loomed and he spotted Mr Cuthbert at his usual desk, marking some books and finishing his cup of tea. Eric knocked at the door.

"Afternoon, Mr Cuthbert" said Eric "Mum asked me to ask you if you're going straight home tonight" he lied, with his heart beating fast.

Mr Cuthbert looked up, over his half-rimmed glasses and spoke "Oh, hello Eric" he said in his usual quiet and unfaltering manner "Yes, yes I am, but aren't you meant to be going back to the boarding house this evening"? he enquired.

"No" came the instant reply "I've got a hospital

appointment first thing in the morning. It's my ears again. Dad was meant to come and get me but rang to say he was held up in a meeting".

"I thought you said your mother rang" came the response.

"No, Dad rang and so I had to ring Mum and Mum asked me to ask you" wow, he was proud of how well he lied.

"Well, actually" Mr Cuthbert said tidying up the books "I was just about to leave, so you've timed it well. Come on".

Eric couldn't believe his luck, unfortunately the opposite would be the case the following morning when Mr Cuthbert was called in to see the Headmaster.

OOPS !

This was to be Erics first funeral, though he didn't know it yet and at the age of 9 his grandfather was dying of Lung Cancer. Spring had sprung and almost gone and his mother said they were going on a visit to his Grumpy at hospital, where he had been for a couple of weeks, ever since they had taken him for a drive around the top corner, of where Kensington Gardens meets Hyde Park, to see the beautiful, breath-taking crocuses.

They arrived at the hospital and were led into a quiet room where two strange, elderly ladies sat, weeping, talking to a very frail, small looking man, who didn't move or seem to register anyone. The ladies reminded him of a time when he had been ill some years ago. He was always ill with something or other, often bronchitis, sometimes worse.

He had been in bed and the doctor in black had visited him and sat by his bedside. Eric liked the smell of the large black square case the doctor opened, something reassuring and friendly about it. He turned and looked back at himself, he was standing at his bedroom window and saw his parents, sister and doctor gathered around his bed as he lay there, though they were all in Victorian clothing. It reminded him of the time he saw the White Horse come through his bedroom wall and the skeleton trying to open his eyes.

His mother looked the same way now, at this wasted figure, as she had at her son then and Eric wondered who he was. He sat down on the floor and pulled out his little scribble pad and pencil and started drawing some monsters, he liked drawing monsters. The teacher didn't. She even talked to his father because she was concerned about his painting and drawing sometimes, thought something bad was happening at home.

Eric sat, using the chair as a rest, and went into his dream world until it was interrupted with "Don't you want to come and say hello" his mother asked. Eric frowned" No" came the direct reply, "Why would he want to talk to a stranger" he thought.

They were there for a while, not as long as they would be when his Grandmother was in hospital though. That time would trouble Eric for years. His Grandmother and Mum never saw eye to eye, though eventually they would be peas in a pod and when she came to stay, circumstances would cause her to die of pneumonia.

But that was a long time off, and for now it was time to leave and Eric wanted to see his Grumpy. Instead, they left the hospital entirely, his mother in tears and Eric asking "Aren't we going to see Grandad"? and "Who was that you were talking to"? "That was your grandpa" came the answer. The funeral was two weeks later and Eric was still convinced his Mother was wrong.

The ceremony was a very black affair. The church was filled with very well-to-do people who Eric didn't know and would never see again. Cassandra dabbed her face all the way through the service, but would scorn Eric for it years later at his Grans funeral. But today he was interested, looking around at the different hats and outfits, all the cars outside and where all these people had come from.

The service ended and invitations were issued to meet back at the flat for drinks whilst Tess and Eric were led away to a waiting limousine. The driver was asked to take them on and return as soon as for the rest of the party. The long vehicle pulled away with Tess and Eric looking out of the back window at the shrinking scene and couldn't believe their luck. A whole stretch limousine just for themselves. Wow! They rolled around on every possible surface going, much to the amusement of the chauffeur, "Carry on kids, it'll be your turn one day. Make the most of it"

CAS

Despite her sudden outbursts of violence, lies, inability with confrontation, jealousy, secrets, emotional breakdowns and general madness, Cassie was a loving Mother. Desperate for attention and affection, flirtation was a handy, well used tool as well as her acting background, giving her the ability to lie convincingly (a trait that Eric would adopt and excel at, bringing him a lack of satisfaction of his own).

There would be occasions of bills or shop credit that would need to be paid, often leading to hiding behind the sofa when the milkman came calling or sending her 5-year-old son into a shop, where credit was already exceeded, to purchase some goods, to spin a yarn and look innocent. It often worked and Eric learnt the skill quickly to make his life easier.

Tess would often take on responsibilities during one of Cassies "moments" (Dicky being away as usual) having to tend house, cook and call the Doctor. On one such occasion, Robert was out playing cricket, a regular event, as well as golf or polo, any sport activity except on Saturdays when an afternoon of fixtures was displayed on the box, and Cassie was distraught.

Tess rang the doctors, as per instructions, and relayed how bad her mother was, as per instructions, and emphasized the lack of paternal aide, as per...The family physician appeared within the hour and checked on her patient, lying dramatically in bed, too ill to raise her head and wipe her own brow (though, oddly, thought Tess, fine not 10 minutes before, reading her book) and was furious that Tess had not contacted her father, and should do so immediately "Do you not realise how ill your mother is" she said.

A faint murmur emitted from Cassandras lips, and both Tess and GP turned, the destination was given weakly again. "Go on then girl, ring your father". Was barked. To a young 9-year-old, already confused and injured, she tried her best, with the doctor leaving and mother shouting demeaning comments, she sat on the downstairs sofa and waited for the rest of her family to return and ease some of the pressure from her small shoulders.

Apart from her usual illnesses, Cassandra had experienced two miscarriages, potentially harming to any psyche, one requiring a fortnight stay in hospital and an erratic couple of years to follow that would entail disappearances from the family home in the middle of the night, only to return days later, hair dramatically shortened or coloured and dressed in unrecognisible clothing. It was always a stressful time for the family, constantly walking on eggshells, which came to a head (at least one of many) when a month's hospitalisation occurred, with no visits allowed or contact made (it would later be speculated on, though never talked about, that sectioning had taken place).

For a while after Cassie felt better, new medication was prescribed (and shared with Eric) and she started applying herself in new directions, for the first time in years, life seemed on the up. The new fall was around the corner.

The Centre had been doing well, attracting international buyers, especially from America and Japan and a sales meeting was taking place in Scotland, organized and presented by Robert. She felt very proud of what he had achieved in such a short time and with so little, and was already reaping the legal rewards from all his hard work and long hours. It was a ten-day event, but she felt prepared enough to handle the shop and children, especially as well behaved they now were. The time went quickly, with no hiccups and Robert returned with an abundance of positive feedback, potential contracts and possible investors and contacts. He rang Harry, his business partner with the good news and received devastating news in return. Robert put down the telephone gently back on the cradle. He was no longer a part of the business, Harry had bought him out for £1, "...a legal loophole" he said, "Sorry to tell you" he said. Roberts face drained white as he faced Cassandra to tell her the news. "What would he do now" he thought, terrified.

MR LUTON

It was late evening and Eric was enjoying the evening. He had been disturbed from his slumber by the flashing lights outside his bedroom window, not for the last time, and, bleary eyes being rubbed while pulling up his striped cotton pyjamas, stumbled to the window (yes, the same window) and peered outside behind his curtains.

Much to his young delight, it was a most impressive scene. A large red fire engine, illuminated by its own and street lights, was trying and failing to manoeuvre around the tight corner into his cobbled road, with fireman shouting orders, dashing this way and that.

The last time he had seen an active group of firemen was when he had got his head stuck in the local public gardens railings. It was another lovely summer day, so himself and Cassie had gone for a walk to the park and, at the front entrance, spied the Balloon Man selling his wares next to the Flower Lady. The black balloon looked particularly interesting and attempted to persuade his mother to purchase one. Today, however, was not his day, he was going to have to find another way to amuse himself.

Walking along the low brick wall, with arched railings above, Cassie suggested (though I don't think literally) that Eric should stick his head through the railings. Eric couldn't believe his luck. He had always wanted to try but always got told "Don't be so stupid". So, with invitation opened (and checked, just to make sure), obliged.

It wasn't as much fun as it looked. Easy going in, not so much coming out, actually, not at all coming out. Stuck. A few kindly passers-by tried to assist and offer helpful suggestions, but all Eric heard was "why would you do something like it" and, yes, even "Stupid boy".

He tried telling them it wasn't his fault but no one listened, not even the kind fire chief who brought a hacksaw and laughed saying "Which do you want me to cut? The railings or his ears". Hmm, very amusing. Eric called downstairs to his mother from his bedroom and was soon joined by she and Tess. Cassandra explained that a television had been left on by one of their neighbours, in a drunken stupor, and, being old and faulty had set light to the sitting room. Eric pushed up the window for a better view and was disappointed that he could not see any flames dancing about, though plenty of smoke was puffing away, which alarmed the firefighters more as their hoses would not yet reach from their stuck engine.

Eric enquired about the safety of Mr and Mrs Luton, a funny couple he thought. Mr Luton, a large, rotund, red-faced man, always wearing a caracul hat (no matter what the weather) could often be seen pedalling his penny farthing, with great gusto, looking the worse for wear and on Sundays would return, from somewhere, with a car full of children in his convertible Rolls Royce Phantom.

Apparently, no harm had befallen to any party, much to the disappointment of Eric, not that he wanted anyone hurt, it just would have sounded more...entertaining. Unfortunately, the first love of his life, a young girl down the end of their street (who, with her sister, would attend a series of "secret" midnight feasts with himself and Tess) would one day soon sadly die in a house fire, leaving a large gap in his life and his first introduction with real loss.

But for now, the smoke carried on billowing as did the excitement of Eric and the fireman, as the truck kept going backwards and forwards, slowly edging its way around the corner. Eric hadn't seen this much commotion since a time near the Tower of London, except for the Dalek (and the man who threw a case of money in the air), when, walking with his Dad, stopped to witness a crowd enjoying the stunts of an escapologist.

He had managed to escape from handcuffs and had done a spectacular dive from a ladder into a paddling pool (some years later, re-enacted by Eric, knocking his front teeth out). Now was his Grand Finale. Straitjacketed, chained and tied to a rope, was hoisted, upside down to wriggle like a worm on a hook. Not satisfied with this foot of expertise, fire was added to the rope and the countdown was set. Lots of "OOHs" and "He'll never do it" was heard…and, they were right.

Shouts started coming from the upside-down man "I can't undo the lock, Steve, I can't undo the lock"! People were running everywhere.

"Now, this is getting interesting" thought Eric, hopping up and down, trying to make sure he didn't miss anything, yet at the same time getting pulled in with the excitement. The burning rope was lowered in time, the flames dowsed and The Great Escapo freed, it was all a bit of a disappointment thought Eric.

RETURN

Robert returned to London after six weeks convalescing back in South Africa, trying to come to terms with his life and experiences after his breakdown and shock treatment and was greeted with welcome arms back into The Company. He wished he could have said the same about home. His brother was as cruel and brash as always, fervently machoistic, domineering with unflinching superiority and a general buffoon. His mother on the other hand was as lovely as she was good. Patience, understanding, sympathy and beauty fell easily off her shoulders, he could understand why his father had married her. The farm was in good order, though the stables had been torn down and replaced with a large open garage, his Dads old motorbike covered with a dusty tarp at the back, and new trees had been planted where some of the older ones had been chopped. His mind was taken back when out working with Timo and Julian, a couple of land servants with a group of others, out at a part of forest that needed some scrub and timber clearing. When chopping and felling, you had to have your wits about you and always call out warning to avoid harm. A young inexperienced local was taking a break, eating from a cloth bundle his mother had prepared for him of dried mealie pap, while sitting on the root end of a downed tree. A call went out and he turned to see a tree falling in his direction, but would clearly miss, so returned to eating, not realising his predicament. The two trees, fallen and falling, made contact with each other and projectiled him into the air with devastating circumstances, falling himself, hard and broken, the vision staying with Robert for a lifetime.

He had stayed at the farm for most of his time, revisiting favoured landmarks and hideaways, but found nothing except for the knowing that these places were used as escapes and not attached to happy memories. On one hand he loved his home and country that bore him into life, the vast open spaces where early man would possibly have marvelled at the beauty and abundance on offer, yet if offered him no solace, no escape and no promises for the future, he had to find his own path. So, with weight in heart, he decided to leave and resume as soon as able, as not to miss the early worm.

The Company were in full swing of a run, but rehearsals were also taking place for a matinee production of Maria Marten (Murder in the Red

Barn and the lead had not yet been allocated, so a possible opening for Robert), a melodrama, an unusual choice for this group but a crowd pleaser nonetheless. Robert walked quietly to the wings of the evenings show, receiving hugs, kisses and pats on the back by passing cast and crew, and saw Cassie on stage. She turned, on cue and unflinching, contact was made and she smiled at him, whether it fitted the moment or not, neither cared, but the connection was remade.

The performance ended and bows given and Cassie fell straight into Roberts arms.

"Oh Darling" she said, resting her head against his chest "I've been so worried about you. Have you missed me"?

Robert kissed the top of her head "Of course I've missed you darling, you're all I've thought about".

"Oh, my Darling, do you forgive me? I do love you so". She continued.

"There's nothing to forgive" he said feeling slightly confused, like he had forgotten something inside, possibly important, though couldn't be otherwise he would remember "I love you too".

They embraced and kissed and received more slaps on backs.

Make-up and costumes needed removing and

congratulations and suggestions given, so Robert waited by the Stagedoor for the ensemble to depart, thinking “This time, this time. This time I’ll make it right”.

He turned to hear the voices coming closer, the first wave, normally the ones who hadn’t been on stage last or the ones hurrying off, furthest to go, or the ones, like Cassie, rushing to see her beau.

He stood upright as she came into view and noticed she seemed hesitant or not so confident. She took his arm, as she had so many times before and exited under the old light, it still watching yet not being able to tell. Robert went to lead the way to the little passageway out to the front and Cassie pulled at his arm.

“Let’s go a different way tonight” she said softly “I haven’t seen you for so long, I do want to catch up”. She said “There’s a new café round the corner that will be open. We could go there”.

Robert faltered slightly, but smiled and kissed her once more and they turned and walked into the darkness of the night, leaving Tommy out front, waiting in his car.

EASTER AT ROOKS END

Tess and Eric (Dicky being otherwise engaged) were excited as always to be visiting Rooks End, especially now that it was Easter and the promise of an Egg Hunt around the gardens. Pulling into the drive way, they looked out of the car windows searching the hedgerows and bushes to see if any eggs had already been concealed. Alas, none.

Pulling to the usual handbrake stop, Tess and Eric dashed off with permission to their first port of call. Running through the house, shouting hellos, they headed upstairs to their favourite corridor and bumped into Great Aunt Jane coming down.

"Ooh, mind where you're going children. Where are you off to in such a hurry" she said, knowing full well.

Thwarted, disappointed and not wanting to offend, in unison said "We were looking for you

Aunt Jane"

"Well, come along downstairs and we'll see if we can find anything in the kitchen". That worked.

In a full about turn, the little feet pounded down the stairs and hurried through the door and sat in their trained positions, at the breakfast bar, like good puppies they were, awaiting treats.

Moments passed slowly, dishearteningly and droolingly as they heard Great Aunt Jane saying hellos to Cassandra and Robert, how was the drive, how was Dicky, how was work, blah, blah, blah. They looked at each other and decided action was called for, so slid of their seats and sidled into the corridor to chance their luck.

"Oh, sorry children" said Aunt Jane smiling "I forgot all about you, lets go and get you a biscuit each".

A biscuit! They had hoped for more, but supposed a homemade biscuit might mean two...or three. Tess couldn't help but lick her lips.

"Don't worry about biscuits Jane" interjected Cassandra "They won't eat their supper if they fill up on biscuits".

"So"? thought the two, now desperate tummies.

Being steered away from the house (and away from their prizes) and led back to the car, they were handed their bags and told to take them in.

Begrudgingly doing as they were told, received

an update.

“You’re sleeping upstairs” stopped them in their tracks. That meant the attic. They turned, enquiringly silent. “Tristan and Blanche are staying tonight as well” ended the sentence.

“Yuck, not nasty...” (freckled, permanently runny-nosed, spoilt little brat) “...Tristan and smelly...” (oh, so smelly, whiny...) “Blanche” retorted Tess.

“Now Darling” replied Cassie “They’re not that bad”?

Tess turned and signalled to Eric to move “You don’t have to play with them” she thought, whilst Eric pondered “I might get on the roof again”.

The evening was a bit of a sleepy blur, that consisted of lots of food, people coming and going, lots of grown-up talk, a snotty Tristan and a not smelly Blanche who had ringlets and a white puffy dress, she seemed “quite nice” thought Eric. “No” said Tess later “Still yuck”!

Morning came soon enough, after the usual ghost stories, the night before, of Great Uncle Crispin that kept them awake, each taking guard, in case he came into their room with his candle and ate them alive. As per house rules, they had to wait in their rooms until the gong had struck three and then the stampede could commence.

A full breakfast was laid out this morning. Bacon, eggs, sausages, tomatoes ("yuck" again from Tess), Tea and, as it was Easter, Coffee (with a secret six sugars) was allowed for Eric, a special treat (he actually drank three unbeknownst to the adults, but much sniggering and icky snorting from Tristan).

Filled and content after fast breaking, children were directed to amuse themselves for a couple of hours before luncheon, which would be a light affair of salads and cold meats, which were always fantastically cooked by Great Aunt Jane (Ruby).

Orders given, the parents stayed talking, tidying up and drinking "Bit early isn't it Robert"? "No, no, not early" came the reply.

The four children ran outside to the front garden, another lovely day at Rooks End, the magic and warmth never stopped. They all had the same idea. "Let's see if we can find any eggs yet" they agreed upon. Dashing around the beds and trees, not going too far afield, a blank was drawn very quickly, knowing full well that they would have to wait until well after lunch.

"I know" said Tristan "let's go to your bedroom" he suggested.

"Why"? enquired Blanche.

"They've got the window onto the roof".

Erics heart momentarily stopped, changed gear, then went full speed ahead.

"You know about the roof" he swallowed lightly looking at Tristan.

"Yeah, c'mon" he said dashing off.

The eight legs hurried into the house and as quiet as a spider dashed up the stairs only to slow on the wooden flight up to the attic room where the window was beckoning.

"Ooh" said Eric, doing his little jump up and down "Can I go first"?

"No, said snot face "It was my idea, I'm going first". Pushing his way forward.

"Well, I don't want to go out" interjected Blanche as Tristan opened the window and started clambering out. Still doing his hopping, Eric turned to ask Tess if she wanted to go before him and that he might have to have a wee out there, all this hopping. But Tess was nowhere to be seen. "Odd" he thought and went to the bedroom door to peer round to see if she was on the small landing. Instead, he saw his mother coming up the stairs. Mouth open, Eric stood there, defeated again. "No Egg hunt for you, young man" came the sentence as she walked past to collar Tristan, alerted by his sister, desperately trying to scramble back in through the window.

Tristan was sent home and Eric had to sit still

for the rest of the day, even while Smelly Blanche and Tess hunted for the not very well-hidden eggs. “Hmph” he thought “I can see them from here”.

His sister had collected the most, “because of her betrayal” thought the gloomy Eric, head resting on one hand, feet swinging on the garden bench. She came over and sat by him and smiled.

“Ten tonne Tessie, more like” he grumbled, possibly aiding the start to her anorexia.

HENRY

Henry sat on the back of the sofa, his favourite sitting position, which annoyed everyone immensely. It wasn't that it was a small sofa, far from it, at a squeeze, it could accommodate four adults, it was the fact that he would sit in the middle and on top of the cushion, making it very awkward for anyone else who knew him.

Henry was an aggressive, short-tempered toy poodle and he hated everyone.

The problem was thought to be that he had been nurtured by a matronly cat, who taught him the ropes, as best as she could, and made sure that everyone knew where they stood. Unfortunately, Henry didn't have a clue what she was talking about, so made it his mission to alienate one and all.

Hence the problem with the sofa. Even sitting at either end could be seen as an invasion of his territory, with low high-pitched snarling coming from those sharp little teeth.

One day, Eric had been invited to a party. Not a

friend's party, Eric didn't really have any friends. Tess did, Dicky did, but not Eric. He had made friends a couple of times, but they had not met with his mother's satisfaction, so had been readily dismissed with "Nasty child"! (them, not him…I think).

Dickies friends were the favourite, Tess's were just girls (barely tolerated), and Dicky, his mates and Tess used to go to Saturday Morning Cinema, by bus, on a regular basis, which sounded so mysterious and fun, "and no adults" he thought. Eric was very envious. Sure, his favourite cartoon, "The Impossibles" was on T.V on Saturday mornings and he would be reluctant to miss it,, but the sound of the cinema…well, excitement overload. Every week he tried to go and every week rejected.

"I don't want HIM to come" said his brother to his mother.

"He'll get in the way. He's so annoying".

Eric wasn't quite sure what made him so annoying, his brother never had liked him, even when rough'n'tumbling Dicky would get short tempered, but he was determined to keep trying. "Wear them down," said the quiet voice.

Eventually, it worked. The group pilled on the bus, pennies rattling in pockets, with Dicky, Richard and Graham taking the upstairs and Tess and Suzy, with Eric in tow, downstairs…he wasn't a "big boy". As usual Eric spent his time looking out of the window, watching the busy world go by, all the different vehicles, buildings, trees and people you see in one of the planets largest cities, centuries old with highlights of the modern touch. He especially liked to see the old alley ways or unusual feature, tucked between, or on, unassuming buildings, but offering a glimpse of life gone by, as the pedestrians walked past, oblivious, of their ancestors.

Tess and Suzy rang the bell for the bus to stop and they all bundled off into the crowd of expectant, noisy children all waiting for the doors to open. Eric had never seen so many bodies in one place before and was quite excited already. A stern looking man came out of the cinema at the top of the steps and before he could finish his first sentence was stormed by the throng of pushing and shoving and shouts of joy. Tickets paid, the pushing and shoving continued to their seats. They had lost sight of Dicky and Co., no doubt somewhere amongst the full cinema of noise and activity, so many excited and ill-behaved screams and shouts. A momentary hush descended, as did the lights, but resumed to fever pitch as the organist arose, playing his wurly music, from out of the stage and a hail of popcorn and sweets hurled through the air, directed at the poor unsuspecting man. He tried to turn and shout condemnation, but was drowned out by the ridicule and confectionary, so retreated below, never to return again. Years later, Eric would often lie on his bed, late at night and listen to "The Organist Entertains", often feeling remorse but enjoying where the sounds would take him. After the man descended, they were treated to an array of serial films, Flash Gordon and Champion, the Wonder Horse, a couple of cartoons, a news reel and a main feature about some children finding a Dragon egg and hatching it. Never once did the volume and food throwing abate, but Eric was focused on what unfolded before his eyes, escaping into his own world of safety and daydreaming and wondering what it would be like to have friends.

The party, as always needed a present, so magically, one appeared that needed to be wrapped. Cassandra and her youngest son sat on the unmade double bed, scissors, tape and paper at the ready but no gift in sight.

"It must be under the blanket," said Cassandra.

Eric slid his small hand under the bulging blanket, eager to see what had been bought, only to find a warm lump of fur that proceeded to clamp its sharp teeth onto the inquisitive hand.

By the time the hand had been cleaned and dressed, tears wiped and present wrapped, dog admonished, the party would already have been in full swing, but Cassandra was adamant that he should still go. A miserable walk followed, still with the occasional sniff in tow, they arrived and coats were taken, with sympathies poured onto his mother for her terrifying ordeal, as Eric was given a glass of squash and told to go and join the others.

MONTE CARLO OR BUST

The day didn't come round soon enough. Tess had left home about a year before and Dicky had had the sense never to have returned, apart from a brief spell after returning from his tour of South Africa and his attempted foray into joining the forces in order to win the hand of a lady. Since Tess's departure, the onus fell more on Erics shoulders to be more persistently reliable (not that Tess had performed many duties or chores herself) without fiscal recompense (food and lodgings were considered payment enough), forcing him in the end, to seek out a full-time job as an apprentice in a local builder's firm.

The work wasn't the problem. He enjoyed the outdoor life and found manual labour instantly satisfying and enjoyed the challenge of learning. No, the problem lay with his parents, as with any teenager.

His father had become dourer and easily tempered, working longer, unfruitful hours with little reward with a wife who, with possible good intentions, hampered progress or was a drain on valuable resources. And that was his main drive to leave. He realised that he no longer needed to put up with the, what he considered at the time, erratic and crazy behaviour of his Mother, and nor did he want to.

The deciding factor came a few months before. He had already declared his intentions of departure, having seen his Mother attempt to throw stones at horses in a field, or find her hiding one day, preparing to run away, with a fanciful idea of making some money to send back to the family. One morning, sitting at the breakfast table, innocently eating his bowl of cornflakes, his mother strode in, that look in her eyes that he hadn't seen for years, but not forgotten.

"How dare you read such disgusting filth" she shouted at him, picking up the box of cereal and striking him over the head with it, cornflakes exploding everywhere. Confused, a switch flicked inside.

"I don't have to put up with this anymore" the small voice said inside and he immediately stood up and pushed Cassandra.

She stumbled back, shock in her eyes, incredulous at the response. At the same time, Robert arose and punched Eric full in the face.

"Don't ever do that to your mother again" was shouted.

Mother fled sobbing to go and have a lie down.

" How could anyone be so horrible to me" Eric heard as she went.

He no longer cared, enough was enough, though was still confused at what she had been going on about. It was then that he spied a book he had been reading, a standard yet very popular, semi-fictitious, risible, American crime novel about the New York Police Department and had passed it on to his father. Pages had been torn out, a mild yet humourous sex scene and another concerning a donkey.

Erics face throbbed, but he really didn't care. The years of abuse had piled up and he wasn't going to take it anymore, though not realising that nature abhors a vacuum, the void left by his mother was going to be filled by years of damaging hedonistic behaviour.

And so, his determination to flee the nest manifested.

His bags were packed into the car.

Robert was going to drive up, with Cassie, not wanting to be left behind (more likely wanting to keep an untrusting eye on Robert) to lead the way and carry the luggage, as Eric rode his motorbike on the longest journey he had yet to make.

Familiar lanes and roads soon disappeared with the arrival of the rain, and as the roads became busier and wider, Robert's speed increased also.

Eric, though a competent rider, had no experience or desire, to ride at such excessive speeds as his father (often above 80 miles per hour) in the rain, especially as he only had two wheels compared to the dry, warm comfort of four, in addition to not knowing which directions to be taking, relying of his fathers' bluster of "you'll be alright, just follow me".

Eric wasn't "alright". Far from it. The rain had been insistent and wintry cold and traffic as steady as his Dads foot on the pedal. A window ("if only he had one" he thought) arose. Stonehenge came into view, marking a rough half way point of his sodden journey and his parents' car slowed to allow Cassandra a view of one of her favourite landmarks. Old churches, brass rubbing, ley lines, dramatic skies, they all featured heavily on her list. Eric flashed his lights at his family and signalled to pull over, indicator flashing and arm gesticulating, all to no avail. The rain was as hard as ever, as was his resolve. Eric opened his accelerator and pulled up alongside the f"*|^£$g ...sightseers, shaking his fist with a tirade of expletives.

Fortunately, and coincidently, a small roadside

café loomed and was manoeuvred onto, with Eric still doing his Captain Haddock impersonation as he got off his bike, striding towards his bemused looking parents.

It took about an hour's rest to go from drenched to damp (a wonderful difference) and calm down. Thankfully the rain eased to a fine drizzle and they resumed their uneventful journey.

Eventually, the first address of his new life was reached. A picturesque two-bedroom house nestled quietly (for now) in a pleasant back road of student town.

HOPE HOUSE

Weeks of worry and searching had proved fruitless. Work for a man in his late 40s, with plenty of valid experience in sales and marketing, though no formal qualifications, was far and few between, especially when coupled with pride.

The weeks turned into desperate months, causing a shoe string existence and pulling Eric from public school life (much to his elation). It happily, or unhappily, coincided with a call from the college, asking his parents to attend a meeting due to some undesirable behaviour. The conference was held with both parents, Eric and House Master, who laid out the seriousness of events which had involved streaking after lights out and Eric being witnessed on the House lawn by the Headmasters wife. The story omitted the circumstances of clothes being tied together to form an escape rope, thrown out of the window and the victim being towel whipped while trying to retrieve them. House "pranks" were common. Ranging from Apple Pie beds, where the top sheet is removed and the bottom sheet folded in half to represent a fully made bed, to wet flour in pyjamas, not fun to be made to sleep in. All the while the Housemaster was extolling healthy virtues and unwanted miscreants, Erics mind wandered to an event a couple of weeks earlier and how three fellow pupils had raided the secure arsenal, housed behind the Captains lodgings, and borrowed some rifles, ammunition, smoke grenades and flash bangs. They proceeded to terrorise the local village in the middle of the night and caused much commotion (and hilarity to the admiring, innocent understudies) until eventually being caught, absconded, then caught again by the local constabulary. Only one was expelled, the other two told off (with no parents having to attend "a stupid meeting" thought Eric) as their parents were too wealthy to attend.

Meeting over and "drivel" talked, Erics parents took him for a drive and "a word". The word was:

"Eric, if you don't behave, they'll kick you out of College. Then, when we move, you'll have to live with us in the countryside. And you don't want that, do you"? was delivered intermittently by both parents.

"What"? said Eric "We're moving"?

"Yes" Cassie said.

"We're buying a small place in the country, a few

cows, chickens…" said Robert.

"Oh Great" came the unexpected, enthusiastic reply "when are we moving".

"Don't you want to stay at College" his mother nervously asked looking at Robert.

"What"? came a shocked exclamation "No, thank you..." emphatically came "farming sounds great". He said sitting back in his seat smiling, free at last.

Things began to move very quickly from his point. For Eric it was to be a new lease of life, opening up a whole world of possibilities, but for Tess, it would be leaving all her beloved friends behind to an existence she did not want or care for.

The contract completion was being held up by the sale of their house in London and Great Aunt Janes family solicitors, who were helping in part, with Cassandras "one day" inheritance, raising some funds now, sooner than later.

The new school term was looming and it was decided to send Tess and Eric ahead, in order to get settled in with their new education and get to know the pupils and the area.

They were introduced to the large Hope family, a friendly 5 boy family who sometimes took in waifs and strays and directed them on a new course of life, with them popping in, out of the blue, years after being given a chance in life to succeed. It was a strange period for both Tess and Eric, happiness and communal efforts not marred with suffocating seclusion was a refreshing change, as was the ability to cycle around tall hedged lanes, smelling wild garlic and cow muck instead of car fumes, and nothing more dangerous than a slow-moving tractor chugging along with a wurzel at the wheel or a wellie-wanging competition.

MY FUNNY VALENTINE

Tommy was devastated. He sat in the quiet of the club, last man out, with a bottle of scotch in front of him, half drunk and an ashtray fit to burst. Cassie had stood him up again, he couldn't believe what a putz he had been. She flitted between men, depending on what they offered, tiring of commitment, seeking the thrill of the chase and the attention it brought. A month ago, he had gone to meet her outside the theatre, only to wait forever and find she had walked off with that Robert. It stung. He took another swallow, that stung too.

She'd come back, mind. Came running back like she always did. "Oh Tommy, I missed you" she said, "how could I be so foolish" she said. Again, another hefty glug.

He leant back in his chair and wiped the hair out of his face and reached for a packet. He pulled out a stick and put it in his mouth and struck a match. The end fizzed as he drew in a smoky breath and exhaled, blowing out the match at the same time.

She only stayed a couple of days before disappearing again, only to reappear at that same weekend. "Why was he such a mug" he thought, tipping the bottle to refill his glass. He took another drag of the cigarette and blew out its blue smoke hanging low over the table.

Ron and Jay had told him things would end up bad. He just hadn't wanted to believe them, he had faith in the old girl. "What a mug"! another slug easily gulped down his throat.

And now this evening. Well, this evening was a beaut. One of The Girls was in, gossiping away like they do, and word gets out. Only it's a word that's not his. Pregnant they say. Cassies only gone and got herself pregnant with Robbo's baby. Two hefty swigs from the glass followed by an "ahh" and another puff. Glass empty, Tommy reached for the bottle for a refill only to find another bottle was called for. He stood and wobbled slightly and staggered for the bar, more difficult than he thought. Rather than going round, he leant over and just managed to fumble a bottle off the shelf and told a chair to get out of his way as it threw itself into his path on the journey back to his table. He fell into his seat and reached for his smoke only to find it had disappeared, so lit another. He unscrewed the lid of the fresh bottle and chucked it across the room "won't be needing that" he said. The liquid sploshed over his glass wetting part of the table.

With glass now well topped up, Tommy drank heavily and refilled again. "I can't believe my Cassies gone and got herself pregnant" he said to the bottle that stood there ignoring him. "Why would she do that to me" he said again, but no response came. Another puff of the cigarette was followed by a hum of F, Dm7, Fm, G7 which made him laugh. F, Bm7-5, E7, Am, C7 which made him cry. The cigarette was almost out, it had had too much whisky, but it tasted okay. That reminded him, more whisty. "What was he going to do now"? he thought as he drank, "Cassie was my life" another slurp, "I wanted to marry her not him" refill again.

Silence fell like a heavy brick as he already knew what he was going to do. His Uncles World War 2 revolver sat also on the table. It was what it was for after all, thought Tommy, his hand reaching out to feel the cold metal. He picked up the gun in one hand and glass in the other, wet cigarette in mouth. For a moment he contemplated what a mess he must look. He put down his glass and gun, lit a fresh smoke, tidied his hair, shirt and tie. Put on his jacket, kissed his trumpet and had another large swallow of scotch. Another puff and gave out a laugh as he pulled the trigger goodbye.

TOM THE MILKMAN

The stables doors often had the top left open in the quiet cobbled mews, allowing the noises and smells of the city to come and go as they pleased, but bringing the scent of the ivy (growing up the front of the house) in along with what plants were blooming in the small flower boxes.

When Cassandra and Robert were first married, they rented a quarter of an unimportant mews house, a glorified, but rundown bedsit, the Belfast sink with dripping tap and haphazard gas cooker sat in a partitioned off corner by the window and the rest of the room had a small, Formica covered table (with two straight back wooden chairs), a china wash basin and jug and a small double bed. Each time one of the other tenants moved out, they were able to expand their living quarters with agreement of old Mr Coxton, the owner and landlord, a kindly chap, though tired of life. Eventually, as time passed on, the longterm tenants and proprietor became good friends and the house was sold to them on condition of him being allowed to stay in his humble abode until his time came to fly to pasture new.

Life grew quickly for the newly-weds. 9 months after their happy day their first son was born, two years later their daughter and another two years would pass until their final, though not last child.

Life, in the unassuming part of the city, was like living in a miniature town of its own. Everything you needed was within easy walking distance, shops, transport, doctors, carpenters, park, casino and brothel. In fact, the last two were actually opposite the front door of the small residence and someone had very kindly daubed, in big white letters, BROTHEL, on the side of the building, just to make sure you didn't miss it. By the time Eric was three it had been painted over, looking a bigger eye sore than ever, and a trailing plant was attempting, and failing to hide it. Clampdown came on criminal activities after a celebrity was found dead, in the back of a car, down a quiet alley way, too close to common folk, moving away from the East End where trouble and strife were more noticeable.

The Rag'n'Bone man was a regular visitor to their area. Hearing the shouting from a distance there would be a dash around the house to find either a sugar cube, mint, or apple to feed the cart horse as it came clopping along, pulling its cart, but appreciative of stopping to put its head over the stable door and snuffle at the offering from young hands.

There was also Tom the Milkman. A thin, tall, kindly man, ex-services, always well dressed in his uniform and blue and white striped apron, leather satchel at side, mimicking the angle of his cap, which was supported by his round spectacles.

He would lead his horse for a few years more, until it was sadly replaced by an electric three-wheeler milk float, full of rattling crates, loaded with the day's deliveries and empties of the 1960s housewife. The wooden slatted flooring, studded with brass tacks, the hum of the motor sang to the rubber tyres, who tirelessly carried the load and the solid bakerlite steering wheel all struck an encompassing picture to Erics eyes.

The children of the street would often dance around the delivery vehicle, sometimes being given short rides and sometimes allowed to help steer. It was one such day that this would end. The big round pedal on the floor was a stop/start affair. No acceleration or braking, it was either going or not and Eric had been watching carefully for some time, growing in confidence and ability. After considerable nagging, Tom relented and let Eric take control of the whole cart. All went smoothly enough to start, sitting next to Tom, being allowed to press the pedal and steer, chasing Dick Dastardly and Mutley, catching the pigeon, "look out Cavey", Zoiks!

There wasn't too much damage to the car.

SUMMER AT ROOKS END

Pulling into Rooks End already felt different, change had occurred and not fully understood or explained, but to Tess and Eric part of the heart had disappeared. The car pulled up with its usual crunch on the gravel and everyone got out of the vehicle and stretched away the journey and inhaled another beautiful day. It was always sunny at Rooks End.

The heavy-hearted children carried the bags into the house, calling out hellos to Aunt Jane and made their way past The Cavalier, nod, past the wooden cabinet of curios and dolls house accessories and put their bags in the large middle bedroom. The big windows and curtains giving a cruel reminder. Before heading back down to the kitchen, they looked at each other in mutual agreement and headed toward the narrow twisty corridor which led down to the back of the house and the magic chamber of Ruby's. Walking along to the rickety stairs, their hands trailed the walls and they stopped at the end to look out of the tiny window that peered out onto the orchard.

Tess asked "Are you coming"?

"No, what's the point" replied the gloomy Eric, sighing.

Tess went to the door and turned the knob, which didn't open the door, it was locked, so came back up.

"It's locked" she said.

"Hmm" said Eric, turning and heading back into the main house, "perhaps there might be a biscuit somewhere" he thought to himself as if in a dream.

The house felt emptier, as they entered the kitchen, where drinks, soft and not so, were being consumed and a plate of, not home cooked, biscuits sat waiting.

"Now children" directed Great Aunt Jane "I've got a surprise coming this afternoon".

Interests perked, Tess and Eric were brought out of their malaise.

"Ooh" said Tess "what is it"?

"Well, if I told you, it wouldn't be a surprise any longer, would it dear".

Eric stood listening, mind tumbling, a surprise, hmmm.

The afternoon rolled on into early evening and

nothing transpired, despite all the pestering.

"You'll just have to wait until tomorrow, won't you dear" Great Aunt Jane said to the now tired children. Disappointed, they dragged themselves to bed, only to be reminded by the open curtains, that there would be no morning ceremony of curtains being thrown open by Ruby, to awake them with the words "Lovely morning, breakfasts waiting" now that she had left after all these years and they never got to say goodbye. It just wouldn't be the same.

Morning came and greeted everyone with a fresh "Hidey Ho"! the children stretching awake in the large open room with the Victoriana sink in the corner. After a cursory splash, they trotted downstairs to be greeted by the three adults, smiling, the smell of bacon and a glint of sun on metal through the large bay window. Saying their mornings and ignoring food, they stepped toward the glass to get a better glimpse. Outside, parked next to the car, gleaming silver and chrome, was a homemade go-kart, complete with crash helmet.

Great Aunt Jane explained that her next-door neighbour had built a couple and knowing she was to have visitors, suggested she could borrow it to have some fun with. Eric thought "Fun" would definitely be a good word to use.

Breakfast was very quickly consumed and

with eagerness and enthusiasm proving good incentives, beds were made and rooms were tidied (though teeth weren't brushed).

By the time Tess and Eric appeared outside, they had already heard and smelt the engine being primed and warmed up by Robert, who was a little disappointed that he would not fit, but was already making up for it with a glass of whisky in hand.

Tess, being eldest, was to go first, with a few steady laps around the circular gravel drive outside the front, while being watched by father and son. Around and round she went, slow and steady, with Eric watching, contemplating the toilet. Robert and Dicky had been to Brands Hatch and Silverstone on numerous occasions (once taking Eric) and had also been to see the James Garner movie Grand Prix, which had, according to Eric "...some very exciting bits, but I don't understand why it's called Grand Pricks".

Tess pulled up smiling and got out of the Kart, engine still running and removed and passed the helmet to Eric. Sitting in the Kart, Robert explained the controls and directions to the ever-impatient child, who was already envisioning the starting grid, at pole position, awaiting the chequered flag to fall.

As soon as he heard the word "Okay"? he was gone. Tearing around the corner, foot almost pressed flat on the accelerator, gravel flying, he saw his opening. Rather than going around the roundabout, like he was supposed to, the straight part of the drive looked more preferable. Off he shot, in the lead, he'll be bound to get the cup, no overtakers. It was at this point, realisation that the track ended and the road was about to start to hit home. "Brakes" he thought "What did Dad say about brakes"?

Too late to worry and hearing plenty of shouting behind him, he decided to turn into the long grass and head towards the pavilion. Not being able to remember where the brakes were, he lifted his foot (still happily pressed) off the accelerator and glided to a bumpy halt. "Gosh, that was fun after all" he thought.

...AND AWAY

The years of self-medicating had at last caught up with her. Depending which decade, there had been prescribed antidepressants, tranquilisers, statins, beta-blockers, pain killers, antibiotics, pills for the heart, liver, kidneys, colon and a profusion of ointments and powders, the list was as long as the varying ailments. As her years on the planet progressed, so did the number of illnesses she suffered and with, each came a different treatment, with surplus medications being squirreled away to some hidey-hole, the same treatment met out to unwanted bills or communications.

On visits, one could turn over a sofa cushion and find a final notice or a spare tablet, years out of date, yet kept for special occasions, depending when or where you were in the house at the time.

Despite what was occurring in her life at any time, you could always be sure to find a healthy selection of ProPlus in the cupboards and even towards the end, a venture into energy drinks.

At one time, when moving to their poor choice

of bungalow, the garage-cum-scrapheap had to be sorted and cleared. Years of official letters (denied at the time), Christmas presents (not sent or given), canned food (thought to have been disposed of from their last move) and vast collections of expensive cosmetics (some trialled, others untouched) were all found, carefully hidden and forgotten.

But now, she lay in the hospital bed, one mix of pills too many had taken its toll on her liver, though the blame was being squarely directed to the G.P for misdiagnosis and incorrect remedy.

The three children, now, most grandparents themselves, stood around as their father sat holding Cassandra's hand, convinced that all she needed was a good holiday to get over this current malaise.

The nurse came in to check on the situation, since the intravenous had already been removed, it was only a matter of time. For once, for Eric, this time felt different. His parents had been taking it in turns over the last few years in hospital visits, each possibly more serious than the last, though each time coming back, weaker than the last, like a sculpture being chipped away at by its creator, or going down the stairs, each step progressively worse, never being able to attain its previous height again.

There had been plenty of hospital visits

for his mother in his youth, broken leg, thyroid operation, car crash, bumper car crash, the miscarriages and possible sectioning, but mortality wasn't visited until his father's drinking overtook his ability to work it off and an induced coma was called for. Last rites were administered, with the family present, though Eric felt this was presumptive but was rebuked for this train of thought.

He left the hospital, well into the night and started his long journey home. In the emptiness of the roads, he lit a small pre-rolled smoke and put the radio on. Time and road passed and he threw the spent roach out of the window, thinking about death and lines being etched in the sand being drawn by the pulsing sounds coming from the speakers. Sudden ethereal awareness punctured his thoughts. He had travelled some miles, and over twenty minutes had elapsed in a semi-hypnotic state, yet the radio was still playing the same track. Unheard of in '91 and disconcerting, almost panic set in. Thankfully, before sanity was lost, if it had ever existed, John Peels reassuring voice informed Eric "Well listeners, that was The Orb, and the longest track I've ever played on the radio...". Normality resumed and his father didn't die that time.

Their mother was lapsing in and out of sleep, waking to tell her spectators of visits from long gone friends and how she felt a lot better about dying now, knowing that they were waiting for her.

Robert was somewhat alarmed, saying "You're not dying darling, you just need a good holiday" looking at his children for confirmation.

Dicky was the first to depart, taking the father home, who was in need of a drink and cigarette, knowing that left to his own devices, would head for the nearest ward toilet and light up accordingly, causing alarms to wail and nurses and orderlies frantically dashing around, trying to locate the outbreak (as he had done so before, unfortunately, not once). Dicky left instructions to be notified, no matter what the time, of imminence and pushed Robert quickly out of the ward in his wheelchair before temptation got too much.

Tess, in tears and distraught (and still slightly drunk from breakfast), chatted briefly with Eric when Cassandra came too again.

"Oh bother" she said "I'm still here". Which made Eric burst out a laugh. He recalled two of his mother's favourite comedy quotes and ongoing joke that he had shared when younger. "Funny he never married" by Marty Feldman and "I'm getting better", a great piece in The Holy Grail (I'll let you discover them).

She explained that she visited them all again and

she must hurry up, and in mid-sentence saw Tess crying. Her hand reached out and comforted her daughter, reassuring her and thanking her for all her years of support, but for Eric, there was no apology for the untold abuse and violence and she died in the early hours of the morning, no family by her side. Different reasons were for the lack of tears shed by Eric, not malice or resentment, but those attributes did disappear from his being once his mother had died.

YORICK

Robert had returned from working in Cambridge after a number of weeks, on a short-lived production, and as usual, fallen easily back into city life and The Company.

Cassie and friends had written plenty of times, keeping him up to speed with the latest gossip and found that, at times, stories differed. It was great to see everyone again, a pleasure to feel recognised and accepted, though was starting to tire of possible unwanted attention.

Perhaps too much water had gone under the bridge, too many comings and goings or too many variations of the truth being spun, he felt that maybe, maybe, it was time to cool things off and perhaps, change direction. He had certainly found a sense of freedom since being away, had found it quite liberating and realising a new self-confidence.

Despite his lack of trying and his disinterest, Cassandra pestered him more and more for recognition and attention, holding onto his arm at any given moment and making sure an available seat was always by her side.

On a couple of occasions, he relented, but each time, sooner or later, found her back in Tommy's arms, which no longer left him feeling a fool.

One evening, he spurned her advances totally and for the first time, witnessed the venom rise from pits unseen. Vitreous and as black as pitch, spat from the depths and flung in all directions, unleashing fury untold from hidden nadirs. Shocked and unable or un-wanting to tackle such a creature, left to protect each other from harm or further onslaught, only to be greeted the following morning by beauty and serenity as if the demon had been chained and forgotten.

A short time later, at his small flat, life would change for good (or bad). Cassandra knocked at his door one evening and immediately informed Robert that she was expectant and the child would be his. Feeling incredulous, he took the news lightly and inferred possible other candidates or scenarios and reflected the allusions that were being directed towards him as fanciful and untrue, quoting "to thine ownself be true". The demon was released again, but Robert let the harpy fly its course and when exhausted, calmy suggested that "Perhaps we shouldn't see each other anymore"? and escorted her out.

Two nights of silence came, yet on the third,

returning from his new part-time job, he found Cassandra and her Mother waiting for him outside his rooms, waiting to be invited in and waiting for justice.

“Well Robert, what do you intend to do now you’ve got our daughter...pregnant”? the word being forced out with discomfort.

“If I knew it was mine, I suppose we would have to get married” he said out loud, half thinking to himself, half not realising that these were the words waiting to be heard.

“Well, good then” carried on Cassandra’s mother “I’m glad to hear that you’re going to do what is right”.

“Now I never...” Robert replied, getting cut off as both ladies turned and walked away down the stairs.

For the next few evenings, each time he returned to his flat, he found Cassandra with her Mother, waiting for him to return, her mother doing the talking and Cassie silently being submissive, slowly eroding his resolve and convincing him to “Do what is right” and for him to accept “What he has done”.

Eventually it worked. News was heralded to one and all, the bells rang out in the land for each soul to hear of the forthcoming ceremony. Happiness was to be shared from John’O Groats to RooksEnd for the ecstatic couple.

It was to be a brief engagement, a mere 2 months, as the young couple were eager to be betrothed and life was but a fleeting blink in the eye of the universe (and no parents would want their bride "showing" under the white of the gown).

They were married at the beginning of the new year, symbolising new starts and new beginnings, their son would be born in October.

DICKY DOES

Going through the motions and jumping the hurdles was important for Dicky. Life was no joke, as he had experienced through the violence of his father growing up, and in order to succeed he needed to take things seriously and professionally to ascend the ladder. Unbeknownst to him, the ladder didn't really exist and if it did, there were plenty of rungs missing to stop people climbing too high, after all, those at the top didn't want to be toppled from their comfortable position. So, the endless game of cat and mouse continued, with bored "executive" onlookers chasing their own dreams, seeking out distractions or power whilst the minions strode to what they believed in.

Dicky had always been a serious and studious child. Tess tried to focus on being a girl, though looking at life from two steps away, unable to run but skip, not really having a reliable role model to copy. As for Eric, he was the joker in the pack.

As the children grew, Robert would issue ideas:

"Why don't you three form a band".

Admittedly, Dicky had learnt guitar and flute, Tess guitar and piano and Eric...well, he tried piano, but found the drums more to his taste though the noise did interrupt his mother's "rests".

Then there were suggestions like:

"I think you'll make a fine writer one day" to Dicky (despite no encouragement or direction, 50 years later did).

To Tess "I'm surprised you never became a Tennis Player" which astounded all as she had ever, barely, lifted a racquet in her life.

And to Eric "I thought you'd become a Racing Driver" confused everyone. Instead, Dicky had turned to the Music Industry, diligently working in many areas, sound libraries, mixing and editing, publications and most recently, management.

It was this last foray that laid the path for Eric to springboard away from home (becoming a roadie and engineer for one of his bands) and into a place he could call his own, not in a way he expected, but might have seemed obvious to an outside spectator.

Eric was settling in to his new life, in the compact yet attractive two-bedroom house. The floor was comfortable enough, as the small bedroom only had room for a single, and that was mostly occupied by Tess (though, when spending time away, allowed Eric the comfort of a mattress), the larger room was being rented by John, a friend of both the owner and old school chums of Dicky's. Tess had kindly persuaded in her boss of a local Bar/Restaurant/ Bistro to give her brother a go and they worked well together, with a free hand all aspects of the Bistro, including the music. This delighted Eric considerably. Mix tape after mix tape was provided, even if the record had stuck and the bistro was packed every lunch time, from opening to close, with a vibrant mix of office staff and public, enjoying the sounds and food offered fresh each day.

It was here that a regular group, all of similar age, attracted his attention one day. Bringing a plate up to the bar, Eric was verbally pulled to the side and shown a slug in their salad. Immediately and automatically, Eric unfortunately, burst out laughing but quickly extinguished it, it had reminded him of his mother's antics when young, but quickly and honestly apologised and rectified the situation with recompense for the whole party. They were a pleasant group and would one day become his brothers he never had and loves of his youth, but for now, they were looking for a drummer for their newly formed band.

And so, his life was filled. 9 to 3 was spent cooking, baking, slug bashing and serving and evenings was juggled around either band rehearsals or being taken off to set up for gigs, and such like.

It is the "such like" that started to take a hold of Eric, for a number of years. Distorting and warping reality, almost ending it on a few occasions, but almost certainly always being a learning curve.

FIRST DAYS

Life had changed dramatically for Eric. His past had been shaken off and puberty had attacked his body with gusto, empowering him with super strength and invulnerability, at the same time as taking him from inner-city habitation and the confines of male dominated public school, to open fields and pastures new of the rural countryside and mixed comprehensive education.

The picturesque village of their new home fed his senses every day, so many new things to take in fuelled his natural curiosity as did the local pub that lay 100 metres from their front door.

The quaint pub, far older than its name implied, was fitted perfectly with dart board, bar billiards and both types of skittles, along with both types of farmers, either the cap wearing gentry or down to earth, who would be more accepting of a shove 'aypny challenge and pint of dry cider, though admittedly you rarely saw the cap wearers in the bar. It was most frequented by the people that Eric learnt to admire the most, the hard workers and day to day poachers, who would teach him how to fork hay and make ricks, lay hedges, milk cows, wring chicken's necks, shovel shit (properly, it is a skill) and most importantly, how to drink (especially at lunchtimes).

The house stood emptied of Mrs Harris's life, but now was a strewn with tea-chests and boxes, all waiting to be emptied and contents fitted into their new places. Dicky was in attendance for once, with an ulterior motive though, having rescued a dog from being drowned, had brought him to the farm with the intention of giving it a new life, though not governed by him.

The two, family cats, that had been caged and driven down carefully, were suitably disorientated and were let go in the upstairs area so as not to be able to flee as activity progressed with the unpacking.

Cassandra, having her afternoon lie down suddenly stirred, concerned about the two moggies and needing to check on their welfare. Searching around the bedrooms she found no sign and called her sons to the rescue.

Dicky took the bedrooms, rechecking under beds and in wardrobes (just in case), whilst Eric went up the creaky and rotting stairs to the attic, where at night, what sounded like a body being dragged across the floor would be heard, but fancifully dismissed as rats.

Carefully walking across the beams of the floorless floor, in the dark and misty gloom he thought he saw a movement in the far corner. Instinctively, Eric stepped in that direction, only to suddenly plummet through plasterboard, his feet and legs appearing right before an astonished Dicky. With inherited reflexes, he had caught a cross beam on the way down and stopped his descent, abruptly and almost fatally. His brother, laughing out of surprise, called.

"It's okay, you can let go. I've got you".

Sensing that all was not well, Eric replied "Yeah, don't think that's a good idea. I think you better come and pull me up" as he stared down at a long protruding nail that had skimmed his chest and wanting an excuse to plunge deeper.

It would be later that day that the Witches Bottle was found and removed from its decades or centuries long resting place, from that night on, noises would be heard and things would be seen until, some weeks later, the house would be blessed and peace would descend until they were to move again (but, that's for another time).

For now, everyone was getting used to their roles and finding their feet in village or school life. The shire people being friendly and welcoming, especially as the newcomers were adopting their ways and not trying to insist on the tried and tested communal life, unlike some who move to the country and complain of cockerels or the church clock striking at 5 in the morning to call out the workers, or buy a house near a runway and grumble and protest about planes. No, here the status quo would be kept and humbly added to, grateful for the new life and new loves.

THOMAS AND TUPPENCE

The small farmhouse stood in the middle of thirty acres, the highest field giving a glorious view down the southern valley while sitting under the perfect tree, its arms symmetrically proportioned and roots forming a lover's seat, admired by each person who saw it and even the cows, who like to use the base of the tree as a rubbing post.

Needing more acreage for the increasing herd, the decision had been made to move again, more rural than before, no village life here or pavements here, just a dirt track to walk on for ten minutes to reach any sign of tarmac and then a ten-minute drive to the local post office-cum-community store, nothing like keeping away temptations and focus more on mere existence.

The dilapidated milking shed, attached to the back of the house, had touch and go electrics, you touched a switch, then didn't dare go anywhere near it, particularly as a small stream ran by your feet, through the centre of the barn and whether you were wearing wellingtons or not, the idea of checking a shock near a cow* wasn't the idea of Friday night entertainment.

*electric fences are more effective on cows for one main reason. Cows have four legs rather than two. If you're still not sure what I mean, next time you're near an electric fence for cattle, touch it. "Ooh, hmm, not bad" you'll say. Now try it while on your hands and knees…yeah, big difference.

A lot of work was needed doing to improve the place. The rats had had time enough to overrun the hay barn, holes in the walls could easily be used as climbing footholds, and the range, in the tiny kitchen was hazardous enough to poison the residents within a week of being there, with the coke fumes permeating the whole house.

Ramshackle repairs were done, though more were needed and as Robert was no DIYer, had to rely on outside help, a bigger drain on resources on top of the high phone bills created by Cassandra trying to keep up with the latest with her ageing friends. Being now in their 50s, it wasn't the best time to be accelerating, especially with Cassandras back.

In her teens, Cassie had been a promising ballerina, performing for the future Queens Mother, and receiving accolades and recognition, widely regarding her as another Fonteyn until tragedy struck. During one tragic rehearsal, a trapdoor on stage had not been properly secured, causing her to fall and fracture her leg, hip and damage he lower back. Recovery was hampered by sitting in a curled position on a sofa, rather than legs straight, as her parents each vied for her attention, an only child getting all the things she wanted at the cost of her parents' marriage was a good starting point for decay and only fuelled he distaste for her mother.

On occasion, Cassies mother would come to stay, insisting on being driven and bringing her two feline friends Thomas and Tuppence, both of which had never set foot outside her London flat and lived mostly under her bed when staying, obviously terrified. A small bedroom by the downstairs bathroom was created, solely for her use, as the stairs to the bedrooms were steep and only had a rope rail to hang on to.

The routine of the farm rarely changed, nor can it, when the ladies need milking and feeding twice daily, morning and evening tide.

The girls were, mostly, a friendly bunch. Well looked after, loving eyes, good coats, pleasant manner and each as individual as they come. A large proportion of the herd were home bred, raised from cow to calf to cow, Annabel and Seven being the original two, had sired many a calf, thankfully mainly cows and Seven liked to sing to them all. At nights, after milking and being settled in their barn, fresh straw laid down for their beds and fresh hay put out for when wanted, the cows would settle, chewing their cud, snorting softly and getting ready for a night's rest, Seven would start her song. She would be the only one to make the rhythmic melody, soporific for any listener, possibly telling tales of days gone by or just reassuring the ear, that they were in good hands.

During one afternoon, between the milks, Robert was attending the land when a desperate Cassie appeared waving her arms for attention. He drove the tractor to her.

"What now" he muttered "Can't I get any work done".

Pulling up alongside her, Cassie was shouting.

"Wait until I turn the tractor off" he shouted short temperedly.

"Its Mum" she shouted "she's fallen down the stairs" in a fluster.

Robert jumped out of the cab and rushed into the house to find Cassies Mother lying at the foot of the stairs, unconscious.

"Have you called the ambulance"? he urgently asked.

"No, not yet, do you think I should"? replied his wife.

He looked at her incredulously “Straight away”.

Despite their location the ambulance arrived within 30 minutes and rushed the old lady to hospital, where, after x-rays, a broken leg and hip was diagnosed, only to die a short time later from “unforeseen complications” and pneumonia.

Questions lay unanswered and officially unasked. How did she fall, but most importantly, why was she upstairs, yet at all, on her own as stated by her daughter?

“I was in the kitchen and I heard a crash and found her lying there”.

Whatever the reasons, the truth will never be known. But Thomas and Tuppence became farm cats, preferring to live in the barn, roaming the land and excelling a reducing the rat population. Its never too late.

ROOFTOPS

The dreamy spires were a magnificent sight, much of the architecture reminded Eric of parts of his hometown and he was getting familiarised with the alleys and secluded courtyards dotted around the city.

Most of the pubs had individual characteristics of their own, each lending themselves to different styles, but predominantly catering for the student market. One pub in particular didn't favour the establishment, instead offering a safe (not really the appropriate word, considering) haven, where punks would accumulate, thanks to an excellent juke box, ability of underage drinking, the turning of the proverbial blind eye and being allowed to "smoke" in the back room. It would see its fair share of "busts", since "Operation Julie" had only recently taken place and it would only be a matter of time until it died, but being a student town of the elite, there was little impact on the other venues where the wealthy still floated the laws.

Many young "gentlemen" to be, maybe from

Harrow, Eton or Winchester, who already, prior to Uni. life, had jobs and careers lined up for them, would be dallying with substances and nuances, buying, using and selling as common knowledge. This is what made people dislike them more, whereas, at the time, the lesser folk would be targeted as easier to prosecute.

The mix of lesser people was immense. From Skins to Bikers, Soul Boys to Rasta, Townie to Punk, they were all there and more. And into this cauldron, Eric found himself fully immersed, a whole new chapter and set of experiences to be sampled and sample he would, but that was still to come. For now, work was unfolding its opportunities, and during a break from prep., coffee was to be had with the boss on the rooftop overlooking the High Street.

The roof was large and flat, easily able to hold a kick around, though probably ill advised. Looking down over the pedestrians, going about their daily routines was a comforting and enjoyable sight, them being mostly unaware of being watched and talked about, at the same time seeing how they behaved when not realising scrutiny.

Erics mind took him back to his childhood bed and the skylight that lay above his bed, fitted with misted security glass. He would often stare up it at night, seeing shadows of movement, scared of vampires or werewolves' visits, until one day a pigeon would die, spreadeagled on the glass and over the months of decay, leave its forever imprint. But still he saw the shadows flicker, often calling his mother in fear, only to be told not to be silly and given another pill to help him sleep. But one night the shadows were different and had sounds as well. The big black figure, hunched over the glass, made the young boy scream in terror. Turmoil ensued and police were called. The next-door neighbours had been burgled and they were next on the list.

Eric entertained his manager of the stories of various rooftop exploits, not knowing that they weren't yet over, and told of how, when at school, his most dangerous stunt, to date, was performed.

In the main class area, an old courtyard, with a tithe barn that was used for gym, services and movie night, was the large red slate roof that covered the semi-circular building. No one had ever achieved a whole circuit of the roof and not been caught, so to Eric and one other, the challenge was open to be had. Speed was of the essence. Spotters were sent to strategic locations, ready to shout the ridiculous "Cave" (K.V), giving the game away instantly, rather than a subtle bird call. With the help of a boost or two, Eric and comrade found themselves scampering quickly along the ridge, occasionally slipping, almost falling, with much hilarity and goal coming quickly in sight, only to be halted by a loud, severe, masterly shout from below.

Busted.

The lookouts, had failed, but were now joyful spectators, cheering the fact that people had been caught. Standing upright, instead of scurrying position, the two assailants could no longer escape Colditz and were bound to be shot by the guards. Fortunately, there was only one route down from the position they were in, they would have to complete their journey, making the mission a success...of sorts.

RETURN TO ROOKS END

It had been a long and hard 9 months, but the news came through, Great Aunt Jane had died. Tess, the only family member, had visited her a couple of times in hospital, brushed her hair and reminisced about days past, the last to have seen her in almost 10 years.

As Eric was living, with family, near Robert and Cassandra and she had just come out of hospital, following one of her "episodes", it was decided that Eric should accompany his father to the funeral, helping with the arduous drive, despite having a new born at home. Assurances were made of only a one-night stay at RooksEnd and they would be home before they new it, hopefully comforting words to a convalescing wife looking after four children.

The drive was demanding, in more ways than one. The most challenging part was the excessive speeds and erratic driving of his father, who rarely dipped below 100, unable to see the near misses and getting side tracked by his cigarettes. The hours rolled by and as dark started to set in they arrived at the familiar entrance to RooksEnd. They drove past the almost disintegrated pavilion and tennis court and noticed how the apple orchard had all but been chopped down. Only two lights were seen in the house, the kitchen and porch, lighting their way to one of the last times they would arrive at this house. The car pulled up, though no characteristic gravel crunch was heard, and the two men got out and stretched their muscles looking up at the building, each in their own memories, each in their own thoughts.

The front door opened and were greeted by Meredith, the latest housekeeper who had cared for Aunt Jane the last year or so, her lack of warmth disappointed Eric, not for himself, but for his Great Aunt. The house felt empty, even the echoes of the past had left, he was surprised that the walls themselves had forgotten who he was now that Jane had gone. It was a that moment he realised, it had been Great Aunt Jane herself who had kept the place alive, every room and everything had a piece of Great Aunt Jane in it, and now she was gone. The house, regardless of familiar furniture, was empty.

The morning of the funeral came quick enough, after an uncomfortable night's sleep and it felt peculiar making coffee and toast for his father in a kitchen where Eric had only been allowed to be bystander. But now, breakfast had, they changed into their mourning attire with Eric unfortunately tearing his trousers and having to wear his black jeans instead.

It was a short drive to the church, which was packed with the influential and affluent well-wishers that had been associated with the family, one way or another over the many years, but no recognisable faces were see. The service progressed, formal and to the point until the eulogy. To both his and his fathers surprise, Dicky took the dais and delivered an unsentimental speech about his aunt and the work she had done during the war and its after effects on global commerce and business.

Back at RooksEnd the after service do was held and Eric seemed it right to offer his help with the serving of drinks and canapes to guests. Circulating around, cold shouldered by Dicky, but trying to be friendly to all, despite having just buried his great aunt and memories, received a rebuke for his attire "Hmm, bad breeding stock no doubt" came the gruff, pompous voice from a man he'd never seen, but certainly directed fully at him. He smiled and passed on, looking forward to be going home once Robert had had his fill.

Unfortunately, time dragged on and Eric pulled his father to the side and informed him of the time and how they ought to be going soon. “Oh, we can’t go this evening, I’ve already arranged to stay another night” said Robert filling his glass, “it’d be rude to go now, besides I want to talk to... Ahh...hello Andrew, good to see you...”. It was probably the most fun Robert had had in ages.

Eric was speechless, he tried to intervene again but got cut off again by his father’s drunkenness. He left the soiree, nauseated and angry and called his wife to break the bad news. Upset but understanding was all she could be. He sent his love to the children, one already tucked up in bed and wished them all a goodnight. He always missed his children and didn’t want to be the same parent as his. He went to bed, listening to the people forget why they were here, to mark the leaving of a Great Aunt Jane who he never told he loved her and if he had? She probably would have said “Nonsense, silly boy” x

BEGINNINGS

Having left London for the rural idyll of self-sufficiency, Cassandra sat in her new kitchen, now all unpacked, and picked up her guidebook, from The Ministry of Agriculture, on how to farm.

They already had been visited by some of the very friendly and accommodating locals, welcoming them to the village and letting them know of do's and don'ts, why's and how's, when's and where to's and buggers an' rascals.

There was the Major who lived on top of the hill, the Captain who lived by the church, the new lady (who didn't mix much with village life) lived by the pub (and had pigs), the geese "mind" up the road ("best take a stick, when going to Post Office"), the ghost up the lane and "mind youself with that young Billy Hunter".

There was a lot to take in, Robert had already thrown himself in head first, organising chickens, buying a cow and the basic equipment needed for milking, sorting out an old red Massey Furguson and working out a timetable for the year ahead, pruning, feeding, planting and harvesting, of both veg and grass alike. It was going to be hard. With no machinery, except for the tractor, everything was going to have to be done by hand, from cutting and stacking the hay, to the milking of the cow (soon to be plural), it was going to be an arduous task and a steep learning curve, but "as long as everyone (meaning Eric, Tess, Cassie and himself) got stuck in" thought Robert, "it should be easy enough". Unfortunately, only half the task force was up to the job.

Cassie sat at her kitchen table with her cup of tea leafing through her book and chuckled when the Min. of Ag. mentioned that "Jersey Cows were right little sods".

She suddenly realised that the Aga hadn't been attended to and had once again gone out, meaning one of several situations were to occur.

1) She could attend to it straight away, probably get dirty or worse still, chip a nail.
2) Leave it and act surprised later either confessing that she forgot or didn't know how to do it, or tried and it didn't work
3) Call Robert to do it for her.

Cassie contemplated what food they had in the kitchen cupboard and wondered which she would prefer: a hot or cold supper. Looking at the clock she realised that if the range got lit straight away it probably wouldn't be hot enough anyway to get an evening meal ready, so stood up, pushed in her chair and went off to be busy lying down with a headache, so, option 4.

Meanwhile, outside, Robert was giving Eric a lesson in the importance of cleanliness. Having thoroughly cleaned all the milking equipment, churn, bucket, sieve and muslin with sterilising fluid, it was onto the importance of milking parlour hygiene. Robert handed Eric a shovel. Looking at him, his Dad explained "That's a shovel son, that, over there is a wheelbarrow", signalling behind his son "you need to shovel that" pointing to a fresh pile of cow dung "into that" pointing to the wheelbarrow.

For a 13-year-old boy, having never done physical labour and, essentially, only used to city life and the over protectiveness of boarding school, there was only one reaction.

"What, me? Urgh. Why"?

"Someone has to do it. We'll make a big pile over there" his Dad said pointing behind a wall "and when needed, spread it over the fields as a natural fertiliser".

"Oh," came the reply "do I have to"?

"Yup" was the emphatic response with a big smile.

That was the first of many wheelbarrows. And after barrowing away the manure, the clean up (spraying down the yard) would follow (Erics favourite bit), leaving a wet but pristine canvas for the dears to mess on again.

Over the years, as the herd grew, the wheeling would be succeeded by a manual scraper, a large curved rubber type broom, and then a tractor with a drag scraper attached to the back. This wouldn't be until the next move and the muck would be scraped into a slurry pit, a large swimming pool sized hole in the ground, about 8 foot deep, at the back of the cow shed where all waste was collected.

Unfortunately, the sluice ramp wasn't steep enough for clear drainage and would often need to be manually cleared with an old two-pronged hay fork, sometimes a risky job. It was on one such occasion Eric found to his cost.

Standing on the bank, to the side of one of the ramps, Eric had climbed out of the cab and was attempting to shift a large heap of muck and straw that was refusing to slide down the slip, despite the plentiful rain that might have helped.

Nothing was shifting. Taking the calculated decision, he stepped onto the top of the ramp to try and push the pile from above. With the first effort, it worked, dramatically.

The ground underneath him slid instantly into the waiting pit taking him with it. He was instantly "dipped in shit" up to his eyes. It filled his ears, mouth and nose as he, fortunately, managed to heavily scrabble a foothold and save himself from being fully submerged and drown in the stuff.

Clambering out, like something from an old Tarzan movie, escaping from quicksand, he made it to the bank, spitting and blowing out of his nostrils. Squelching his way back up to the farmhouse, the cows gave him a wide berth, a look of surprise in their eyes as he sloshed and sploshed his way across the yard.

Cassie saw him coming and rushed to the door, stopping in her tracks.

“What on earth happened”? she called.

Eric raised his arms and shrugged his shoulders, still spitting out large chunks and trying to clear his breathing. “I fell into the pit” was all he wanted to say, not wanting to swallow any more.

“Well strip off here and go and have a shower”.

Eric stopped and kicked off his boots and pulled of his overalls, amazed to find how much had made its way through the layers. Once down to his underwear he was allowed inside and made his way to the bathroom. It took a while to get fully clean but it would take weeks for the smell to go.

BATH TIME

The bath was run. It seemed like a good idea to have a bath before going to bed, "Try and get a bit sober before going to sleep" was the logical thought processed by Erics once again alcohol induced brain.

It had been a lonng day. Sitting on the toilet next to the bath, ears and head still ringing from the gig, he wondered whether the last drinking session had been that a good idea. Last night was still very present when the morning started, but being followed by a coach, ferry, then another coach journey, all with proportion of drink, well, he did feel drunk. "Ha" came from somewhere.

"Wow, it had been loud. I think the loudest yet" he half said to the bath. The bath wouldn't have understood what had been said, since only some of the words came out, more of "Wow, loud, think, yet", perhaps to some, a deep philosophical problem trying to be posed by someone who could barely crawl.

The room was certainly spinny, so the bath really was going to be a good idea, the next serious decision forming in his head was “Am I meant to get undressed”? it seemed like the right thing to do, but it felt odd at the same time. Eric couldn’t actually remember the last time he had taken his clothes off, it had been a while, he knew that. He tried thinking, very hard, perhaps if he “Hum”ed or even “Err”ed while tapping his chin it would look like he was thinking and, who knows, might help. It didn’t. he just forgot what he was thinking about and got side tracked by the three double gins and fizzy orange he had recently consumed at the little night café round the corner from the 4star hotel, where the two coach loads of Motorhead fans were staying.

Licking his lips, needing fluid, he scooped up a handful of bathwater, with bubbles, and had a drink.

“Ooh” face wrinkled “Too warm”.

And bumped his way to the waiting courtesy fridge, door open and waiting and already plundered, to see if anything left was worth consuming.

“Ah, peanuts” he said as he spied a can of salted nuts not yet open.

“They’re mine” came a distinct yet muffled voice from a pile of upturned furniture. It was his travelling companion and second drummer of the band, who had also come to Brussels for the weekend, but was now crashed out in his own fort, a result of raids committed earlier but at least thirty metal fans on all rooms.

Eric popped open the can with a swift hit of "eau de penut" and a shout of "Bastard" and decided his bath was more important. He didn't understand why he felt so drunk, after all he had eaten before they all went out to the red-light district, apparently where the best bars were to be had, but he couldn't for the life of him remember how they got back to the hotel.

Back at the tub he turned the taps off, he guessed it looked full enough, so automatically stripped off, wondering whether he should put his DMs back on or not and climbed in regardless. He sunk down under the bubbles and had another slurp.

His mind started to wander as soon as the warmth spread into him, soothing and relaxing.

More recent flashes of the past, namely Tess's birthday, flew by, "Boy, he had been drunk" he thought, he'd gotten in the bath with his pyjamas on at that party (long story), "Man, the water was dirty" he mused.

"Then" he said, talking to himself "school... Being made to fill the bath with a milk bottle" he continued, remembering have to run to and from the river to the boarding house with bottle after bottle to fill the bath as punishment meted out by prefects and masters alike. They were all sadistic. One master came to mind at the top of the list. This English teacher doubled up with P.T

(Physical Torture, not Training). At boarding, the afternoons were put aside for all sports (except for Fridays which were reserved for C.O.R.P.S training and punishing) and a usual 3-to-6-mile run was required to start the session if one came under the jurisdiction of this Mr Walsh. The run itself was easy enough for Eric, who always enjoyed long distance jogs, finding a natural rhythm of music in his head, but more often, couldn't take sports seriously so got sent on laps around the pitch instead of following rules.

On one such day, Mr Walsh was particularly smiley, disconcerting in itself, and a 9-mile run was set, the maximum the route allowed, along the river to a lock and back, so flat all the way. It started well enough, the keen and determined at front, dashing off with eagerness, already wasting their energy in wanting to climb the ladder of success, whilst Eric put on his internal hum and drifted away on the beauty of the scenery with Elvis for company.

A few miles of gentle jogging brought you to a small woodland with little twists and turns, jumping logs and sploshing in undrained puddles. Rounding a bend, he heard calls from behind and looked and saw a halted group who had decided they had had enough and were going to wait there for the leaders to return, then follow back.

Eric halted to try and encourage continuation,

but by the time the conversation had been had, the pack was probably a mile away, with no chance of catch up, so he resolved to stay and wait. An unfortunate move.

As the pack returned from their turning point, the remainers tagged on behind and looked suitably exhausted at the finish line. One by one, names were called out of all who didn't complete the full run and beaten, severely, with The Plimsol, kept for such occasions, by being hoisted over the boathouse workbench, wrists held and pulled by two pupils to ensure the feet left the ground. Sadly, for Mr Walsh, the days of such punishment was limited. Not because of reprimand, but when adjusting the tension of his motorbike chain, with the "help" of a favourite pupil, mistimed instructions caused the amputation of the fingers on his right hand, above the main joints. "It's a funny world" Eric pondered.

The bath was very relaxing. Even the reminder of his Mother trying to strangle and drown him in their bathroom, with Tess banging on the door after hearing the terrified screaming and the beating didn't phase him. Instead, he slipped into peaceful unconsciousness, comforted by the bubbles and warm water...and an incredible amount of booze.

Something didn't feel right?

Cold.

Cold and wet.

Cold, wet and a funny smell.

Hard…

"Oh, I'm still in the bath" flashed through Erics brain as he stood up. "Odd"?

There was no water left in the bath to speak of. Just a couple of inches of reddish-brown liquid and dried spaghetti stuck to the sides with plenty clogging up the plug hole.

Still in an alcohol stupor and limited brain function, Eric quickly surmised that he must've fallen asleep, his Bolognese from the start of the evening came to pay a visit, somehow, he kicked the plug and water drained. "Ta Dah" he thought brilliantly.

Climbing out of the bath he realised he looked very red and greasy, so attempted to dry himself off with a very soft and luxurious towel and climbed into bed, gone in seconds.

Morning came too soon. Breakfast missed, room in total disarray and waking up in a slimy orange bed was an experience too much for the brain to fully comprehend. Baz was already up and smoking and suggested they depart to the waiting coach, quickly. Quickly wasn't available at this time, so Steady had to do. Carefully making their way down the stairs, the lifts were somehow broken, they made their way into the foyer, where management and staff were trying to cope with 60 leather and denim types trying to avoid payment of consumption and destruction. Keeping eyes to the ground, it was too bright anyway, Eric and Baz slipped out to the waiting coach, not looking forward to the ferry back or the comments concerning the smell.

MAURICE AND THERESA (AND ALL)

Morris and Theresa lived at the far end of the cobbled Cul-de-Sac, the narrow door tucked neatly between two others, almost unseen, but when opened, certainly noticed by the smell of cat and air freshener.

Both Italians, even to younger eyes, how they became a couple was a guess in itself. Theresa, dark hair always in a tight, compact beehive, pencil skirt and polo neck, was an attractive older lady with a beautifully friendly smile, relaxed and at ease with herself and nothing being too much trouble for her, even Morris (and boy did he challenge her).

He was sharply dressed. As sharp as a stiletto blade. As sharp as his tie was thin. His light grey suits with very subtle black trim were always tailor made and came with matching trilby, pulled down at the front, but not so low as to hide his pencil moustache, but enough for the need to walk with head slightly tilted back. An amiable gentleman in his twilight years, but would not look out of place in a dodgy, backstreet market or with switchblade in hand. Neither would he be seen dead in, for his main occupation was cat collecting, a passion shared with Cassandra.

Everyday had its routine. After his breakfast and morning coffee he would take a walk to the nearest newsagents to buy the mornings paper. Only located a few hundred yards away, as the crow flew, it might take him an hour or so to complete his task, yet somehow managed to return most days with a cat under his arm.

“Maurice”! Theresa would exclaim “Watta you got”? “Ah, *another* CAT”! she would shout exasperated “Where you find it this time”? would be asked but definitely not wanting an answer.

No sooner had one cat been turfed out, another one or two would arrive. And so, the game continued. Occasionally, Cassandra would receive a knock at the door. Either Maurice trying to hide a new discovery “Cassandra, my love” would be the opening line “I found this poor creature abandoned, would you look after it for me, while I buy some food for it, please”? (Once, she agreed and got stuck with the animal for several days) or it would be Theresa in tears, wanting to go back to Italy and get away from the ever-growing pride.

The quiet little backwater of the hustle and bustle of city life, lay nestled amongst the tall surrounding buildings with hundred-year-old cobbles still in place. It was home to many a character. The aforementioned Mr and Mrs Luton, she small and stout of stature, possibly of Cossack descent; Wol and Phil the carpenters, who owned the corner property, with its double floor doors that could fold open like a giant dolls house to expose the full workings on its insides, workbenches, sawdust and a plethora of timbers. Many a time as Eric grew, he would wander in and be allowed to watch them work, sitting on a saw horse, legs swinging, twirling the ringlets of freshly shaved wood. Offcuts scattered the floor, swept into piles, or fallen from shelves and would often be given to him to take home where he would imagine himself hard at work nailing and chiselling, or fashioned into some nondescript item for Erics imagination to fill in the gaps.

The small community had its benefits. Dickies closest childhood friends lived around the corner, as did Tess's in the flats of the neighbouring square and her Godmother living next door.

She was an elderly lady, who had also driven an ambulance in the Second World War, losing her fiancé in battle, at a tender age, never married, but had the company of her two short-legged, black and hairy Griffon dogs, Topsy and Turvy. In the early evenings she would sit in her chair and listen to the wireless, a favourite being Radio 4's The Archers and Topsy and Turvy would howl along to the music, not stopping until a small treat arrived in their mouths to quieten them.

There were many characters and buildings that stood out to a young boy's eyes. The ivy-covered corner builder next to the tall double doors of the beloved carpenters, the sloping road that ran the power station and flats, the cobbles and manhole covers that Eric practiced his brass rubbing skills on, the external metal spiral staircase in a front garden, the squirrel monkey kept in a large cage, the noise of the tube trains rattling on their tracks and the embankment full of daffodils in spring that could only be reached climbing the wall.

The old Russian Orthodox church lay nearby, opposite the small private garden, and Eric would pedal his little, chunky, red bike to be able to watch, from a distance, the austere and sombre, yet incredibly attired priests arrive for ceremonies.

The stream of clergy and patrons fascinated the small eyes, wanting to know where they kept themselves, what they ate and how they prayed. A tall and dark-long-haired clergy man acknowledged the young onlooker, making him feel exceptionally privileged, yet witnessed an exchange of words with a elder, who seemed to be rebuking his juniors behaviour.

The square (triangle), of which they lived off, was a mix of creeds, and Eric would enjoy the smells as he cycled around, sampling some more interestingly than others, yet all creating a homely feel to his little microcosm. Whether it was the biker's fires and 'erb in the recess of knocked down buildings rubble, or the fragrant earth of the Norwegians abode, or the tang of spice from the newly arrived Indian family, whose patriarch would sit daily on their step, reading the Financial Times in his lopsided turban.

MUSIC

Eric sat in front of his laptop, slightly amazed at what he had found out but still uncertainty lived, to hover about like some curious bee looking for a plant to settle on, yet none fulfilling the brief.

For years his mother had spun yarns about her brushes with the famous and her exploits, many not being uttered to the family directly, but to outsiders who admired her achievements and varied life.

When very young, skipping around the streets or pulling along his metal truck, just big enough to hold a loaf of bread, Cassandra would point out, with great affection in her voice hinting at a more than casual acquaintance, the house where John and Cynthia lived, or how Lady Madonna was written about her, or the nearby church where Eleanor Rigby had worked and died. As thanks to her, when leaving the area, Cynthia and John gave Cassie a beautiful blue and gold tea set, which stayed boxed and hidden in the kitchen cupboard for years, all confirmed, dismissively, by Robert, but never knowingly witnessed by Eric, which, over the years, grew in suspicious speculation of authenticity.

Being brought up with parents who had been actors and living in the nation's capital, it seemed natural to rub shoulders with the rich and famous (sometimes infamous depending where you were) and very soon became humdrum and meaningless for the youngest of the family (whose early years consisted of being plugged into either the radio, t.v or record player, with a possible crushed pill to keep him quiet) who saw them all as just people who sometimes behaved in odd ways.

The flamboyant Glam Rock star (looking just as he did on stage, leaving him instantly recognisable) sat across the busy and now fashionable Italian restaurant with its sunken garden styled seating, with large palm fronds and gold tinted mirrors around on the split levels, as the large circulating fans in the ceiling cooled the already "chilled" clientele. For the first (and only time) in his life, Eric was in awe. He was sure he was gaping at the smiling face (who gave a friendly little wave from across the tables), as he recounted all the times he had stood on the table at school doing his extravagant and flamboyant impression, imagining roaring crowds as he pranced, waving his arms in the air singing, strutting and stamping, tossing his head around with gay abandon and living the moment of exuberant passion. The other kids just thinking he was odd, but Eric was sure they were just jealous. It never dampened his enthusiasm though. If anything, it urged him on to be more and more outrageous as possible (and reckless), glad to have found a niche he could call his own.

Too shy to go and ask for an autograph, Eric turned to his father.

“Dad..., Dad” he said trying to get his attention but unable to take his eyes off his namesake, he understood what it was like to be him. “Dad, would you go and get me his autograph please”?

“What, Who”? replied Robert, unaware of the world that his son had just been in.

“Gary Glitters, he’s sitting over there”. Eric signalled with a movement of his head, still SO much in awe.

“What”? came the reply “That creep. No, I don’t think so. Ask the waiter”.

Double whammy. Creep? Ask a waiter?

“Dad..., Dad” Eric persisted, not bothering with the creep bit, after all Dad said that about The Goodies “Dad”!

“What”?

“Dad, can you ask the waiter for me”?

“Oh, all right” he said.

Signalling "Gaston" an Italian waiter came over discreetly and words and head movements and smiles were exchanged with the waiter moving off on his mission. Eric watched as the waiter approached the table of his task and brief were had, another big smile and wave, a scribble, third wave and the waiter returned with a card saying "All my love Gary Glitter".

"WOW" thought Eric "bit heavy on the love bit" thought his mature voice inside (one that would often pop up), but never the less "WOW".

He could not look in that direction for the rest of the evening.

Eric collected many autographs over the years, some easier collected than others. By way of an example was John Cooper Clarke, a Manchester punk poet whose first album made quite an impression on Eric, was giving a lecture at the Oxford Union, a discussion hall predominantly for students, but a place he would often go, blagging his way in, like so many others places. After the lecture he dug deep in his trench coat pocket, only to find a condom packet (and a newspaper fold of "seeds") for Mr CC to sign, which got a seal of approval and an amused comment. Amazingly, their paths would cross again about three years later.

Dickie was working hard and seriously for a London based music magazine (most of Dickies work had to be taken seriously), and was organising a celebratory birthday bash ("No, it's an event"), hosting an array of bands at a well-known Victoria club. Being a roadie for one of the performing bands, Eric was roped in to help with the whole event, much to his delight. Eric enjoyed the work, but the bigger the "event", then bigger the after party, which he was seldom invited to, but it did mean that more people would be milling around backstage and more people meant a wider variety of drugs available… and that could only be a good thing.

Setting up was pretty straight forward. The first job was to hoist the giant backdrop for the stage, a giant Happy 100th Issue banner needed attaching to a large pipe running the length of the stage. Normally a boon would be lowered, banner attached, then hoisted in position, but new regulations meant that a non-electrical engineer was not allowed, by union law, to operate the equipment, so a ladder and Eric was called for.

Eric strolled onto the stage, slightly worse for wear, to be greeted by an enthusiastic Dickie.

"Right E, I need you to take this corner" (signalling to the immense banner) "and rope and climb up the ladder" (easily 30 ft tall) "and tie it to that pipe up there" (pointing) "it'll been fine".

Eric wasn't quite sure what was meant by the last bit, but not being of sound mind, Eric agreed, as usual, trusting his brother.

Hands full and climbing up the ladder, the very long ladder, he decided that, yup, he didn't like heights. Especially on wobbly ladders. With his hands full. He nervously reached the top, which was good and bad. One: he couldn't decide whether it was his knees or ladder shaking and Two: he could hold on to the pipe. Now this too was good and bad. One: the pipe was definitely robust, but Two: it was very hot. Obviously, a hot water pipe.

Carefully tying the corner of the banner onto the pipe he started to make his way back down, until...

"Don't bother coming down" came the unwanted command.

"Grab the next loop, hold on to the pipe and I'll jig the ladder along"

"What"? shouted Eric in disbelief.

"I Said" Dickie called back.

"I heard what you said, I just didn't believe you" shouted Eric again, feeling that he had only just started his life.

"It'll be quicker this way" called back the ever mature and knowing older brother.

And so, the exploit began. Once Eric had

managed to burn his arms by clutching to life too hard (as he was only wearing his Motorhead TShirt) and almost soil himself on at least three occasions when the ladder almost disappeared, it wasn't so bad, and after all Dickie was right, it was quicker.

By the time Eric was allowed to come down there was only a short time left until the opening. Time enough for a few beers though. The first two that were gone in seconds, as they were only cold half lagers (with brandy chasers, especially good when taken with Whiz (Speed/Amphetamine Sulphate)) just to bring him back to normality, the third being Guinness, to level him out (and apparently, to protect him from BeriBeri). Black glass in hand he wandered over to the pinball machines, now with a slight fuzz starting to soften his edge, to eek out any other lingering stress he had suffered.

Coins in, lights and noise commenced, the now familiar ping ping of the machine, instantly recollecting memories of his first attempt playing at an amusement arcade and failing, unknowing about flick buttons and bumps, only to be embarrassingly tutored by a well-meaning older lad. He also recalled getting banned from his local, until repairs had been paid for and apology made.

Eric noticed he had been joined by a competitor, on the identical machine next to him, and they spent the next ten minutes or so in a head-to-head, enjoying the simple diversion. Glass emptied, Eric decided on one more shot before retiring backstage for duties and offered his now partner a drink.

“Can I get you one”?

“Nah, it’s alright, thanks” said the tall hatted man in a gravelly but smooth voice.

Eric paused and momentarily realised that he recognised this bloke from somewhere. Not surprising though, he covered a lot of ground and when gigging he tended to bump into fellow roadies and engineers etc. all the time.

“I know you from somewhere, don’t I”? he innocently enquired, still not managing to find this person in his stored data banks.

The man grunted and left. Totally perplexed at this reaction and standing like a confused lemon (trying to figure what he’d done wrong), he heard the doors open and people came flooding in.

“Wow” someone excitedly said to their friend “That was Lemmy, did you see him”?

Now just a lemon.

Unfortunately, Erics stay at the foyer bar lasted a bit longer than intended, mainly wasting time, chatting-up possible conquests.

Realising that time had passed, he headed towards the soundproof doors of the main auditorium and pushed one open. He was instantly transported to a totally different world. The heavy tribal, rhythmic thud of tight drums chocked and pounded out a fierce energy. The skins (Skinheads) were stamping hard to the beat and a flame thrower, only clothed in a loin cloth and dreads, was spitting out flames above the masse of bodies. The earthy, chemical smell of fumes filled the air as did the palpable feeling of threat and danger. He was glad that Todd (a skinhead friend, filled with dubious exploits... we'll come to him later) was not here, because as he made his way through the crowd, violence erupted all around, with the band still playing, fuelling the hatred and animosity of the pit.

Dodging the conflicts as if they were "someone else's problem", he made it back to the wings of the stage in time to be ordered to help clear the stage for the next act, as it had been advised to pull the band to calm the existing clamour of angry bodies and bouncers.

Within minutes the atmosphere changed, as John Cooper Clarke stepped out and administered much needed dry vitriolic humour against cider and simplicity, and boots and brains. The roar from the crowd signalled their agreement just as Eric was sent out again on stage to move some cables, unfortunately located behind Mr Cs swinging gesticulations, resulting in a fist coming beautifully in contact with Erics jaw. A huge burst of laughter erupted as he was sent backwards and Clarke, not missing a beat, delivered another poetic put down, to the delight of the audience.

A real lemon day.

One of the main advantages of being a roadie was seeing so many bands, for free, but Eric soon realised that he preferred to watch from out front, as it was the magic of the performance he enjoyed and not how the trick was done. He loved music, from Mozart to Zappa and often went to gigs with his mates, some enjoyable, like getting in through the Stage Door, by some other kindly bouncer, to see The Skids, or disastrous times like the Ramones.

The day started well enough. Erics rubber lipped mate Andrew, who was the bassist of the band that Eric drummed for, was an enthusiastic Ramones fan, having seen them once on his sex-fuelled exchange trip to America when only 16. Funnily, he never seemed to stop smiling. He was like a brother to Eric, the brother he never had. Both enjoyed practical jokes and would often plot various scenarios to shock or startle the rest of their friends. One time, in their local watering hole, they lit small smoke bombs and convinced punters that the pub was on fire, unfortunately the smoke generated from such small tablets filled the bar with heavy white smoke in minutes, causing evacuation and the calling of emergency services. The landlord never did find out where the smoke came from...thankfully. Many times, what seemed amusing to them wasn't always regarded the same by others.

Andrew and Eric had gone to buy tickets for a Stiff Little Fingers concert (where Todd, a stocky [muscly] not tall chap, but with a broad, cheeky smile and personality that would charm all mothers and make him somehow irresistible to women (despite his violent and wayward ways), would decide to make a clear passage in the crowd to enable him to run up to and leap and hit an unsuspecting bouncer. All hell would break loose, resulting in Andrew and Eric missing the last bus home and walking back, 20 miles at 12.30 at night, because the concert was held up for half an hour) and drove to the venue (only to discover later that they could be purchased nearer) on Andrew's bike with Eric pillion. Again, unfortunately, if they had known about purchase location or if they had watched the end of Tiswas (a raucous Saturday morning kids T.V programme) and The Bucket of Water Song finale (like they always did) they would have missed the elderly 85-year-old gentleman, with virtually zero vision, on medication, pull out in front of them causing the crash which resulted in Andrews arms and hands in cast and a bump to Erics nose. For Eric it all happened very slowly.

It was a lovely clear summers day, the road

straight and clear, except for the one oncoming car, which turned suddenly across their path with no warning. The motorbike slammed into the front passenger door, front wheel pushed its way under the bike tank, while Andrews hands were crushed between the handle bars and door, gauntlets giving some but not full protection. Eric, wearing only an open-faced helmet (for the last time) had his head thrown forward, smacking his nose on the back of Andrews helmet and elegantly swung his right leg up and over the back of the bike in a manoeuvre between a pirouette and a pas de deux. His mother would've been so proud (being also an ex-ballerina).

It would take some time for Andrews arms to heal and boredom would set in, giving him plenty of time to come up with a jolly jape that seemed good on paper. Blood capsules bought and plan devised, a visit to the pub was called for. The usual crowd was there, and they settled in for a friendly evening of drinking, surreptitious drug taking and mutual banter. Eric would often recall these moments as the closest he came to having true friends and would always miss them. The session started with Eric and Andrew at odds with each other. Andrew blaming Eric for causing the motorbike accident and Eric blaming Andrew for his reckless riding. They bickered all evening, escalating tension and disharmony while quietly sniggering to themselves. It culminated with a fight outside the pub, Andrew's plaster caste arms flailing and feet kicking out while both had blood streaming from mouths and noses. Their friends rushed to separate the children, who instead of staying aggressive, couldn't help but laugh as they explained it was a big wheeze and it was fake blood, not real. None of the girls found it remotely funny and called them babies, it was the last time they, though unfortunately not Eric, did anything like that.

As for The Ramones…

The morning started with trepidation. The three bandmates were looking forward to the gig. One had already seen them before, one eager for the experience and the other…well, who knew. It is here, background on the third member needs clarifying.

Todd was much loved by all who knew him, a truly loveable rogue, you wanted to love him more, but…

Which was worse is hard to say. The violence, drink or drugs. His mum would often ask his closest friends to keep "an eye on him", meaning "don't let him drink too much, don't let him take anything". For, when he did, trouble would ensue. Break-ins, vandalism, punch-ups (a mediocre term) and general mayhem would unfold, often resulting in early morning raids by the police or tracking Todd down in hiding. Having an often-absent father and a childhood of dipping in and out of 'prove school and borstal would ultimately end in prison, after one particular innocent night of visiting his girlfriend, which resulted in him requesting "36 other offences to be taken into consideration" at court.

It unfolded like so:

Pub...lunchtime...

"Blimey Todd, you look rough, what have you done to your hand"? asked Eric.

"I'm on bail" came the reply.

Shocked, incredulous silence hit the group of friends.

"What the F..K"?

They had all been together the previous evening, and when they parted company at closing time, all seemed well, nobody too drunk or stoned.

"I went and saw 'Chell last night".

Confusion set in all round, but alarm bells started ringing. Michelle, Todd's girl, was at a girl's boarding school, they didn't allow visitors, especially by skinhead boyfriends at midnight.

Apparently, having an urge and missing her, he broke in to the dormitory, got caught by the headmistress, exposed and pleasured himself, refused to leave and attacked the police.

His friends sat agape at their grinning friend. Only Todd.

The trio arrived at the bus station to take them down to London and met with Todd's brother, one of his mates (both skins) and the unnerving Alan. Al should have had "form". The crimes he had committed seldom got reported, due to known reprisal, and because his illnesses helped him elude incarceration. If Alan walked into the bar, you walked out. And here he was now, waiting for an hour's bus journey. Both Eric and Andrew were determined, but uncertainty or awareness had dropped into their laps.

The journey started easy enough, but as soon as the cans and bottles opened, the trouble started. Complaining passengers, an abused driver and an escalating argument between the three skins and Al, with both Andy and Eric trying to keep their heads down.

Pulling into the Victoria Bus Station, passengers disembarked and an elderly gentleman was pushed by one of the drunken groups, causing everyone to scarper in all directions.

By the time they had stopped running Eric and Andy were relieved to find themselves alone and walked on to the tube station, looking forward more than ever to the concert. Rounding a corner of a leafy green square, they joined up with the two brothers and Alan, the fourth member having been detained for his callous act.

No sooner had they met up, the fight erupted. Some disagreement had started on the coach between the brothers and now was the time to settle the score. Fists and steel toe-capped (the only type) DMs flew between the siblings. Alan stepped between meting out well placed headbutts, with Andrew and Eric watching, then turning their backs on the melee, figuring there was nothing else to do, occasionally turning around to see if the fighting had stopped…it hadn't.

Both performances were the same, hit, after hit, after hit. They were glad they made it.

SECRETS & LIES

One of Erics mothers many other professing's (apart from being a BBC scriptwriter) would be being a member of Pans People (which, when growing up as a child, remembered clearly her disgust of “”that” type of dancing”), a regular dance group from the BBCs light entertainment music programme, Top of the Pops.

The “scriptwriting” wasn't discovered by Eric until very late on in Cassandra's life. He, having a need to visit her Chiropractor of 20 years, arrived to the general welcoming chit chat which was interspersed with a curious question:

“Did your mother get her typewriter”? asked the ageing practitioner casually.

“Typewriter”? came the uncertain and befuddled response.

“Yes, typewriter”.

“I think you might have my mother confused with someone else”. Eric said genuinely.

This was followed by an indignant look and pause.

"No. I know <u>who</u> your Mother is". Came the emphatic and terse reply.

"Er, well, no typewriter, no. I don't see why she would want one"? Eric followed.

"For her scriptwriting of course, the Beeb want her back for some specials or other" came the surprising reply, only concreting the fact that this gentleman really had the wrong mother.

Eric stared blankly, then the penny dropped. "Not heard this one before", he thought, feeling "that" familiar feeling he felt when discovering one of his mother's lies. a bit like sitting down with a sudden groan, but the groan didn't want to be sat next to and didn't know where it came from anyway. A nauseating memory of a time when Cassandra had tried to pass a children's book off as all her work. She had written it, just for him, (this occurred decades ago), an inane adventure (even to a ten-year old) of a wizard, filled with Eric relevant details. The story was quickly upturned when Eric discovered the back page for people to fill in and send off, to make a "special" connection "for you child".

"Yuck" thought the already cynical internal speech of Eric "vomit inducing".

Eric's inner voice had always been much older than him. He enjoyed listening to it and it would often give very good advice, not that he took any notice of it.

Eric remembered two special occasions when the voice had been very present. Once, when Cassandra was battering the hell out of him in the bathroom, her favourite place of attack or subjugation, where it took him to the side and talked calmy and quietly to him, taking Eric away from the onslaught. The other, when walking through the peaceful Georgian houses of Lexham Gardens (the tall pillar fronted buildings hiding so much history), with Tess, stopped by a grating in the road by the path and started dropping ha'pennies down the drain (as instructed).

"Eric" came the rebuking voice of his sister "Stop that".

Eric stopped for a moment and wondered.

"What are you doing"? she dumbfoundingly enquired.

"Dropping pennies in the drain" was the matter-of-fact response.

"Well, don't do that. It's a waste".

After a couple of moments listening, he replied:

"No, it's not. Someone might find them one day and wonder how they got there" then dropped his last coin in. Satisfied.

Eric and his "imagination" or "voice of the future" were becoming best buddies and he enjoyed taking a step back and watch the world and its people unfold in front of him, as his imagination conjured up their lifestyles and abodes and his voice explained how things worked.

The most dramatic observation, where Eric saw himself watching others (without the use of drugs or illness), was when extreme life patterns collided, when Bill and Suze came to visit. This was also a turning point for Cassandra, where her exaggerations and lies would start their journey on another level.

Many of his parent's friends and early "thesps" had stuck with acting, or such like, and some had achieved considerable success in their adapted or chosen fields, leaving the glee of envy and pang of jealousy, especially on Cassandras shoulders, and more so when awkwardness reared its ugly head.

As you know, there are many variants of people, one such are Townies. The true to life, live and die surrounded by concrete folk, who feel out of water when even not putting on their heels.

Cassandra had altered somewhat to rural life, she coped with no pavements, the geese attacks while walking (an umbrella came in handy to shoo them off) to the little post office shop that hadn't changed since it opened, tractors flicking up large clumps of muck as they drove past and the bus, running three times a week to the nearest large town. The positives were that she had done more creative cooking than ever (marmalades, casseroles, pates, crumbles and wine (the magnificent Golden Pansy, thick and syrupy, as good as any dessert wine and the truly potent Wheat and Raisin, not for the feint hearted)), learnt how to look after chickens and not "pop" as many pills as she did before (a true exponent of "Mothers Little Helper"), mainly due to her new G.P who only believed in paracetamol and chicken soup, for all ailments.

On top of this, there was less call for dressing to impress as the cows were more occupied with in one end and out of the other. So, when the call came of a long weekend stay by two of their dearest "darlings", the stops were pulled and drawers opened to search for the cache of emergency pinks, yellows and blues, but unfortunately knowing she would find no blacks, would have to purchase a new discovery of hers, ProPlus (which would be a standard "go to" until her death).

Another glorious day in the Dorset countryside arrived. The fresh field air, the rolling hills of time stamped beauty and wisteria, lazily draping itself, in full bloom, from the twisted limbs leaning against the thatched house, whose stone was as old as the hills that lay behind.

Both Robert and Cassandra (more so) were looking forward to the weekend reminisces of cricket, names and catch ups, though the current of, and acute awareness of how the lack of money had changed their standards echoed in both their minds. Eric had removed himself from the scene via his motorbike, tootling around the windy, narrow lanes knowing the routine of stress and ang...uish/er of his mother, that would peak moments before expected e.t.a., nothing had changed there.

Perfect timing had him coming down the road as Bill and Suze were pulling up gracefully in their brand new, prestigious Mercedes. They both looked astounding, for many a reason.

As Eric parked and took of his helmet, he noted that Bill was dressed for сaж (caj). His white Yves Saint Laurent slacks were topped with a white Lacoste polo shirt, while a white and blue yachting jacket hung fabulously off his shoulders, whereas, Suze (on the other hand?) was dressed to impress. If the cows had seen her (and some neighbours did), they would have stopped chewing their cud and, even Eric thought, would have gaped in awe (or incredulity).

She looked sensational, especially to a fifteen-year-old boy. If she had been in the middle of St.Tropez in Autumn, I doubt you would have noticed her amongst the other glamour models, but in the middle of a sleepy Dorset village...

Eric saw Suze swing her legs out of the car, the six-inch stilettos trying to find solid ground under the gravel, followed by the waft of expensive living and a pair of incredibly smooth and tanned legs. Bill had already ventured to her side of the car, taking in his surrounding as he went and wouldn't have missed the accompanying smell.

Taking Suze's hand, she gracefully rose out of the car sporting a large fur, that matched her hair and large sunglasses. Eric remembered to close his mouth. F.C & N.K he dreamt and gulped. He re-introduced himself and led them up the path to the house, where they were duly greeted by his parents with genuine warmth with a hint of contrivedness.

"Darlings" and welcoming's were boomed around for all to hear.

Eric again made himself sparse and put his bike away into part of the long barn, next to the chickens, who he dropped in on to bring them up to date with events and see if they needed food and water.

By the time he exited the peaceful warmth of the softly contented birds and made his way up the small slipway to the back of the house, he heard the chattering's of the four adults out front and assumed "tea" would be served on the lawn. Entering the kitchen, he found no kettle on the stove or tray set, so made his way through the house only to be met by his mother and father coming the opposite way.

"Hi," said Eric, "Where's Bill and Suzy"? looking over their shoulders, heaving the start of an engine.

"Oh, they're not staying" they both replied "they were just dropping in to say hello". Silence followed.

It transpired that Suze had a "splitting headache" (couldn't stand the smell) and "needed to get some medication" (somewhere cleaner and more chic to stay). They were never seen again, sadly, but Eric wondered if tales would spin at their future gatherings, he hoped not but did feel sorry for his parents, for at last, they seemed to be grounding themselves in reality…or so he thought.

KNOCK, KNOCK

Eric had always seen them, they had always been there, always out of view, peeking around the corners, standing in the shadows or behind the doors, or hiding under the bed, but once or twice caught in all their glory, watching him, out of the corner of his eyes.

The bedtime ones were the scariest, for a young mind, perhaps not helped by his sister's macabre fascination with cartoon deaths, of the reveal of pictures of tombstones on eyes, when lids raised. Tess would creep to her brother's bedside when asleep and open his eyes to see if he was dead or not, her thin young fingers giving him imaginings of skeletons scraping his face, waking him in terror. The doses of morphine and such like probably didn't help.

As Eric grew out of childhood scares, he had his own experiences with things that go bump in the night, being chased by a dim light in a boarding house playground, the sounds of a body being dragged across a floorless ceiling, a piercing yell from the downstairs in a secure and empty house, the shaking of windows and doors as if a wind blew hard, yet all was still outside. Many other trivial incidents which would eventually become insignificant occurred, until the dark figure stood over him, by his bedside, feeling threatening and ominous, paralysing the older Eric in fear.

Two other events stood out, as they played out longer than the others.

The first occurs one dark and lonely night...

The bakery stood in the middle of a terraced row of businesses. An Aquatic shop at one end, a couple of empty units, a driving test centre and a hairdresser at the far end, all having separate properties above. It was a pleasant residential area and the newly acquired business was building well, despite the work needed to revive it, but was helped by the heavy footfall of examiners and visitors to the centre.

Eric had arrived at the property just before midnight (in the late 80's of the popular seaside town), and had seen the last of the drunks reel their way home on his journey there and started work as others were already far in slumberland or nestling down to sleep.

Work progressed routinely, mixing the first batches of dough and the first turns of puff pastry, with the night radio chatting in the background, interspersed with that certain quiet of the night and the thud of the dough hook.

As the hours passed, he made himself a mug of coffee, helping himself to a newly baked piece of shortbread, and sat down on the stack of flour bags for a moments break. Sipping and nibbling, staring into space and listening to the drone of the radio, he suddenly leapt up, feeling a sharp pain on where his buttock met his seat. He brushed the area to see if a pin or something was protruding and checked his whites likewise. Nothing to be found he passed it off as one of those things and finished the drink and resumed work, checking the floor in case anything might have flown off. The next hour ticked by quietly but steadily, all forgotten. He was just bending over to pick up another bag of flour when he leapt a mile, thinking that one of his fellow bakers had come in early. As he was bending over, what clearly felt like two definite fingers slid into the back pocket of his trousers. He jumped and spun around. No one was there. He ridiculously called out, but naturally none replied. Totally unnerved, he checked the doors, still locked, looked around, then made another coffee.

Nerves not calming he continued uneasily in his work, and by the time other staff arrived, another couple of hours later, no more events had occurred and nothing was said, not wanting ridicule for something so foolish…

9 a.m. came, and apart from opening time, it was

also the first delivery of the day. A selection of biscuits and cakes to the hairdressers. Today the duties fell to Eric as he was off home anyway, so wandered over and walked through the door to the smiling ladies ready for their elevenses already.

The manager greeted and thanked him and asked "How you getting on next door? You settling in alright"? him being new to the area.

"Yup, fine thanks" he smiled.

"Have you met the bum pincher yet"? she said.

"What"? was all that he could say.

"Oh, the bum pincher. He's always at it".

Again (feeling a bit stupid) "what"? he replied (man of many words, bang goes his credibility).

"Isn't he girls, always at it".

A resounding "oh yes" and "always" rippled through the salon.

The "sightseers" were a very different affair and were spotted on one of the many drug-filled nights of his 30's, in the front room of a quiet residence of a seaside town.

As usual, friends had come over after work and they had smoked and chatted and ate and drank (and smoked some more), until, as usual having to be kicked out so the day could start again.

Once gone, Eric settled down to a final smoke (or two) before retiring himself, so rolled up a couple of joints, sat back in the quiet of the large and comfortable sofa and inhaled himself away. He had quite a high tolerance. Drink, drugs, pain, he was sure his day would come though.

Lying back on the seat, staring at the ceiling he suddenly realised he wasn't alone. Not moving, pretending he hadn't seen them, he noted that there in front of him was a group of about seven figures. All different sizes and heights, all dressed differently, but they seemed to be standing behind a rope barrier, like at a cinema, watching him.

He casually got up, not paying them any attention and lit his other smoke, trying to watch them without looking or giving the game away. They were still there. They seemed to be chatting to each-other. Panic suddenly spread through the group as Erics eye caught the direct vision of one of the tourists and they were gone.

Both of his parents and siblings exhibited the feelings or awareness of other things, though his father never discussed such matters until his final days, whereas his mother was a different story.

Cassandra had always had an intuitive and uncanny perceptiveness to know about forthcoming events. The complexity of single child rearing, war shock, emotionally competitive parenting and being bred into money that was no longer there, along with the confusion that was created by "second sight" created a confused and damaged mind that would be a lifetime user and abuser of prescription drugs in all their glory.

While Cassandra was having her numerous "breakdowns" and miscarriages, enough for any single person to bear, her "episodes" would also play out, revealing themselves more vivid and traumatising in times of duress.

The mid-week late lunchtime weather was warm and pleasant and school summer holidays had only just begun for the 12-year-old, and he sat at home on the sofa, under the window, eating a crisp sandwich, watching his dad smoke his pipe (a habit that phased in when trying to give up cigarettes) and read a newspaper in his black leatherette reclining rocking chair. The smoke danced on his taste buds as he crunched another mouthful and found it more warming than the greyness of the cigs that his Dad normally smoked.

Tess was sitting, with her back to everyone else, up to the groovy, round, white table that had recently been bought from either Habitat or Harrods ("...somewhere beginning with H..." thought Eric), humming a tune to herself whilst she ate and flicked through her latest copy of Jackie.

Cassie was pottering in the small open-plan kitchen (the majority of downstairs was open-plan, kitchen, sitting room and dining area all in one) and had been experiencing one of her "headaches" lately, which tended to last a few days, so was in one of her "moods". These made for erratic behaviour, but if you kept quiet and undemanding you could probably escape any venomous retribution.

Much as Eric was enjoying his food, a drink of milk was called for (and maybe a doughnut later if they went out).

"Mum," called Eric gently "could I have a glass of milk please"?

A simple "okay" and "hang on" came in response as Robert looked out from behind his paper and puff of browness.

A silence seemed to hang in the air, as if drifted in on a breeze and momentarily froze everything. It was loudly followed by the shattering of a dropped milk bottle and the terrifying scream that came from Cassandra. Robert leapt from his seat and dashed to her aid as Tess turned to watch, rising slowly as Eric stayed sitting, figuring that "no milk today".

The screaming slowly stopped only to be replaced by:

"What..."? "...the blood", "so much blood" she shook, gasping sobs looking around herself as if in another place, trying to wipe her arms away, all the while saying "look at the blood its everywhere".

Robert stood, his arm around her, consoling.

"it's alright darling" he said softly, "its only milk, we'll clean it up".

Cassandra looked up at him, the wildness and confusion in her eyes "What...what was that noise, that explosion"?

"You just dropped a milk bottle, that's all, don't worry" calmed Robert.

"What"? replied the more aware Cassie, now looking about her at the white liquid and broken glass a strewn on the floor.

"But there was a huge explosion and then blood everywhere and the silence, and the screams began" she said, still confused and disorientated.

"No, everything's fine" said Robert "go and lie down, rest, we'll take care of it".

"But the blood" she said again, more softly and unsure "I saw so much blood.

Robert led Cassie to her bed and made sure she took a sedative. Tess started cleaning and Eric carried on crunching, though more slowly.

It wouldn't be until later that day that the news was known. A bomb had been detonated at The Tower of London that afternoon, severely injuring dozens of people, many children, causing facial damage and limb loss and one direct loss of life.

BLACKOUTS

Being in Bournemouth had been an unexpected turn of events. It had been a few years since leaving the full-on lifestyle, which had climaxed in the loss of his stomach lining, a combination of acid poisoning and months in Yugoslavia where he discovered his second home. The friendliness and warmth of its "one" people only enhanced his desire to fully absorb the water and wine at lunchtime and the home-grown apricot brandy and coffee all afternoon and sitting with the old folk, reminiscing about German occupation and trying to compete with the chili eating sessions.

From Ljubljana to Skopje and Belgrade to Dubrovnik they travelled, visiting Milo's vast family, not once using their tent (which had been bought especially for the trip, but had been utilised journeying through France and Italy in Erics white V.W Beetle which had "Lenin" sprayed on the green, back passenger wing. Lenin served them well, though once, needing an oil change, they stopped at a small garage in

France. It was a hot lunchtime and a student had been left in charge and was eager to help by putting the car on their ramps to make it easier. Once up, he pulled a portable drain system in place to catch the oil and took over task, much to the surprise of Milo and Eric. Job done, the lowering of the hydraulic ramps needed all hands as flaps needed to be deployed and kept out of the way at the same time. With Eric at the front of the car and Milo at the back, Jean-Paul controlled the descent by means of a joystick located on the far wall.

A sudden scrunching sound of metal crumpling shot out and shouts of "Merde ! Oh, Merde"! were heard.

The oil drip tray hadn't been removed from under the car as it lowered, and now leant at a buckled angle, obviously feeling very sorry for itself.

In a matter of minutes, the tray was moved, the car was off the ramp, doors and shutters of the garage locked and they were on the way, looking in the rear view mirror at a fleeing body of a worried young man.

For their excursion across the waters, Eric and Milo had been advised to take plenty of coffee, both roasted and instant and a varying range of jeans and denim jackets to give as valued gifts to those they visited, being the most sought-after items of the then unified country.

Ironically, one storming evening in Beograd, they were taken to the cinema to see an old Warren Beatty and Natalie Wood movie, Splendour in the Grass, with mixed Croatian and Macedonian subtitles and girl that Eric sat next to, tried really hard to translate the subtitles for him, even with her broken English. He thanked her for the efforts she was making, and fellow patrons didn't seem bothered, but, nevertheless, he tried to dissuade her but failed to smother her enthusiasm and persistence, so sat back and enjoyed the film despite the constant narration, the film was subtitled true, but not dubbed.

When all was over, they said their fond farewells and vacated to the parking lot only to discover the beloved beetle quarterlights had been broken open and car ransacked. Standing in the pouring deluge, Milo and Eric frantically checked their travelling home on wheels and were amazed in their findings. The passports and traveller cheques were still in the glove compartment, though sunglasses gone. The thieves had been very considerate, only a portion of the valued coffee had gone, as had only half of the denim clothing, but what was most odd was the two half-filled bin liners of their dirty laundry had been taken. Always a silver lining.

Neither the rain or event did anything to dampen their experience of such a beautiful country and its kind and friendly people, everywhere they went strangers welcomed them and were interested in their lives, whether it was sitting on a large shared table, in a busy lunchtime café/restaurant in the capital, or at an outdoor party/festival, deep in the southern countryside. Jokingly named "prvi engleski" (first Englishman: someone who, possibly conceitingly, believes he is the first to discover something, even though he isn't, though his new friends knew he wasn't, but enjoyed the ridicule), it filled Eric with such sadness at the events that would befall the land, even though tell-tale signs were already in place and fall-outs between Serbs and Croats were not uncommon, now Tito had died, who left could hold the country together.

Returning to England was a hard knock. Arriving back in a country that was filled with unrealised aggression and selfishness was a shock to the pair and they went their separate ways, Eric to Devon, to his parent's new farm, to try to recuperate and get back on his feet.

Thankfully, for his body, being in the middle of Devon, with no contacts (and no stomach lining) and little money, he could focus again on clean living and hard manual work, milking cows and looking after the 30 acres with his father, but that would just be the eye of the storm.

He would find himself having to leave the pleasant seaside resort some years later for two reasons. One being work, the other to escape the grasping claws of heroin that were taking his friends and to trying to attach themselves with their grasp.

The opiate comes with its story of romance and intrigue, sinister yet mysterious, one of the big highs, yet as rotten as maggot filled meat.

Heroin fools you in many ways and you listen to it, knowing the lies and lying to yourself all the way, knowing the full truth, yet ignoring all, trying to block out the hurt and pain of your pathetic and worthless existence, sponging and stealing off friends and relatives when you've become too inept and only focused on your own interests.

Eric had once been shown a film of drug abuse whilst attending a Young Farmers meeting, trying to ingratiate himself into a new environment, by the local Drug Squad. The film itself was a confused affair. The first half showed the entertainment factor of various drug taking in all its glory, using "real people" in the roles followed by the sudden, in full, autopsy of one of the participants who had died of a drug overdose. Unfortunately, the message that seemed to linger was "drugs are great… as long as you don't overdo it". Not the intended message.

Bournemouth started smooth enough, slowly reintroducing his body to the pleasures of booze was quickly accepted and soon happily having a few lovely, cold half lagers at lunchtime, not too bad you say? No, not in themselves, but each one had a double brandy chaser, just to keep company. Even his girlfriend joined in, to an extent, having Dubonet and Lemonade for breakfast, not realising it was alcoholic, and finding it particularly refreshing and a great way to start your day.

*After settling in to a new job, new acquaintances arrived on the scene and with them, more and more outlets to shop at. Admittedly, the selection and availability weren't as extensive as in the Uni. City where Eric had lived, where at the time, even after Operation Julie (a big set of busts, nationwide), you could order or request what you wanted and your dealer would normally be able to supply your shopping list, though relatively clean opium itself was harder to come by. On occasions, Eric had brazenly (and worse for wear) walked the corridors of various colleges, randomly knocking on bedroom doors trying to score and succeeded.

One such evening of success, led to a heavy night's session and he woke up, suddenly and early, still sitting in an armchair of the pleasant, little, two-bedroom house he was living in, in the attractive part of town.

Being a Saturday, and still morning he would soon have his visitor, ready for her weekly fix of

Tiswas.

Erics next door neighbour was a pleasant elderly gentleman, very hard of hearing, thankfully, considering the quality, quantity and loudness of music played in the household, varying from Baroque to Throbbing Gristle. One time, whilst still at school, in Social History, taken by a relatively new teacher, the pupils were invited to take a record of their choice into class in order to open up a discussion on diversity..." or some other bollocks" thought some of the kids.

Mr Chapman was in his thirties, with a wife and recent child, a pleasant chap, informative and enthusiastic, trying to pull people out of their predestined ruts and give them food for thought. He gave Eric two albums, From the Witchwood and Grave New World (the pun instantly sticking with Eric having just read the Aldous Huxley novel), both of which were taken away and played with nurturing appreciation (...and Eric sold him his woodwork project of a rocking chair, which collapsed after a few uses).

Eric never fully appreciated his width of musical awareness, it had grown with him, sometimes incidentally, from the soothing tones of the unknown harmonica player on the hot summer nights of the city and South African rhythms to Flanders and Swann and war time pub songs. Robert had attempted (and failed, due to being tone deaf) to be a jazz trumpeter, favouring Trad and Dixieland and Bing (often sung to nut no one else knew the tune). Tess was more into Roberta Flack, The Who, The Stones (which Cassie hijacked), Donavon then David Essex and Peter Skellern. Cassandra, well… she said: Modern Jazz, The Beatles, Ella and Louis, Cleo and Johnny and a bit of Frankie boy, though plenty of 60s pop was enjoyed and popular 70s music was embarrassingly danced to. Dickie was a more serious affair. Renbourn, Fripp and Williams where the top with easy listening was left to Feliciano and Arlo Guthrie, all topped off with a plethora of classic. And Eric…he enjoyed the simpler things, My Ding-a-Ling, shaking like Elvis, Streakers in the Sun, Jerry Lee and watching The Doors concert perform on T.V. the young Eric, who already was inappropriately being given the likes of Valium, sitting there, opened mouth, as Jim Morrison writhed on the stage floor, humping the air with his microphone, telling the world he was going to kill his Mum and Dad…Eric smiled… "Wow, awesome !" he quietly mused "Mum, this man wants to kill his parents" he shouted excitedly.

Years later he would try to offend as much as possible, taking in an Ian Dury record in to class, to play the intro of a track "Plastow Patricia" to the class.

As luck would have it his track was chosen amongst a few others, being lesser known at the time. Mr. Chapman lined up the stylus to the rotating grooves and lowered the needle just as the headmaster knocked on the door and walked in with some prospective parents being given a tour of the school. Smiles dropped as the words "Assholes, Bastards..." and other profanities burst forth onto the unprepared ears, followed by, without batting an eyelid "...and here we have Social Studies, where we're not afraid to question stereotypical thinking" followed by a smile and guiding the parents back out.

Again, thankfully, Erics elderly neighbour would be spared from hearing the modern take of music and the hullaballoo that was created at the end of the Saturday morning ritual of The Bucket of Water Song, that was the ever finale of Tiswas, normally re-enacted, with gusto (and sometimes ketchup) by Eric and his chums.

Their little visitor was the gentleman's Granddaughter, who came to stay every weekend and broke into Erics house every Saturday to watch telly. As far as he knew, the 10-year-old had been doing this for a while. her grandfather had no television, so hearing the neighbours, snuck into the back garden, through the rickety fence divide and opened the window into the sitting room (this was very easy as no locks or catches were on the sash window). Once in she would make herself comfortable and watch the morning T.V before returning for lunch. Initially startled, the tenants became used to the routine and soon settled in as a matter of course, though never "partaking" whilst young persons present.

It was on one of these mornings that Eric stirred in the armchair and found the television on and company already arrived.

"That's a lot of zips on your trousers" she said pointing.

"Yeah, I 'spose. They're called bondage trousers". Replied Eric.

They were actually black Boy bondage trousers, very comfortable and bought from the Kings Road.

He'd had a notion to get some and a knuckle duster, not to do damage but it seemed like a good idea at the time. Kids! So he figured he would start in the Kings Road and if that failed he would head over to Kensington High St. and go to the basement market, which always smelt so good...

Back at Kings Road the search was proving useless and he almost gave up until he spied a small collection of alternatives, yet fashionable looking shops. Wandering around the arcade he noticed some descending stairs, so wander casually down. Bingo! He couldn't believe his luck, "plenty of leather and studs in there" thought the 1979 Eric. In he wandered and without wasting time, asked the two guys behind the counter if they had any knuckle dusters (not realising they were illegal).

They looked at each other.

“Well, no” said one, looking at his companion.

“I suppose you could use this” said the other, producing narrow leather strap with a set of studs on and fastened with metal poppers.

Eric tried it out for size, the biggest setting fitted fine.

“Is there anything else you might like” smiled the first assistant leaning forward.

A bit taken aback from such a friendly request and the strange nature of the phrasing, Eric declined at the same time as noticing, for the first time, the black and white pictures that adorned the boutique. Lots of men, with big moustaches, leather caps, naked torsos and very tight leather trousers covered the walls.

It wasn’t until he was walking down the street, after a hasty exit, he pulled out his purchase, to try it on again. Fitted fine, but who would have such small wrists when done up on the tightest setting...ohh.

So, sitting in his chair, bondage trousers on, and young girl pointing.

“Are they all pockets”? she enquired.

“Well, yes, most of them” he replied.

“What’s in that one” she questioned, again pointing.

Eric had to go through all his pockets, even

though he knew nothing was in them as he had a faint recollection of emptying them last night, but to his surprise...

"Oh," he said, producing a small paper packet from one of his pockets.

"What's that" she said.

"Er...I don't know". He honestly replied, having no recollection of the item, though his brain was scrambled, again.

He carefully unwrapped the package, only to discover a few joints worth of weed.

"What's that" she said again, pointing.

"Erm, some seeds...for planting...my friend gave them to me...I forgot" he truly had forgot.

This wasn't unusual or seldom. Excess was his "go to" and he would frequently have recall flashes of staggering into someone or something, car horns blaring, or admiring the night sky from a peculiar and probably illegal position. One such of these events had left him confused and dumbfounded for a long time.

The evening was nothing unusual. The four elements, a combination of powder, pills, smoke and liquid had been consumed, his friends telling him ease up and to do less (except for Todd, who enjoyed the encouragement), but Eric only tended to stop when his conscious brain said bye-bye.

His hedonistic, addictive and self-destructive lifestyle was a resulting combination of many factors. A mother who showed sympathetic love, emotional fracturing, psychotic outbursts, narcissist attributes, flirtatiousness, the intelligence of B.A student with the naivety and stability of a scared and insecure child and a whiskey and nicotine addicted father who was as distant in himself as to anyone else, awkward, despite his inappropriate handling of women, in his emotional and physical connections, having being "buggered senseless" as a child by his overbearing elder brother and competing for his mother's affections with an archetypal South African alpha male husband.

His early introduction to mood and mind-altering pharmaceuticals in the mid and late sixties, undoubtably helped, with the music and colours of the time, especially the vibrancy of cartoons and comics combined and flicking through pages of the shelves of books, finding Huxley, Blake and Shakespeare, all leading to other lands, a real eye opener for a child still in single figures. It wouldn't be until some fifty years later, twenty years after deciding things had to stop, that he realised the more he imbibed, the clearer the sadness became, though not understanding what lay behind the title of that book, he had to obliterate his presence, to rid himself of the conflicting feelings, not knowing how to face himself.

Now in adulthood, he recalled standing up from

his chair in the side room of the pub, where the Asteroids game, his companion, was, possibly saying goodnight to everyone, then...blank.

He woke the next morning, feeling very comfortable, on his back, in the middle of his bed, naked (he always wore pyjama trousers in bed, except when...). He sat up suddenly and looked around and stupidly called out "Hello"?, feeling as if someone was or should be there.

Being a small bedsit, there was no hiding place, but what was even more bizarre was his clothes. At the bottom right-hand corner of his bed sat an exceptionally neat, folded pile of clothes, fresh underwear included. He looked around the room again, just to make sure he hadn't missed anyone in the 20ft by 20 ft space and called again. No reply came, obviously, as it was a one-bedroom bedsit which, literally was, just big enough to swing a cat in.

He searched his memory for any hint of how he got home and got up the six flights of stairs, that would have been a feat in itself, yet alone the tidy stack, coming to the conclusion, someone must have helped him back. He'd had quite a bit last night, even by his standards, mixing his intake heavily to prove a point, and considering, he felt pretty good...except for the total memory loss... not a hint of anything existed. Confused and befuddled, he checked the time and noticed that friends would already be congregating at the lunchtime local to prepare for the evening and reflect on the previous.

Eric quickly got dressed, still unnerved and still feeling remarkably refreshed, and left, jumping down the flights of stairs, eager to find out from his compadres the previous night's events.

He entered the pub under the watchful eye of the landlord, giving him a look of incredulity mixed with "behave", though his wife smiled and, disturbingly, chortled.

He went to the bar and ordered a pint.

"You feeling more yourself this morning" she said while pulling the bitter.

"Odd thing to say" thought Eric, replying "Yup, fine thanks, never better". A noncommittal and hopefully appropriate response he thought.

He made his way through already crowded hostelry, students galore, as you'd expect to find in most places in a university city. The mix here was about 60/40 in favour of townies, though some establishments would be 90/10 in favour of the ya-ya's. The 100% of either type was never a good idea to frequent, it would result in a lot of "Oh, yuh, of course, Father had to buy the villa" or "Do you want your fuckin ed kicked in". Eric never understood the politeness that preceded the violence; odd bedfellows. He got to his group of friends who all smiled and laughed when he appeared.

"You're alive then" said Elle, smiling, causing a

ripple of amusement.

“What happened to you last night then” interjected Todd.

“One minute you got up to go to the toilet” said Milo “the next, gone. How the hell did you make it home”.

“Yeah” said Todd “we were actually worried” laughing.

Eric explained that it was all a blank, though did now have a recollection of forgoing the toilet, for some reason seeing the pub door instead, but then went on to recount his waking etc... to his beloved small group of friends.

When finished there was silence. Then laughter.

No one had a clue what had occurred, it was going to be one of life’s little mysteries that would hang around for a long time.

THE LAW

Flouting The Law was instilled at an early age, not disrespectfully, just a matter of casual collision of cultures, sometimes literally.

Living near a major highway, leading into the centre of the nation's capital city, there were obvious restrictions and instructions for motorists to adhere to, for example, no u-turns, something Robert did on a daily occasion to avoid an extra two-minute detour, almost the amount of time it took to execute the about turn to their turning.

Always thrilling, Eric loved to get a chance to sit in the front seat of the old, two-tone Rover P4, which often had to be crank started, and watch his father manoeuvre the city's traffic at speed and to slipstream emergency vehicles up close, to get through red lights without getting caught.

A special treat was driving up the circular ramp of the West London Air Terminal, that serviced Gatwick and Heathrow, a speedy fly past of the startled doorman with a wave, whilst watching pilots and trolley dollies in all their finery, coming and going, carrying their PanAm and BOAC bags.

As the years progressed and engines got bigger, Robert's foot got heavier on the accelerator, making the most of company cars, especially when the head turning spectacle of the first Range Rover came on the scene. People stood and stared at the large, white, angular vehicle, so tall off the ground that Cassandra had to be helped in and out, attracting the wrong sort of attention she desired.

Robert was a spectacular motorist, thought his youngest child, handling the vehicle with ease, parking where he chose, sticking fingers up at parking wardens (which Eric never understood, at first, until he tried it out on a teacher at school...), the most impressive time was when the two of them were caught in a heavy London fog.

It had been one of those occasions when Eric had decided school was horrible, so threw himself out of the moving train, executing a truly magnificent double roll, he was always impressed until he felt the kick up the backside. As a result of his exploits, he had to tag along with his dad for the day, arduous meetings, waiting in the car...he learnt how not to get bored by watching, so the day passed eventfully, imagining people's lives and homes. Time came for home and twenty minutes' drive from home, the fog dropped. As thick as it was grey, visibility was zero, about a foot in front of the headlights could be seen. Thankfully it was already night, the roads were quiet and Robert knew the area well and incredibly, continued driving home, at a crawl, not hitting a single car or kerb.

Unfortunately, later in life, Robert hadn't slowed his speed to match his ability, or intake and recklessly drove as fast as possible on motorways and careered down country lanes, avoiding dusk and night driving, only to Nazi salute the arresting officers and get tackled to the ground when in his 80s for drink driving...not that losing his licence made any difference. He was even a demon on his mobility scooter, bumping into cars and crashing into shelves in the small, narrow convenience store. Cassandra had never driven, trying to ride a bike had proved too hazardous enough.

Moving to the university city, Eric came into his first contact with people who had very different views about the powers that be. Typically, at school and briefly after, there were those who professed dislike of the system, but with like so many others, confused the boundaries or painted everything with the same brush without the awareness of the many layers and angles that existed. Having had few minor and relatively innocent run-ins was inevitable, especially when riding a motorbike, wearing a leather jacket and, to be truthful, probably behaving too exuberantly at times. But he did enjoy enjoying himself, the wide openness and beauty of the Dorset countryside touched his green personality and innocent ways.

City life in the early 80s offered an eclectic atmosphere, about to be taken full advantage of by someone eager to expand his knowledge after a suppressed childhood, despite the recent freedom of the rolling hills, his two wheels and haybarns.

Despite having an easy nature, Eric found aggressive conflict quite quickly from the boys in blue. At the time, the Sus Law was still in effect, an understandable, though possibly heavy-handed piece of legislation at the time it was introduced and now utilised to its maximum limits.

Cheffing and being a roadie had one thing in common: Unsocial, actually, totally the wrong word to use, hours. Eric would often find himself walking the streets in the early hours of the morning, normally after work, admittedly, sometimes, all night sessions of Monopoly or Colditz and Scrabble (with the obligatory puff added to the mix) and get "pulled" by a pair of overly threatening enforcers, demanding information and a search. Ironically, they tended not to like the truth. When questioned about where you're going, where have you come from and what have you been doing is responded by "I've been playing Monopoly until 4 in the morning", it was pretty common to be instantly pushed onto the bonnet of their car and searched.

Eric learnt quickly to remain pleasant, something some of his friends failed to, or didn't want to grasp. Much to their expense. One evening, after a usual session at their favourite watering hole, Eric offered to walk Elle, Andrew's girlfriend, home, as And. was visiting his mother in Reading. It was about a 45-minute walk out of town to Elles parents' house, where she still lived, but that never bothered him, frequently having walked miles across the Dorset countryside to meet up with mates, when either buses were not available or having the need to stretch his legs and admire the tranquillity.

Living in a small rural village, getting to and from one predominantly relied on Shanks's pony, especially at night, walking down the narrow, sometime haunted lane and hearing strange noises from behind the hedges. At first, unnerving, but soon became comforting, hearing the wild animals of the night about their business, occasionally walking through fields as a short cut, and surprisingly, meeting a fellow traveller, normally with bulging pockets, a heavy looking sack and a mischievous smile, the wink standing out in the moonlit nights.

Walking along with Elle they chatted and laughed, making short work of the footsteps and soon enough left her safe in her doorway, silently waving goodnight. Eric jogged for a little, not only to fill the quiet, but also to cover some ground, eventually settling to a comfortable steady walking pace after about 10 minutes.

He was coming to the first main road that intersected his route and noticed in the distance a cyclist headlight heading towards him, slowing his pace to see clearer, he noted it was none other than a female police officer on her night duties.

"Excuse me" called out a soft and slightly nervous, but authoritative voice "Could you stop there, please".

Eric stopped and then checked over his shoulder, just checking to make sure she wasn't talking to anyone else on the empty street.

The slight and diminutive person, was just doing her job and Eric was impressed by her courage.

"Good evening, Sir" she said "How are you this evening" she continued.

Eric instantly decided to empty all information concerning his last hour, and more, making it clear he wasn't a nutter or a threat, noticeably, much to the relief of the cyclist, who seemed to relax a bit and laugh. They stood and chatted for a bit, finding out that she <u>was</u> a new recruit and had cruelly drawn the short end of the stick that night. They departed on their separate routes, Eric kicking himself for not getting her phone number, another trait he'd picked up from his father.

By this time Eric had already moved from his first house, though had already, usually thanks to Todd, had quite a few dealings with raids.

The evening turned to night as Eric and a couple of friends had gathered, as usual, to joke and smoke, and tonight it was Linton Kwesi Johnson's turn to set the mood, telling it about Winston getting high, when, suddenly, Todd burst through the front door and into the sitting room, hands covered in blood, out of breath, followed by a panicky Billie, his girlfriend, clutching at a large bloodied poster. Billie shot upstairs, locking herself in the bathroom and Todd exited via the backdoor into the garden with no explanation.

The group were a little startled, but this was Todd after all, their main concern was hoping that no one had been attacked.

"Erm" said Milo "What just happened"? being snapped out of his sunken state.

"Er..., not sure," said Eric.

As if the shock of the bizarre interruption was enough, there came an instant heavy banging on the front door.

"Police. Open up" came the order.

Before anyone could rise, momentarily again

stunned by their new situation, in burst a small wave of authoritative uniforms, instantly filling the quaint sitting dining room.

This was the first-time experience of such an intrusive encounter, though as mentioned before, not the last, especially involving Todd.

One morning, Eric would be awoken at 5, his room, which he was renting from Todd's Mum, and house filled by the raid, looking for and not finding their assailant. Apparently, Todd and cohort had broken into a supermarket in the early hours, having previously damaged a few phone boxes and fleeing with the proceeds. At the shop, for ease of carrying, only stole cases of soft drink. How did they get caught or why did the finger point so quickly to Todd?

Stacking the cases on a corner, around the back of the ringing alarm, one of the perpetrators went to an undamaged phone box and called for a taxi to drop off Todd and goods at his home address.

When interviewed the cabbie stated he did think it odd at the time, but he was convinced by the fact that they paid his fare all in 5pence pieces.

There would be other brushings, especially at parties, where raids usually were followed by violence, normally meted out by those few goers who always looked out for an opportunity. Unfortunately, normally a given if one would attend those types of parties.

To a mentally growing lad, things never seemed to amaze Eric in the complexities of life around him. Sitting in a quiet room, away from the main party, he sat with about 10 strangers, chilling back, chatting and playing pass the joint. There were definite types of tokers. Some preferred smoking other people's stuff, some hogged the spliffs (called Bogart), some were canny, and to some, like Eric, rolled quickly to override the others, just wanting to get wasted.

Everyone was friendly enough and the conversation soon ventured onto what people did for a living, and one guy caused a big laugh when stated:

"I'm with the D.S (Drug Squad)".

The laughter was free and easy, the D.S always a word your ear would be hoping not to hear shouted at parties.

"No, really" said a bloke sitting next to other "what do you really do"?

Putting his hand inside his jacket, he pulled out a small wallet and flipped it open.

"Really" he said "I work for the Drug Squad".

Silence slammed into the room as if air was no longer needed.

"Don't worry though" he said again "I'm not on duty" laughing.

That put a downer on that evening. It's funny how a few words can change the atmosphere so completely.

Paranoia is one of the negative attributes connected with a drug lifestyle, though sometimes reality can be strange enough.

Eric found himself living in a small be adequate property, a kitchen sitting room and bathroom on the ground floor, tucked away, down some steps, at the back of the main house, with a door with a single, small glass window that led up two flights of stairs to two, well sized double bedrooms.

He was sharing, at the time with his girlfriend, a trainee beauty therapist and fellow baker, whose main hobby was Karate (and trying to chat up, unsuccessfully, girls).

The maisonette had previously been rented to psychotic nurse, who, apparently, brought work home with her and had many unusual visitors, day and night (which still carried on visiting even after she had left). When they first moved in, they discovered that a good clean was in order, discovering what seemed like dried blood sprayed on the inside of the cupboard doors. The little window, in the door that led upstairs, had an unnerving nature, often catching your eye and expecting to see a face peering through from the darkness. The strange feel to the property was enhanced one evening playing Monopoly (always a favourite goes to) and each player threw about three double sixes each in turn and in succession.

About 5:30 one late afternoon, the usual turnaround was occurring.

Erics girlfriend had just returned from college, still in her purple uniform, Eric just about to leave for a shift, so garbed in his bakery whites, and their mutual friend kitted out in his Gi or Dogi, ready for a session of open hand training.

Sitting around, tea and chat, all three gasped as they saw a face appear at the little glass square and door slowly open towards them.

Frozen in amazed shock, the front door opened and again police poured in, looking rather bewildered at the three costumed figures.

A momentary pause.

“Mr Forest”? came the stern query.

“No. he lives at the main house at the front”.

“Oh…sorry. We thought this might be the back entrance”.

A slight shuffling, followed by “Do you know where we can find him”? Then leaving, with slight awkwardness and obviously wanting to ask, but confused about the whole affair.

As a footnote, and to complete this offshoot, Mr Forest had been involved in a car accident… of sorts. A young acquaintance, whom he hadn’t seen for about a year, turned up unannounced to take his old friend out for a spin in his new car. They only managed to get to the bottom of the hill, when the car caught the corner of the pavement and rolled. The young lad then ran, leaving a bemused and confused Mr Forest to wander off to the pub, as per usual, to nurse his wounds. The vehicle had been stolen.

As was the scrumpled and bloodied film poster in Todd's girlfriend's hands.

They had been walking to Eric's, past the ever-busy cinema club, when Billie said to her beau "I like that poster".

Ever the roguish gentleman, Todd proceeded to smash the external display with his hands to win his prize. Sadly, the proprietors didn't agree with this process and decided to explain their displeasure, receiving skin on skin contact for their efforts. Todd being Todd didn't flee the scene immediately, he kindly waited until the panda cars were in sight, up for a merry chase and high jinxery.

It would be considerable years until Eric had any serious involvement with the enforcers of The Queens Regulations, apart from the occasional motor theft or accident, spending some hours in a cell, listening to the cacophony of his neighbours, one, young, continually abusing his captors, the other, older, wailing his unhappiness until silence again came to visit.

Escorted from his cubicle, passing the "other"s open door, he saw him still and lifeless, surrounded by activity, trying, uselessly, resuscitation.

"Move along. Nothing to see here Sonny" came the order.

NEAR MISSES

In his first fifty years, Eric had been considerably lucky in avoiding serious injury, considering the risks and foolhardiness he partook in.

Apart from his mother's attempt on his life, he had almost drowned on a number of occasions, once, at a crowded swimming baths where he was dive bombed by accident, a couple of times at schools due to cramps and broken toes and again at a primary school friends country house, a party left him pushed, literally, into the deep end, leaving him out of his depth, physically and emotionally, possibly for the last time.

Evel Knievel became a big influence on his desire to become a stuntman, with Tess and friends putting on shows for the family, or anyone else who could be persuaded to watch, and Eric being used as the clown or acrobat, falling over invisible hurdles, pratfalling into walls and doors and spectacularly falling off chairs, much to the alarm for the onlookers.

As age progressed, his desire to outperform previous exploits also grew, learning how to jump of first floor school windows, blazer flapping in the upcoming draught like Batman, climbing towering T.V masts that swayed in the lightest breeze, then onto activities such as abseiling and rock climbing, parascending and parachuting, but the thrill of motorbiking didn't need speed in the quiet, narrow Dorset lanes, just the meeting of a milk tanker coming the opposite direction was sometimes enough to get adrenaline racing. The large, unforgiving lumps of metal, carrying liquid which would push the brakes to their limit and taught Eric the ability to make friends with hedges.

The freedom he experienced at such an important time in his life, was, perhaps, unfortunate and well timed (though perhaps the real unfortunate thing was the tight rein that he had been leashed on for his first twelve years), the subsequent "knee-jerk" reaction would take twenty years of experimentation, resulting in dramatic weight loss and homelessness (being saved by a £10 note and a small bible verse, the only things found in a wallet, discovered in a phone box late one night, wandering the streets for warmth and distraction (saviour indeed).

That event was a pivotal change, instrumental in getting him back on his feet, though, at the time, probably not taken full advantage of, as his habits wouldn't be dissolved for a long time yet, but, nevertheless, it was instrumental in many ways.

Things escalated quickly from the turnabout. A job came first, mobility and relationships followed and the passing of his driving test gave a renewed sense of independence.

Italy was an exciting country to drive around. Banked corners were a delight to speed around and every driver was in a hurry, honking horns and gesticulating and where there were two lane roads, the motorists would turn it into three, and no waiting for your lights to turn "GREEN", but "GO" when the opposing lights turn "RED".

Milo and Eric had been advised to go to a certain Piazza in Roma, for substance purchasing, if needed, so after a couple of days sightseeing the spectacular ruins of ancient history, went in search for the advised beautiful square and statued fountain. Rome, like many other early cities, offer breath-taking architecture, from the magnificent giant buildings, to the smallest, unassuming courtyards, that can be found hidden about the small back streets, unlooked on by tourist's eyes, but lived with like an old acquaintance. Even visiting an Italian bank could be an experience. Housed in some archaic marbled building of a senator, now repurposed, but still as casually masterful in its simplicity yet effectiveness.

Milo and Eric stood in the piazza and looked around for a likely target for their need. A group of seven likely suspects lurked with darkened eyes by the entrance of an alley way, a more residential part of the square and after several minutes of discussion, Milo drew the short straw of contact.

They strode towards the like aged youths and waved with smiles.

“Ciao” they both said.

“Hashish”? came the response.

They were a bit taken aback by the reply, but were relieved at the same time.

“Er, yeah, Prego”. Said both Milo and Eric in unison.

“Opium, heroin…”? came the further question.

“No, no, just some hashish prego”. Again, in unison.

The Italians looked a bit disappointed, but the older and taller one of the groups, who had not spoken yet said “you, come with me”, turn and started to stride off.

Milo turned to Eric.

“Stay here, I’ll be back soon” and trotted off after his quarry down the dark alley.

Eric stood, feeling like a little kid watching his balloon blow away with the wind, unsure of what to do next.

The diminished group dispersed themselves in various directions, leaving Eric totally alone and uneasy. Something didn’t feel right. He felt immediate concern for his friend and realised that him, being the more physically toned of the two, should have gone in his place.

He found an old stone bench and sat and waited.

Time passed.

Then some more.

Too long for a simple deal, Eric started working out plans of action and possible scenarios.

Eventually, a couple of hours later Milo returned and both were relieved.

They had topped up for their journey out, confident that no checks would be made on a ferry from England to France, and had even obtained a couple of tabs (thin cardboard-soaked LSD) from a magnificent and an impressively filled old mansion that look like it belonged to Miss Haversham, but was owned and housed by Hells Angels, one of who sat on a raised throne in a darkened ballroom, next to the hallway an impressive staircase, all of which exuded the danger and paranoia of excess intake.

The acid had been consumed whilst camping, out of season, at Lago di Como, a beautiful lake in Northern Italy, the backdrop of the still mountains reflecting in the calm waters, which was only disturbed by a large fish which, Eric and Milo considered, insisted on messing with their heads, as it kept swimming onto the nearby bank from where they sat, getting extremely sunburnt, flounder around for a moment and then disappear back into the water, only to repeat this process many times over a couple of hours. Fortunately, the acid was weak and the fish became a joke instead of a concern.

They had not intended to stay at this campsite, which they were the only visitors at, but as Eric had decided to almost cause a multiple collision on a mountain road, overtaking three cars and a van, a hair breath away from colliding with an oncoming vehicle, sending many to their demise down the drop of the side of the road, Milo, not for the last time, said "Enough".

A brother and sister owned the campsite, situated on the banks, with the other main road blocked by a rockfall, that had buried a small factory some years earlier, but was not allowed to be cleared, by orders of "Mafiosa".

They set their tent up on the back edge of the site, in front of a spindly wooden fence, with a wide view of the vast countryside and hills. Evening came soon enough and an invite for beers came with it and for the first time, Milo and Eric felt that they had begun an adventure.

Returning to their tent after the fish escapade and slightly sore from being burnt, both by the sun and metaphorically, they spent the rest of the eve eating tinned ravioli, listening to their collection of tapes, Sandinista and Dr Hooks Medicine Show tonight, and smoking and glad they had decided on this excursion. France had been France, but Italy, well, after all, all roads lead to Roma. They settled down, happy and peaceful and sleep came quickly.

Erics eyes flicked open, instantly alarmed. A hand, not his, covered his mouth and in the dimness of the tent, the bright full moon outside, could see Milo raise a finger to his lips, signalling silence. At that exact time, he heard it.

Raising his head, milo removed his hand and they listened.

Outside of the tent, someone circled. They moved stealthily around the tent, checked the car door and carried on moving around in a clockwise fashion, stumble over a guide rope, then resume. Being stuck inside a tent was a dilemma. It would take some effort to get out quickly as there was an inner and outer zip on the small four-man tent, and could easily be trapped or overcome without defence, not knowing where the attacker, or even attackers might come from. So, silent they stayed, listening to the heavy, deep, erratic, yet calm breathing, as theirs had ceased.

A sudden cracking and snapping emanated, as whoever, must have climbed the spindle fence and then silence.

Staying in the tent for a few minutes that took ages to pass, not hearing any sound, ventured, carefully out.

Clouds had started covering the moon, but no

one could be seen and no damage had been done, so cautiously they returned to their shelter and spent the rest of the night half awake and vigilant.

The morning came soon enough, and the previous night's experience was behind them, as now was the broken wooden fence. What startled them though, was what else they saw. The foot trail could be seen clearly in the long grass, leading off into the distance and up into the uninhabited hills of the countryside. They didn't stay another evening, just in case, though mentioning the events to their momentary incredulous hosts.

They say a cat has nine lives. Eric grew concerned, as he touched his 60's, that he had spent them all many times over and then some. Whether it had been falling through a roof and managing to clutch a beam on the way down, only to find the six inches of a nail grazing his upper torso or falling through a skylight of a factory roof (… whilst with Todd), only to land on a huge pile of recycled clothing. The list was extensive. Staggering into the road, in flashback, hearing car horns and lights, snorting unknown recipes of stolen pharmacies causing blindness and pain, the drownings and fights, the psychotic and schizophrenic, the undesirables, and not to mentioning the innumerable car accidents, for the moment.

Everywhere has its toilet. Wolverhampton in the mid-90s was no exception. Following his future wife, Eric found himself working for a company, under a pseudonym, by accident, and couldn't be bothered to change it.

One day, Big John and Bob, his co-workers, were assigned a job in Wolves territory that had a reputation. The previous year, Big John had parked the Land Rover and secured all the equipment in the back cage, and walked along the canal treating unwanted plant growth, spraying from his knapsack. All was going well as he crossed the bridge to return to the vehicle for a top up when he was approached by a stranger in his late 20s.

"Give us a hand with that," said the male.

"What"? said Big John, a bit confused.

"That cylinder, there" he gesticulated to a large gas cylinder on the back of BJ's wagon.

Still uncertain as to what was going on, Big John replied again "What"?

"That cylinder" pointing "Give us a hand with it over the bridge. Its mine" came the reply.

"No' it's mine".

"You're mistaken mate" pulling a machete from his loose jacket "it's mine".

"Alright then" said Big John calmly "Keep your shirt on".

Having re-laid the story to their new fellow

worker, they were advised to work in groups and not leave the van unattended, for any reason.

They drove for a while, through the estates which had walk ways over the roads, where you could see debris scattered all round, broken bricks, bottles, even smashed toilets, unsuspecting cars being target practice for those above.

Arriving at their destination Eric was confused. Why were they working here? The whole estate looked deserted, only the occasional car moved by, and sizeable as the area was, shops and house alike were boarded up, not with wood, but steel shutters, punched with holes, covered every door and window, on every building they saw.

He queried Big John.

"Daft bugger" he said "Course people live here".

Naively Eric questioned again.

"Stops them from being petrol bombed" Big John said, pointing to scorch marks on some of the walls.

"Even the police don't come here" he continued.

Eric considered himself an aware person, he knew about poverty but this, this was in the heart of England, at the end of the 20th Century. A supposedly enlightened and civilised country, rapidly going to the dogs. A country who was turning their backs on growth for cheap distractions, whilst the wealthy grew at the expense of the masses, most of which who were too blind to see, too deaf to hear and too dumb to speak.

The full sentence by Karl Marx, that is often misquoted, as so many quotes are, is such:

"Religion is the sigh of the oppressed creature, the heart of a heartless world, and the soul of soulless conditions. It is the opium of the people".

In the last fifty years, Christianity has been replaced by a new idol in the so-called United Kingdom, a new love, many seeking its glory and shallow rewards, never finding answers, only emptiness, money.

Now opium, cocaine and money are the most popular new religion and the big wheels of the machine keep turning.

Eric had been on the start of his journey when he first tried opium, the sticky brown substance smeared onto cigarette paper and sprinkled reverently with tobacco or grass, rolled, smoked and enjoyed. Though his dealer (who Tess had a major crush on, a blonde version, though more chilled and hippy type, if such a thing can be, of the character Mack, from Green Wing) refused to supply on a regular basis, conscientious in his dealings and responsibilities, a very rare commodity in dealers.

On his second leg, he lost his first in Oxford, of his existential journey, with the Mondays and Roses in full bloom, heroin and its abusers were growing more common in his life and the gap between refusal and acceptance was getting narrower all the time.

Bournemouth, more notably Boscombe, was a bedsit land for a large population of Scots and Scousers, winos and skag heads (not saying they go hand in hand, but a lot of them did), most trying to make a deal or score, to escape the misery that haunted their minds and chased their souls.

The winos normally littered the attractive public garden benches, cadging change or selling petrol-soaked hash, the discarded and failed smuggled goods, whereas the Scousers could be found shoplifting to order or selling Aunties best china.

Driving around the area also had its hazrads, especially at traffic lights.

Pulling up in his old, dark blue Triumph Herald, a wild haired, leather jacket Charlie Manson look alike stepped in front of Erics car and signalled a thumbs up.

The gesture was reciprocated, as a matter of goodwill, but not as a signal of “yeah, come on, bring your mate with his massive German Shepard dog. They can get in the back and pant over my shoulder, while you get in the front and stare at me”. Which is exactly what happened in a flash. Before he knew it, the lights had changed and he had three new passengers. He was as surprised as the onlookers.

Eric didn't mind hitch-hikers. It was, after all, one of his favourite books and he knew what it was like not having a car, but this was... unexpected.

"My names Mantis" said the front passenger.

"I've just out of jail and I'm going to do the bloke who put me there" he continued.

"Ah...right" responded Eric, unsure what else he could say, talk about sensory overload.

"You're not going to tell the police, because I've seen you and I know your car. Otherwise, I'll kill you too".

"Man," thought Eric, "why do I have to always get the weirdos" thinking back on all the occasions, flickering across his brain, like that other guy in the cinema who tried to pick him up, or that other nutter, or...

"Turn right here" came the order.

"Yeah, no problem" came the slightly stoned reply. He wasn't that bothered and offered his now companions a smoke.

"I don't smoke" said Mantis "it doesn't help my head".

The guy in the back did though, not sure about the dog.

After several minutes of left and right turns they got to their destination.

"You never saw me, right. I don't exist. Right" came the emphatic order.

"Yeah, okay" stupidly "Good luck".

Many lessons were learnt in that area. The biggest was another life changer. A realisation that would take almost five years to fully implement and almost twenty years to be fully clean.

They were out on a trip to score some gear. When you're in the thick of it, you don't see what could be construed as sad desperation, trawling from house to bedsit, especially in dry times, where had become easier to pick up heroin than any other substance. Horse was for Matty, a female scouser friend who was getting deeper and deeper into it, and something special for the weekend (normally Whiz/ George (speed/amphetamine sulphate) or, if lucky, some acid) for Eric. All the "stuff" had different monikers, and depending on who you talked to and whether on the phone or out and about, might have extra aliases, depending on the real likelihood of phone tapping (as some had already got extensive form) or just plain crazy paranoia. Even for the most up to date and on the ball addict, name changes could get confusing.

"Hi Bob (Frank) is Terry there (do you have any grass)?"

"Hi Helen (Matty/Matilda), Terrys out (no), he's gone over to Asda (getting some later, good deal coming)."

"What's Chuck (Charlie/Skag/Heroin) doing (how much £) this savvy (afternoon) as I'm coming over in a bit (get some gear ready as I'm gagging for a hit)".

"Wha'? Who the fucks Chuck!"

You get the drift.

After a few calls and drop ins, Matty decided to call on her brother Matty (Matthew) as a last resort, but also knowing he would give her a better deal, if only slightly, than any other.

Whatever you call them: Druggies, Junkies, Addicts, Skagheads (specifically reserved for the dross of heroin users), a lot of them have issues and a lot of them...let's face it, can't be trusted. In order to get their fix, the majority turn to either theft or sex, selling both for a bag or wrap and while they're literally chasing (inhaling) their dream, their life decays around them.

Eric hadn't sunk that low...yet, but he was beginning to notice the rot getting closer and closer in more of his socialising circuit, whereas his work life was a totally different cuttle of fish. By day Delivery Driver and Baker, by night...

He was enjoying his work. The driving was fun and he got to see most of the South of England countryside in a time when traffic wasn't excessive and road surfaces were well maintained.

Accidents were an ill-fated side product of

covering so much mileage, encountering the variety of other road users and the diversity that was offered by the conurbation and rural highways.

Whether it was reversing into a forecourt petrol pump, that jumped out behind him, from nowhere, crumpling like a carton and gushing fuel over the petrol station, much to the amusement of a couple of lads in a mini. Or buckling up, in a fully parked, large white Mercedes van after a delivery only to suddenly leap three feet forward, and on inspection, finding a Mercedes car had decided to wedge itself under the back of the van, crumpling its bonnet, whilst its driver and passenger removed themselves in an alcoholic ether that was still lingering from the night before at 9:30 in the morning. Or even driving into a yearly family outing, including Grandma, while sightseeing. The most dramatic was one of his luckiest escapes.

Eric picked up Betty from his parent's house, on an estate on the outskirts of Bournemouth, having a chat with the parents while Betty finished his Breakfast (6pm). They climbed into the works Citroen pick-up and headed off, chatting. It was a pleasant evening; no hurry was needed to get to work and the back roads into town were always quiet. A sharp right-hand bend loomed, but no concern was needed, as their speed was steady and not at all excessive, so cornering was at ease without any thought, until the van decided to go the opposite way from which it was being steered.

Without hesitation, Eric compensated, but again it had the opposite effect, again and again the van careered on its own course, zigzagging into the path of oncoming car, when suddenly off it shot.

It hit the low hedge and flew into the air, twisting as it went, landing upside down in a field, where the new momentum of height kept moving, windscreen popping out over their now upside-down heads and watching grass flick the roof to a standstill.

The loudness of the silence had been deafening. Ears ringing Betty and Eric looked at each other.

"You okay?"

"Yeah, you?"

"Yeah" smiling "Fine" ..." better get out then"

In these moments of life, one isn't always quite aware as one should be. The seat belts were very stiff to release, this is when the first minor injury occurred. Not thinking, they both dropped, simultaneously about 6 inches onto their heads. Realising that the doors were buckled shut, they had to clamber out of the back, tripping over a tangle of brambles, second injury, and looked at the snapped chassis and driveshaft.

The woman, from the before mentioned

oncoming vehicle was running towards them, shocked and relieved to find two living people. The police eventually arrived and were likewise amazed, a couple of feet in either direction and the trees or telegraph pole would have claimed lives. On closer inspection, it was discovered that, probably a kiddie prank, a large nail must have been leant against the tyre, when stationary, sticking in when pulling off, intending an instant flat, but not actually coming into its own until a sharp corner hit.

It gave Eric a new respect for the road and its hazards, realising he had to take a more defensive stance when behind the wheel.

The same was to be said for his visit to Matty with Matty.

They pulled up to the Victorian block of red brick flats. Eric had always wondered what they looked like from the inside, having passed them many a time, and now his curiosity would be peeked.

Entering through the well-maintained, tiled communal hallway, they climbed the concrete stairs with wrought iron banister, up four flights of stairs. They knocked on the wooden door and waited.

Matty's brother's girlfriend, Sharon opened it slowly, with caution, letting the rancid odours escape from their captors. Her lank, long, straggly once blonde hair draped her sallow[PK1] and gaunt face, sunken eyes and dirty yellowed teeth.

"Oh, hi matty" said the flat voice "c'mon in". opening the door, a fraction wider.

Matty and Eric entered. The darkened room was not dark enough.

Rubbish was strewn everywhere under the dirt and filth. No surface was left untouched, even old needles could be seen amongst the debris. The walls stained and damaged, as was the ceiling and the carpet, what there was of it, torn, pulled up, once a vibrant green, now browned and burnt. Curtains hung torn and nailed in place, furniture broken and sparse as the two tenants walked in circles, trying to remember if they still had a stash.

A noise came from behind Eric as he stood near the front door. He turned his head to see a young child standing in a cot behind him in another room. The occasional pink splotch looked out of place on the grime covered and soiled child, like badly applied camouflage, he would have blended in perfectly with the shit smeared walls had his tears not cleaned part of his face. He couldn't believe he had just stepped into this pit of squalor; the contrast had been so extreme and sudden.

It was then he knew he had to change his life.

OOH, OOH, OOH...

The leaf lined lane, bushes along the sides and trees bending overhead, ran quietly down to the waiting canal and moored barge, waiting for its passengers as the water gently sploshed and lapped when the occasional boat passed by. Ducks quacked and moorhens hurried about their business with the warmth of the summer air flowing idly along the green tunnel of foliage, as Eric skipped along beside his mother, Little Ted in hand, wearing matching red shorts and his favourite striped T-Shirt.

Today was definitely a good day. Not only did the excursion by longboat beckon, but the destination would be seen from a distance, the towering, curved metal frame and, if lucky, some escaped inhabitants might also be spied.

Eric knew this much, and had been taught it from his early steps.

Living in London, he was very fortunate to have so much around him.

"Many people have very little" Cassandra explained to her youngest son.

"Some people live in smaller houses than us, can't afford nice things and can be very unhappy." She told him.

"Can't we help them, mummy," said the little voice.

"Sometimes, but we don't have much to give ourselves, that's why we hide when the milkman comes". Cassie continued.

Eric enjoyed hiding behind the sofa, but sometimes gave the game away by popping his head out over the top to see or by laughing too loudly.

There were many free things to do being in the centre of the metropolis. The nearby park with its round pond (to exhaustedly run around or lose your little boat in) and the tranquil and fragrant orangery of Kensington Palace, or a further walk, deeper into the park, to enthusiastically run up the steps of The Albert Memorial and run your hands along the statues that surrounded the plinth. There were the museums too, the Science, with its rockets and physics displays, the V&A, housing memorabilia of all societies, but the most visited being the Natural History, which was as silent as a library and as reverent as a chapel, only a gentle cough being heard, normally by one of the suited attendants, signalling a dislike of behaviour.

The marble floors, brass hand rails, wooden panelling and large glass fronted displays all held their occupants frozen in a snap shot of time, the many forms to marvel at and wonder of the times they all moved in, with the mighty blue whale suspended above the visitors' heads, exhibiting its vastness and sleek design.

Erics favourite museum though, and one not often frequented due to its further location, was the magnificent British Museum, with its Roman-Greco style entrance already issuing a statement of what was to be found inside. Treasure abounds lay within those walls, Egyptian, Aztec, Mongolian..., mummies, statues and jewellery, the spectacular to the humble, each having had its place in human history and to Eric, each touched by another far distant hand, maybe a simple person had reached out casually, whilst walking past and touched a smooth porcelain monument, or a lover had handed over an amulet to his to be wife. History in its entirety. That is what the beauty he saw, the stories that lay behind the stories, the tales of the unnoticed.

There was a greater prize to be had than a visit to this monumental location. An ulterior motive to persuade his mother of the distant journey. This treasure did not play within the confines of the grandiose or among the throng of tourists.

Sitting quietly, but always enticingly, stone's

throw from the front gates of the museums entrance, stood a small fronted, wood and glass shop, with the words Alan Alans written clearly above.

Entering through the ping of the doorbell, you were accosted with amazement and spectacle.

A glass counter ran along the right-hand side and end of the shop, but the walls were covered with small wooden, shoe box size draws, each with a brass curved handle and a label. But what was truly magical, was the festivity of colours and shapes, ranging from a large red and black, imposing disappearing cabinet to multicoloured knotted hankies, bunches of collapsible flowers, pointed wizard hats and gowns or plastic flies to scatter on your mother's sandwich (snigger snigger).

Every trick under the sun was to be evident somewhere in your vision. Escapology, mind reading, sword swallowing, juggling, everything there to be bought, whatever your trickster needs and whatever your budget. There was one strict condition for purchase. You could only buy if you knew how the trick was done.

However, for those who had aspirations and were new comers to the trade and showed awe and enthusiasm, the diminutive, yet fully skilled Mr Alan, and assistant, would encourage observation. While serving the average punters, who might have called in to buy snapping chewing gum or the ever-popular whoopee cushions, the sales team would be performing sleight of hand or prop ridden tricks, astounding those directly in the frontline, but being a huge sense of amusement to the sideliners.

There was other daytrips Eric looked forward to, but, most especially, the yearly event of November 5th and not just because of the obvious. He did like fire though. Whether it was a chance to try and toast bread on a fork in front of the sitting rooms gas heater, or "accidentally" lighting a whole box of indoor fireworks with his cousin, both gleeful at the fizzes and pops and ever-increasing flames.

The days and evenings leading up to the date in question was spent in dilemma, mainly because of the making the Guy. A pair of old trousers and tights would be found, tied and stuffed with scrumpled up newspaper, as was a shirt, which would be stitched to the legs and a head fashioned by covering a blown-up balloon with papier mache. The quandary was (something he had learnt from school and his from his rebellious father) thus:

1) Guido Fawkes was only one of a group
2) The only one caught
3) Was probably innocent of the accusations
4) Died horribly
5) Those in power probably deserved it

Having all this information to hand, and more,

Eric felt sympathies to the yearly ritual of burning this unknown effigy and made sure that everyone attending knew it, not that it stopped anything.

The car would be loaded with attending personnel, poor old Guy being relegated to the boot with some fireworks (away from his father's incessant smoking, unless Dickie wasn't around, then Guy could be safely placed between Tess and himself for company.

Robert's smoking could be a pleasant and familiar smell, particularly when blended with au de whiskey, but when trapped in the confines of a car, played havoc with Erics travel sickness. On most journeys the scenario was the same, despite the known and impending results.

About two hours before a major (over half an hour) journey was to be had, stress levels would start to rise in Cassandra which would be the same time as extra pill popping and a short rest was needed. Once the meds had kicked in, she would rise, a relaxed, more confident persona, organised and prepared, but not yet dressed for the occasion ahead and the fragility still lurking in the closet.

"Come on Darlings, you have to get ready. Don't forget it's going to be cold tonight, so get something warm to wear" Cassie would say, nurturing her children.

"Ooh, I might wear my purple corduroy dress"

said Tess, thinking aloud.

"Don't be such a stupid girl" Cassandra snapped "I'm wearing purple. Honestly." Walking off into a dark brewing cloud.

Once costumes had been selected and greasepaint applied, the character was ready for the performance, as were the chorus line.

The drive to Cassandra's grownup school friend, Connie (one of the so-called 3 Witches), was an hour drive over the Surrey Hills, always fragrant with bonfire smoke wafting through the cars ventilation system or the smallest open crack of a window that Eric would keep his nose near, rather than face the full and overpowering air of the interior, where Robert chain smoked, insisting windows be shut.

"It'll stop you from smoking when older" came the reply from pleas of air.

Eric would rather have not had bouts of bronchitis and travel sickness, if he had known the consequences of his dad's incessant puffing and nicotine intake. Ironically, all three siblings smoked at one time or other, Eric the most intense, Tess the longest, Dickie the least, this was also the same for their alcohol intake, with Tess never managing to unshackle herself from her prison.

Reaching their destination, the family bundled out of the car being greeted by the other family, Eric dashing off for a fight with his equal, while the others greeted each other with casual luvvie (acting term for "Darling, how lovely to see you... mwah, mwah" etc, barf) friendliness and relaxed charm (yuh, whatever).

Bill, also the youngest of the family, a stocky powerhouse that took delight in inflicting powerful headlocks, showed Eric the tall bonfire waiting to be lit at the end of the garden, through the large lounge windows, only to suddenly choke Eric from behind and pull him to the floor behind the sofa. The games had started. After several minutes of mutual punishment, the Gladiators were told to get up and both behave themselves.

Suitably reprimanded, though still subtly issuing an occasional kick, the visiting family were invited to say hello to Connie's parents who lived next door, who had known Cassie ever since little.

A stillness came over the red faced and sweating Eric. That meant...

The houses were connected by a large garden that had not been divided, so following the gravel path, lit by the large military torch, they made their way to the neighbours. Eric was silent with anticipation. The greetings were standard and short, and to Eric frustratingly long, he just wanted to go and see.

"Hello Eric, and how are you" not waiting for a reply the kind, odd looking gentleman said "Do you want to come and see them"?

"Yes, please" the quiet voice spoke...not forgetting his manners.

"C'mon then, let's see if they're awake". Leading the way.

The door opened to a large, dark room, only the faintest outlines could be ascertained. The flick of a switch sent a jolt of mixed emotions through his young body. Childhood fear, intrigue, nervousness met smiles, leers, eyes, teeth. He was sure, that if they weren't looking at him, then they wanted too.

All about the room, the shelves on the walls, on top of and in cabinets, on the chairs and most alarmingly hanging and dangling from the ceiling, like Vlad the Impaler's victims, were puppets. Every type and colour of puppet you could imagine. Hand, marionette, finger, glove, rod and arm, even the exquisite Malaysian shadow puppets, amazing in their intricacy and simpleness, the favourite to the small eyes that beheld them. For in those shapes, he could clearly see which were the monsters and which could be trusted, something he didn't feel with the painted masks. A cacophony of stories and movement waiting to be told, yet hanging lifeless and macabrely still with eyes straining to see their visitors.

Eric stood and marvelled at the beauty, the sinister, each already belying their intentions, as this elderly man carefully handed Eric his friends, introducing them and talking to each of them as he went, sincerely saying:

"We have a guest. Would you like to come and say hello"?

"Oh, I see, dear me"

"No, I haven't and you don't either"

"Sorry dear"?

"That's frightfully rude of you"

...and so on, all the time, until maybe one or two came to briefly rest in Erics open arms, only to be whisked away again, being told...

"They don't want visitors today, they're a bit unhappy".

The same couldn't be said for a certain well known puppet, with whom its owner had flat shared with Robert, in the days of being jobbing actors.

One of the other yearly rituals would be a visit to the pantomime. A time when the public would put on their finest for cinema and theatre alike and would stand in silence for the national anthem at the end of the night's performance.

The most magical of pantos was undoubtedly The Wind in the Willows, with Moley busily spring cleaning, Ratty being Ratty and Toad...oh, Toad, you are so troublesome...Toot, Toot.

Many a visit to the theatre would involve a boring back stage visit for Robert and Cassandra to catch up with an old luvvie or two, but coming face to face with the fur snouted gagster was something Eric was looking forward to.

Opening the door to the dressing room, they came face to face with Basil in the arms of his handler. A curious situation developed.

Eric knew, as surely everyone did, that this was a puppet, not real, but instead of being shown the furry figure and all its mechanisms, it persisted in behaving like it did on stage, which only made Eric feel embarrassed and uncomfortable. He was 8 after all.

The fireworks after the puppet visit were a good way to end the evening, the fire and guy having already been consumed and would have to wait until next year, but for now the canal was only steps away.

Climbing in, at the back of the long, narrow vessel, the warmth of the sun dappled its way through the trees above and flickered its light that had travelled the millions of miles on a young boy's arms, unaware of the vastness of the cosmos, only concerned with the smiling faces about him and their mutual destination.

The boat chugged easily along, with gentle warm diesel fumes tickling his nose, making his tummy rumble and think about Winnie-the-Pooh type elevenses. Eric watched as houses and roads sailed easily by, all filled with others dashing about here and there, shopping and meeting, working or cycling, a never-ending stream of busyness and variances.

The slow curve in the canal came into view and Eric knew that soon the boat trip would be over. Nearing the end, Eric's thoughts turned to what lay ahead.

"What to see first" he pondered "Hmm..."

"Maybe..."

"Or..."

"Hmm..."

And no soon as these few little thoughts and imaginings had come and gone, the boat was mooring up, and passengers alighting with help.

He was a little annoyed at himself for drifting off into his imagination again, as he missed the towering structure that he liked so much, but walking up the rampart to the main road, he saw the familiar large black, metal ironworks of the turnstiles with the unmistakeable signage saying "London Zoo".

Excitement raised in the young boy's veins with the hearing of macaws squawking their calls and the familiar warm, earthy yet tangy smell of all the animals drifted across the concrete path that led into the myriad of pathways leading off into all directions.

There was never enough time to see all that he wanted, he thought, staring up at the signposts. He mused. A visit to the warm and dark reptile house, with light spilling out from the glass fronted cages, where the inert and docile inhabitants lay, only relishing the chance to strike. The insect house lay near-by too, but held little fascination apart from the industrious ant farms. The penguins would be excellent fun, watching them waddle and splosh would content him for hours, though they were situated far from other possible enclosures and he was unsure whether he could persuade his mother on the venture. “Hmm” he pondered to himself “where first”?

As if reading his mind Cassandra suggested “The giraffes might be a good place to start. Come on darling”.

“Oh, okay” he replied, a bit disappointed “Hippos would be more fun” went unheard.

Strolling along to the enclosure, they passed the restaurant and Eric gently made a hopeful observation which was abruptly rebuffed with “You can’t have everything you want; besides we haven’t got time. Hurry up, don’t dawdle” from his mother.

Eric did enjoy the Zoo. He remembered how, on previous visits, he liked the crocodile, who would sometimes give him a salacious wink, and the furry wombats, but felt sorry about how unhappy they must be, especially as they and the lions who paced up and down their cages, Eric thought, possibly looking for a way out.

Wandering in his thoughts, he noticed they

were passing the chimpanzees and long armed gibbons cages. The tall iron bars were all that separated the out reaching arms, humans and apes alike.

The gibbons were happily swinging about, looking about them, but generally unconcerned and unamused by the outside life of their domain.

The chimps on the other hand were quite the opposite. Their antics were running rings about the two keepers who had entered the enclosure. Running, rolling and hiding under sacks and bins looked like the high light of the day. Treats were being offered for good behaviour and compliance, but as soon as one feigned submission, another would prank their handlers causing others to scarper with much hilarity, apart from the gaolers.

"Where have you been, horrible child" snapped Eric out of his absorbment.

"What"? "Watching the monkeys" Eric said.

"Don't answer back to me you rude little boy", slap, "You're going home straight away" insisted Cassandra, yanking Eric arm.

Tears burst into his eyes and unhappiness shook his body, as he watched distantly from inside, his grown-up voice quietly conversing with him, only to turn, while being dragged away, to see a gibbon making eye contact, directly with him.

"Maybe one day we'll escape our cages".

DULCE ET DECORUM EST

Robert lay in the hospital bed, not for the last time, pipes and wires leading to "machines that go ping". Eric had been warned of what to expect, but found himself unstirred by the sight of his father, lying helpless and vulnerable with the equipment breathing and pumping his blood for him whilst placed in an induced coma.

The whiteness, functionality and sterile surroundings generated their own version of white noise that hissed in Erics head as he leant over and kissed his father's unresponsive temple in greeting.

"He can't hear you" his mother said "though the doctors said to talk to him. It helps apparently"

Tess was sitting in a chair nearby, angrily crying, while Dickie, standing behind her, rested a hand on her accepting shoulder, looking grown up, in charge and in control, yet exhibiting his professional and detached demeanour.

"Poor old Dickie" thought Eric "I wonder if he'll

ever be able to get off his high horse".

Dickie had always separated himself from the family. There were only two years separating each of the siblings, so when an 8-year-old gets attacked by an irritating 4-year-old it takes nothing to swat him aside.

At the time of when they were growing up, Eric had thought Dickie had enjoyed his boarding school days, but years later would only partially discover his turmoiled times, but preferring the isolation and neglect than the beatings from his father and lack of parental empathy, consequentially making him call his parents by their names rather than terms of endearment.

Dickie had been an angry brother, developing a detached behaviour towards his family, wanting less and less to do with them, all the while nurturing a serious and proper disposition, buying tickets for the family to attend classical music concerts for etiquette improvement and introducing them to more socially acceptable standards of living and to acquaint them to people of a better class.

Robert and Cassandra were more than happy to oblige their son's behaviour, having both heritages of coming from wealth and the knowing of how to put on the airs and graces, yet having capital little of their own, Cassies money coming mainly from her aunt and a steady stream, of varying amounts, of mismanaged monies from archaic trusts, for her to spend. To Cassandra, keeping her looks were important, neither she nor Robert liked the idea of getting old, so spent on heavily on expensive make-up, potions and pills, haircuts and dyes and regular visits to massage parlours (...). Robert, similarly had trusts, though with lesser investment, and was canny with his expenditure, though experienced a dyslexion of figures in his proficient attempts to keep the books.

Sirs lay on both sides of the family, family crests on notable public buildings and sizable portions of the City of Westminster belonged in the purse strings, all lost to individuals bad and possibly unscrupulous dealings, but leaving the echo and scent of better times, each generation having their own viewpoint and crumbs to what was left.

The money might have gone, but the behaviour hadn't.

Though he, sister and brother were born of the same pod, the views and behaviour of each were as different as calcium-based products, the divide increasing over the decades, however, Eric would always be treated as "the little brother". Assuredly, as children grow, they will gladly define their ages, with importance:

"I'm 8 and a three quarters and Timmy is only 7".

"I'm actually 7 and 2 months" Timmy would think.

Admittedly, the difference between a year and a half can be huge to pre-teens, especially girls and boys and if you're a proactive parent, but by the time you're all in your 50's...

Their mother was dealing with her husband's possible demise, with, what seemed, great strength and fortitude, something never seen before and somewhat disarming.

She calmly organised her grown children, asking them for unified cooperation and realistic setting tasks for each, while her husband of 30 years lay in a possible terminal state.

Professional prognosis was less than good and each prepared for the curtain call. Tess in tears and turmoil, Dickie with adult thoughtful detachment, Cassie in quiet solitude, possibly performing her finest role, not knowing how else to really behave and Eric, not believing that the time was now, but persistently being told it was and there was nothing wrong with denial. But, no matter how he tried, it didn't feel like the right time to say goodbye.

Sitting by his father's side, alone with the machines, Eric talked.

"This is the first birthday of mine you've missed" he said, his hand resting on his dad's forearm, thinking how lucky he was to have had two present parents, unlike some of the kids he had gone to school with. That rare few who saw their only parent for maybe two weeks the whole year;

who knows what complex issues would develop in those later lives.

He tried to talk more to his father, as he would in Roberts final days, but felt self-conscious and lacking ability, and besides, he was confident his dad was going to be okay, he was sure his time wasn't now.

Two days later, Robert took the first steps to recovery, signalling the future of how he and his wife would take hospitalised turns. Broken limbs, lung cancer, mysterious illnesses (probably drug or alcohol related), were just some of the reasons for the inductions to ward life; some would be treated as life threatening, only for Death to be cheated again and again, eventually, when being told of another grave ailment would sigh and roll his eyes.

It would be some months before Cassandra would take her turn in being administered to a ward, and with each turn, a step would be taken closer to the mortuary, never fully regaining the health they had before, the slow spiral down.

On one visit, Eric accompanied Robert, who, still not totally in tune since his coma, needed to verbally transcribe his experiences of being in his stoic state. He related the intense fires that burnt his skin, and the screams and torment he suffered, remembering the first thing he saw was, what he thought was, his watch, pinned to a nurse's bib and tried to claim it.

"Probably an excuse to try and cop a feel" thought Eric to himself.

They stood together, alone, in the lift to go up to the wards. The doors slowly shut and a hand pushed itself into the gap, causing the sliding shutters to reopen. Two orderlies and nurse wheeled a bed, complete with drip and patient into the now snug confines of the metal box. The prostrate, semiconscious male was of the same age and appearance to Eric's upright and unfamiliarly, nervous looking father, who was trapped by the side of the stranger's forearm.

The doors re-slid shut, trapping all in their journey, Robert looking down as the prone man reached out to touch his hand.

Robert dramatically flinched in sudden disgust and terror, a behaviour his son had never seen. This tall, no-nonsense Afrikaner, who had never shown a weakness (except for the bottle...and tobacco......and women) was afraid of decay.

This was a common factor in both husband and wife, each having the dislike of getting old and neither recognising when they had done so, sometimes with amusing results.

Cassie would regularly visit the hairdressers as part of her regime, insisting that she never dyed her hair, and the stylist only ever touched up her roots. As for Robert, at 80 he would attempt to put his fingers down a shop assistant's blouse for a better look and shout out at a bandaged patient that shared a ward.

"Look at that old bugger over there" pointing, not realising that the entire wing could hear him "looks like his wife gave him a going over, he looks in a bad way".

To which the lady sitting next to the assailed said.

"I'm not his wife. He had a fall" too quietly and not with enough conviction for Robert to take any notice of.

Eric had been fortunate on his personal record of infirmary visits, his illnesses mostly treatable at home or school sickbays, where he would rattle like a battleship because of the amount of various medication administered.

Only one did he recall actually staying in hospital, which was for the removal of his adenoids and tonsils, and while recovering from the anaesthetic, told his mother that he didn't like the lions.

"There's no lions here darling" she tried to soothe.

"Take the lions away, I don't like the lions" would reiterate, if he knew what the word was, "Take the lions away".

Cassandra eventually twigged. Eric had been placed in a cot type bed; bars raised to prevent falls. Bars, lines, lions.

The only other time in his young life that Eric experienced the pleasures of the medical system was for a tooth extraction.

He had suffered a catalogue of bad dentistry practices, now needing to be pre-tranquilised before treatment. The worst had been a visit to a Great Uncle whose hand shook, not steadied by the glass and bottle on his desk, who extracted a healthy tooth (forgetting to numb the area first) instead of applying a filling.

The next tooth removal would be done under gas at the local day clinic, who specialised in child mouth care.

Cassandra and her youngest arrived on foot, one reason because it was so close to home, the other to speed up Valium into his system.

They were led into a colourful waiting room, painted greens and blues, to look like the sea, full of painted fish, seahorses and octopuses and "very childish and rubbish painting" thought the six-year-old.

A nurse came in and talked to his mother as his spinny eyes played whirly games with the tangle of seaweeds and the familiar, comforting, dizzy numbness crept along his body.

"We're going to take you into the room now Eric to see the doctor, okay"? she said in a patronising way that Eric knew was patronising but didn't know the word for it yet.

"Stupid nurse" he thought, smiling happily.

The room was a room. Sparse with plain, pale-yellow walls and a black, raised, operating bed in the centre with the head tilted slightly up and large gas cylinders set behind.

“Here you go” said the stupid nurse, lifting him up to sit on the bed “just get you comfy”.

Eric watched the grown-ups wandering around on their business as stupid nurse said:

“I’m going to pop this mask on you, it’ll cover your nose and mouth for the gas, and then we’ll lie you down”.

As she placed the triangular plastic over his face she added “Don’t speak when the gas comes on, just breathe deeply, we don’t want you swallowing any gas” with added smiles.

“Just lie you back” she said again, helping him into position.

Three large, hard rubber rings, the type a dog might like, had been taped together and served as a head rest and were placed under the back of his head.

He felt like an astronaut. Mask on. Check. Helmet on. Check. Ooh, Gas on. Che..

“Do you like Andy Pandy”? came the interrupting voice.

“Uh” grunted the response.

The gas was cold and smelly and he didn’t like the hissing noise, it was the same noise he heard when he would pass out.

“What do you like to watch on T.V”

“Uhuh uh” came the reply, not wanting to talk

and swallow gas...LIKE HE HAD BEEN TOLD, he wanted to say.

"I said what do you like to watch on T.V"

"Cartoons" came the answer

"OOH, which ones"? still with the patronising tones.

Eric had to think and concentrate hard, short answers he thought, trying to comply with both directives.

After a sentence or two and more questioning he started to feel the rockets ignite. The rumbling increased and the ship shot into space, the pressure pushing his body down as the stars came into view.

"Wow" not for the first time "if this is what gas is like..."

He woke up a while later in another room and saw his mother sitting, reading a magazine, started to sit up and didn't stop vomiting for almost an hour.

"The nurse told you not to swallow any gas" she said.

LAPSANG OR DARJEELING

Andrew and Eric stood in the middle of the freezer section at the local Co-op supermarket. It was a quiet afternoon; the stores security guard was upstairs and Eric had been given his instructions.

And. was doing his weekly lift, a habit he had adopted as he disapproved of any company taking his hard-earned money and, besides, as far as he could see, if they didn't want it pinched then they shouldn't put it on the shelves.

The whole affair made Eric very uncomfortable. Stealing always had.

In pre-decimal days, when pennies were worth ought, he could buy a comic and some chocolate white mice for four pence and still possibly have a ha'penny change.

The comics need a whole mention of their own, too extensive and more worthy, too varied and colourful than I could possibly manage. Let's just say that Eric had a love and fascination for the small piles of paper, such as Buster (and Jet), Whizzer (and Chips), Topper, Shivers, Weird Tales, Astounding Stories, Marvel and D.C., Mad and eventually leading to the likes of Strip and Toxic, all the while being captivated with the likes of Crumb and Shelton, enjoying the kooky and intoxicating images and colours.

On times, when an interesting serialised story line reared, Eric would scour the local sellers, whether it be the train station kiosk, newsagents or paper stand, to find the continuing story, depending on the number of coins in his pocket.

Robert always kept his loose change in a leather tray, next to his side of the bed, on his cabinet with light. Rising early, long before others stirred on a Sunday morning, wanting to catch the only cartoon on television, The (dreadful) Tomfoolery Show, Eric would invisibly move across his sleeping parent's room (like The Vision), around to his father's side, and see how much treasure was available. Sometimes, if lucky, a collection of coinage lay recently strewn, and at other times maybe a crumpled note. Being careful, he always tried to be discreet in his selection, never taking the only coin of one type and never of high denomination, looking at the pile and its design was just as an important move for selection as anything else. Everything had to be taken into for consideration, even listening out for the breathing patterns of all (after all, he didn't need to breath as he was The Silver Surfer).

Once the haul had been secured, Eric would light footedly fly from the room (on his trusty board), down the stairs and out the door, in search for the pesky Bash Street Kids.

Depending on which shop he would call on today (unlikely visiting more than one due to limited finance and carrying purchases from one store to another unsettled the keepers, creating awkward conflicts), was decided upon which comic was needed and which route he wanted to take. Quickness, less public contact or sightseeing.

Today, he had his glove on him, so opted, as time permitted, the more public and longer route. The plan was thus. Glove would be worn on his right hand, no, left hand, just to confuse them more and it would look odd, wearing a righthanded glove on his left hand. "Even better". Thinking to himself "Hopefully, Charles (sounds like a good grownup name, or should it be Frank…hmm, stick with Charles for now). So, hopefully Charles will be asked "What happened to your hand" or "why are you wearing one glove" …hmm… good". He continued in his thinking "then I can say "oh, I lost it in the war (it's a shame I don't have a sling as well). That'll really get them". He finished, satisfied with his plan. Unfortunately, no-one seemed to look, be bothered or ask, much to his disappointment, so fortified himself with the thought of next time he went out with Tess, he would make an extra elaborate attempt at his walk (perfecting a style in the manner of someone with extreme cerebral palsy).

Nearby one of the newsagents, a couple of doors down from the magical sweet shop, (with its counter filled with coloured sugar mice, babies wrapped in blankets, foil wrapped chocolates that looked like cars, ladybirds and spiders, bright swirled lollipops...and an endless amount of glass jars, all shapes and sizes filled with an assortment of drool inducing confection, as well as the latest gimmicks, like jumblees, pez and tictacs) stood the toy shop.

The large Lego pirate boat stood in the window by the door, surrounded by an assortment of other glorious possibilities to buy, just as exciting as the range next door.

Entering, polite greetings made, Erics eyes were always drawn to the shelves of models to build, rarely interested in the military range, unless odd or protype planes, but preferred instead the monsters of film with luminous parts.

He had a love for all things luminous. Stickers and putty were his favourite, hiding under his covers, entranced by the ghostly green light which he found comforting and reliable.

Lower down, under the boxes of tanks and figures were the shelves of novelties and new comers. A glut of potentials, each seeking tactile recognition "Play with me" and "No, play with me" could be heard.

Erics eyes landed on one particular box, something new, never before seen, something he loved drawing (even on the wall).

A box of rubber monsters. Oh, the delight, as he searched through the box. Each one could fit on the end of your finger, but each was a different size and different colour. Blue with yellow bug eyes and green tongue, another was orange with antennae for eyes and sharp red teeth, another… oh, the joy.

"Problem. No money. How much were they? 2D…"

Eric turned his head to see the shop owner busy with a customer, his hand went into his pocket. He turned and left with a smile, a bye and something he hadn't come in with.

The walk home was full of shoulder conversations. The left one telling him not to worry and it was no big deal, with the voice in his right ear berating his behaviour. By the time he arrived home, he confessed all to his mother who gave him two dence and told him to go back to the shop and pay for his deeds.

The shop bell rang and the he was greeted again with politeness and a professional greeting. Eric walked to the counter and produced the coins and stolen ware, explaining his actions and consequences.

He did not expect such a furious response, he

had not expected any response, but was sent out, tail between his legs, only daring to return on occasions, behind his mother's coat tails.

The short, sharp, shock worked at deterring Eric in further thievery, so feeling ill at ease with his friend's exploits was understandable, though he had been given the task of look out, Andrew insisted the deep pockets of his trench-coat would come in handy.

An elderly pensioner walked by as Andrew was attempting to secrete four packets of frozen bacon down his trousers, as Eric, uselessly was looking the opposite direction.

"Honestly, what shocking behaviour" she said as she walked off.

Andrew hurried his selection, disgruntled with his friend's inexperience and incompetence.

Laughing at his mates' serious endeavours, Eric failed to notice the encroaching security guard, stealthily catching him in the act.

The words came emphatically clear and loud.

"Put that back".

With a nonchalant shrug all contents were ditched and scattered on the floor and despite the insistence from the officer that Andy should be escorted to the manager, he turned tail and ran, leaving Eric befuddled as to what his actions should be.

This behaviour had a familiar pattern.

The instance of when his motorbike was moved, whilst locked, during his visit to see the new film from John Carpenter, Halloween, leaving him to walk 6 miles home down dark country lanes. Not that he was particularly spooked, it was more of an inconvenience (he found it later the following day…a "friend" told him where it was), walking down an enclosed by trees lane, at midnight, with a moonless and cloudy sky…Close your eyes, walk around where you are for 5 minutes (you might look a bit silly if on a plane or train), it's a lot quicker with your eyes open, isn't it, miss calculating the curve in a road can prove prickly.

Another instance was when Eric's motorbike was actually stolen, for real…by another "friend".

They had been working together for a number of months in a pizza restaurant, a popular and busy bistro for local office workers at lunchtimes, split levels supplying different needs.

The manager was an agreeable chap, allowing Eric to take in mix tapes of his making, something he relished compiling, as long as nothing too heavy or gratuitous was played. Regrettably, some of his favourite vinyl had suffered from exuberant behaviour, such as dancing on tables or slam dancing, which resulted in a sticking point caused by a minor scratch. This didn't deter the recording however, knowing where the glitch might be, Eric would poise himself over the rotating disc, waiting for the "yeh mun (tick), yeh mun (tick), yeh mun (tick), only for kicks...

The amusing part would come when playing back at lunchtime and a helpful customer would point out that the record was sticking sometimes, only to leave them confused when told that it was a tape.

Erics workmate, we'll call him Knobby, occasionally borrowed Milo's (reluctantly, apparently, they had been acquaintances for a couple of years) dirt bike, to visit his (Knobs, not Milos) sister, who lived the other side of town.

During one of their shifts Knob approached Eric, who was busy prepping jacket potatoes.

"Hey Eric, can I borrow your bike tonight" the knob asked "my sisters having problems with one of her tenants and I've got to go and sort them out" ...being a body builder and martial arts expert.

Being the first time, the knob had asked him, Eric was reluctant.

"Not really sure, I don't like lending my bike" Eric honestly replied.

"I'll only be gone a couple of hours. I'll definitely be back by 8".

Eric thought. Knob had known Milo for a while, seemed trustworthy and had borrowed Milos bike a number of times. Besides, he was working with the band tonight so wouldn't be using it.

"Okay," said Eric "just drop the keys through the door when finished, I'm gigging tonight".

"Great, thanks" he said, taking the keys.

Fast forward to 3 in the morning when Eric got home to find no bike or keys. Concerned and annoyed he figured some good reason must have occurred and half-heartedly went to bed, knowing he would see Knob in a few hours at work.

Bleary eyed, despite the doughnuts and coffee, sometimes they just don't work, Eric stepped through the door to work to be met by a commotion.

Ohan, a fellow worker, a 6-foot 6 muscle bound 21 year old from Turkey was smiling, like he always did (especially after eating 3 pizzas) and said "The place was robbed last night" grinning even more "Knobby took wine, till trays and the safe contents". His smile really couldn't get any bigger as he casually leaned against the wall…or was the wall leaning against him?

"How do you know Knobby did it"? Eric puzzled.

"No forced entry and he had the only other set of keys. They've (the manager and police) already been to where he lives. Landlady says he's stolen her cutlery and owes her 2 months' rent. Ha" … still, smiling.

Eric felt his knees weaken; he felt a bit pale.

"I leant him my bike" he said wistfully.

“Ha. Last you’ll see of that” Ohan said, cheerily, heading back to the kitchen. Afterall, it had been 10 minutes since he last ate.

“Shit”.

Eric walked down to the police station, he couldn’t ride, to report the additional theft. On entering, he was met by a very abrupt desk sergeant.

“What do you want”? came the query, making Eric unsure if he had done anything wrong.

“I’ve come to report a theft” he said, genuinely perturbed.

“No, you’re not” came the reply.

Confused, Eric stupidly said “Yes I am, my friends stolen my bike” feeling like he sounded like a school kid.

“Look, Sonny” said complete with sneer and venom. “You’re not coming in here to report anything...dressed like that” pointing hard to Erics chest.

The penny dropped. He tried to explain that it was a religious symbol of peace, the Buddhists use it, and besides Sidney wore it, it didn’t mean that...

“Fuck off and don’t come back until you’ve changed”. Came the demand.

It would be three years until Eric got his insurance pay out for his bike and he never wore his swastika t-shirt again...it was stolen...by a "friend".

Friends helped Eric lose many things. One time, when letting a friend crash between accommodation, a couple of days turned to a couple of weeks. Having not seen them due to work, he popped his head into the bedroom to touch base, only to find six other people smashed out of their skulls on gear and had been so for days. He wondered where things were disappearing to.

Sometimes he lost more than possessions.

Being young and impetuous, Eric jumped from job to job, trying to find his footing, but more importantly, trying to make a living while committing himself to the blossoming music career, which he felt dedicated towards.

The varying stints would lead him to cross paths with many a varied person, sometimes finding links to people he already knew. One such person was Matt (a different one from before, though those ones were after...). Matt (do we call him #1, being the first in chronological order, or #3 as in reading order...I'll leave it to you), worked in a record shop that Eric had recently been employed in and found that they both socialised, at different times, with the same circle of friends, so received an invite to an afternoon session that was occurring at the weekend at his pad.

Matt's pad was actually a glorified bedsit attached to his wealthy parent's house, who had little to do with their son, and smoking soirees of different sizes were a fixture on some people's calendar.

Eric arrived, not knowing what to expect and was surprisedly greeted by Elle, Andy's girlfriend, with her usual mischievous smile and warm hugs. She led Eric around the back to where he found at least 10 people crammed into a tastefully decorated bedroom, with 60's Americana rock blasting from the speakers and pungent smoke in the air and professional disco lights mixing it up.

Eric waved to the familiar faces and gave a smile and nod to the unknown ones, all of which was reciprocated. Settling down on some spare cushions, of which there were many, he produced his doings and started to roll. Before he had finished, someone had already passed him a joint, which he toked a couple of hits from and passed it on, never wanting to be accused of bogarting (keeping it for yourself, he had been brought up with good drug manners after all).

The room continued to fill with music and a green tinted cloud, even though the number of bodies decreased. The afternoon wore on and as usual, no sooner had one spliff had finished, Eric felt like another, and another. The music started varying more, not always to his taste, until Matt passed over the next record. Eric couldn't believe his eyes. The colourful album cover was undoubtedly the work of Robert Crumb, an adult cartoonist extraordinaire from his childhood, ones he wasn't allowed to read. Cheap Thrills was the title, with Big Brother (and the holding company written beside). It all clicked in place for him. Cheap Thrills is what he searched for, missing out on reality. Big Brother, from George Orwell, a book he had just finished, everything coming from the past, the answers had always been there, needing to be found. The room started to move slowly. Janis started to sing. Eric started to feel very hot and suffocated. He smoked some more, unsure of where the spin was taking him, the ball and chain being sung about hung heavy on his neck, pulling him down, he tried to stand but the floor slipped onto the wall, so he crawled carefully to the bathroom nearby, resting occasionally in the swirl of sound and feeling different textures as he went.

He made it into the cool, oh, that's nice, clean, bright, so bright, bathroom and managed to climb on the toilet. Sitting in an upright...ish position, slumping against the cistern, Ah, that's better. A small sink was at his side so splashed some water over his face and arms, ah, nice he said.

He breathed in deeply his new environment and was at a new peace.

He gently closed his eyes.

Suddenly.Knock. Knock.

"You alright in there Eric" came the familiar voice of Elle.

"Yeah fine," replied Eric, "just needed the loo".

"Well, other people need it too".

"Well, yeah," thought Eric "it's not like I'm going to be long".

He stood and splashed a bit more water on his face and opened the door.

"That's odd" he thought, looking.

"Where's everyone gone" he asked Elle.

Noticing that almost everyone had suddenly disappeared, music stopped, windows opened and aired, wondering what drama he suddenly missed.

"They went home ages ago," said Matt.

Eric obviously looked confused.

"You've been in there for over an hour" Elle said laughing.

"What? No?"

"Yeah, everyone went ages ago".

Eric felt he really should do something about all this time he kept losing. So, he went home to have another smoke to help him think.

SICK

Eric couldn't decide which was making him feel worse, the ear infection or bronchitis. One aggravated the other. Sitting up in bed in Sick Bay, the room used for poorly waifs at boarding school, he vaguely watched Open University (the television set only being allowed on for one hour in the morning and one hour in the afternoon), not understanding it all, but becoming absorbed in the comforting tones and the reassuring neutrality. He especially enjoyed the lecturers who were excited or fully immersed in their subject, their infectiousness grasping the viewers attention, despite how ill he felt.

Matron had already done her rounds, issuing medications and instructions in equal measure, so Eric was left alone, no other occupying the other 3 beds, in the plain white room, window too far to see out of, with a pile of homework for added companionship.

He yearned for a comic or jigsaw puzzle, more for emotional support than actuality, but he wasn't at home now, nor would he be for some time, he had given up counting the days, as some others did, and tried instead to occupy himself with distractions. Regrettably, these ventures usually attracted the unwanted attention of either a teacher or a school bully. A real lose/lose scenario.

He recalled how, before the recent snow, out in the nearby woods, a tree had partially uprooted, making it lean, propped up only by trees around it. An excitable queue of kids would form at the tilting tree, waiting to take turns, with the main despot issuing orders and guidelines, sometimes demanding sweets, but always dictating who can or can't have a go. If some outspoken child refused to be dominated then the consequences could be swift and accurate.

Normally, cohorts would be nearby, waiting for crumbs to be dropped by their master or to do their bidding, and for the disobeying, the made-up rules could be brutish. Tear inducing headlocks, dead legs galore, punches were the favourite, with hangings and body slams (being picked up and thrown to the floor, normally by two assailants and on your back) being left to the more opinionated or smaller targets.

Once you had manoeuvred the gauntlet of the line, the next trial begun. The Leap.

This was split into sections. Firstly, you had to complete the climb of the damaged tree, not an easy task for the smaller child, but fun in itself. It was important to get as high as possible in your climb, not because of what you were attempting, but so as not to get rebuke from your piers or the wolves who circled below.

Achieving optimal height, the sway of the tree could now be felt in the light breeze, its roots wanting to give way fully, only supported by its close-knit colleagues. Eyeing the gap carefully, assessing the distance from tree to tree, branch to branch, heart pounding loudly as calculations for swaying and foot slippage was taken into account. The trunk of the adjacent plant seemed too far to grab onto, but a fall was more preferable than facing the group below with retreat.

"JUMP. JUMP. JUMP" came the chanting shouts from below.

The gibbon swung, jumped and clasped the new friend the other side.

The exercise was however far from over for the performer, though the crowd had moved on to the following possible sacrifice.

Next was the task of descent. Manoeuvring down the upright tree was no easy task as various branches and limbs had been damaged and were now missing, leaving the hapless doer to cling tightly to the bough and attempt to slide down the bumpy surface, scraping arms, legs and face in the process. The most unconsidered part, despite seeing previous victims, the last eight-to-ten-foot drop. Weary from the downward progress most youngsters would just drop, like surprised bricks from a tree, hitting the ground with gentle thuds and, if you looked carefully, bounces.

Minor injuries, cuts and bruising aside, rarely were anyone hurt, more pride damage from laughter of the onlookers than anything else.

The snow fall had cut short climbing activities, replaced with snowball fights and igloo and snowman building, always keeping a watchful eye on bored human trolls, mentally dragging their knuckles while looking for the next target to alleviate pent up angst.

Today was Erics turn.

The pack of juniors rolled and played in the fresh fall of water ice, like young otters enjoying their first taste of freedom, while some flakes, still wafting gently about, looked for suitable landing spots. Eric had dropped his guard, having been distracted by a handful of snow shoved into his face, when the punch came swinging out of the blue cold air and contacted squarely with the side of his head, the blinding black and white light lit up his brain on one side as hit head hit the soft (though not as soft as it should be) ground on the other.

His assailant jumped onto his prey and proceeded to ensure that all visible orifices and clothing were fully filled with clumps of whatever was at hand. A few hefty kicks finished off the ordeal, just for good measure, as Eric remembered winning a fruit cake at this exact point in the playing field only a year ago.

Sated in his glory, Blubber strode off to look for his group of passing friends, eager to retell his exploits, unaware and uncaring of how his actions would not only affect his goal but also of the witnesses.

E.N.T was a weakness for Eric, always coming at an unhelpful or inopportune time.

Great Aunt Janes death came days after the birth of his youngest child, which had been an outstandingly long 9 months pregnancy.

The night was dark. The sparse streetlights in the village themselves giving little light to the distant windows that lay about, with residents, bar one, sound asleep in their imaginary worlds.

Anne knelt beside her husband's side of the bed, hand softly shaking his arm.

"Darling..., Eric..." came the quiet words, but with a hint of concern.

Eric stirred, though was instantly awakened by the unusualness of the events.

"Are you okay" he said, noticing the paleness of his wife even in the darkness.

"I'm not feeling too good" came the reply and as if the last effort had been spent, collapsed, unconscious on the floor, sadly not for the last time.

Eric, wide awake, motor running, grabbed the phone and called the emergency services, making his wife as comfortable as possible and trying not to disturb the sleeping children.

With the bedside light on, he could now see the blueness of her lips and hear the shallowness of her breathing. The slow uneasy thud of her heartbeat was no match for his own.

Despite the distance for the crew to travel, the wait time was impressive and soon enough questions were answered, pressures checked and patient dispatched to hospital for immediate attention, where they discovered internal bleeding and issued a 50/50 nights survival.

The following days of hospital stay was filled with an operation to stop the bleed and an abundance of tests. They were given the news. Anne had been pregnant but had lost the baby, commonly called an ectopic pregnancy, the rupture had been severe. Stunned by the 5 second sentence, the complexity of being blessed with the opportunity of giving life, only to have it taken in an instant was beyond words. Happiness to sadness, relief to grief all in a single breath.

Anne was sent home, needing to report for more tests to check on her progress and ensure healing was going well.

The rollercoaster was along ride, spectators, few, time moved, but normality was not yet in reach.

Returning for her run of examinations, needles and samples everything seemed to be going in the right direction except for the hormone levels. They didn't want to correct themselves. Days passed with worries, more tests, backwards and forwards to the department. Until one day.

"Well Anne, Eric…what can I say," said the doctor.

They looked at each other quizzically, not wanting bad news…it didn't sound like bad news.

"You're still pregnant."

(the sounds of chins hitting floor)

"It seems as if you were going to have twins.

One ruptured and the other…well, seems to be carrying on". he said with a smile.

As you can imagine, it was a long 8 months.

Even up until the night of the birth it was eventful.

Their little car broke down about five times on the drive to hospital at 2 in the morning. All the time, Eric checking on Anne and keeping an eye out for houses with lights on…just in case.

For Eric, the delivery was relatively quick, but the hidden stress of the months, the hiss of the gas (and the need for the toilet) was almost too much for Erics body to handle…there was a definite sparkle of black lights and the weakening of the knees as his youngest daughter came into the world x

He was no stranger to passing out. The kick in the head playing rugby, being pushed over in the playground or hit with a climbing frame knotted rope had all had the same thud sound, just before blacking out. But the ones that were annoying, were the ones that crept up on him slowly.

Over time Eric learnt how to deal with the intrusion, though sometimes they got the better of him.

Sitting at the hexagonal school desk, listening to their Divinity teacher fantasise about Mrs Barrett's (a short, hairy bespectacled elderly teacher) "pendulous breasts", while introducing the class to Derek and Clive, the lads were seeing who could "stab between the fingers" quickest. No knife available, sharpened pencils would do the trick and Eric was doing quite well, much to the annoyance to his mate Dave. So much so, as a joke, Dave snatched the pencil and stabbed Eric in the hand. Being a pencil, the lead snapped of and lodged under the skin and immediately the whishing sound started.

His head sank to the table as the ringing got louder and the beads of cold sweat covered his hot face.

"Sir" said Pete, hand raised "I don't think Erics feeling well, Sir"

Mr Powell strode over and inspected the situation.

"Hmm" he said jovially "you boys better take him to see Sister" sounding like he was relishing the event, perhaps Mrs Barrett was still on his mind.

Peter and Dave helped Eric to stand and started to drag him out of the class.

"Don't walk so fast" came the murmur.

"You're not walking" came the reply.

The incident of being "glassed", smashed in the face with a handled pint glass for bumping into someone or dislocating his shoulder and breaking his thumb, didn't go the full distance of unconsciousness, but almost. Whereas the day operation on his mouth was a surprise, even to him.

With local anaesthesia applied, the operation started well. No nerves were had on the lovely sunny day and the operating chair was comfortable, with surroundings fresh and clear.

So relaxed was he feeling that torpor was creeping in, when suddenly the familiar tingling sounded in his ears, getting louder, washing over him like shingles on a beach. Before he went down he was slightly aware of concern, replaced by activity and his name being called. Then he was gone.

The blackness was fine, in fact quite comfortable.

"Eric. Eric. Can you hear me"? said a voice, loud and clear.

He thought for a while in his own little world.

Hear? Yes, I can hear. Seemed like, odd…words.

"Mr Strong. Can you hear me"?

Hmm…it was cool and dark where he was, everything felt fine thanks.

"Eric, you're perfectly safe. You're in hospital"

His eyes flicked open immediately.

What the hell was he doing in hospital? Had he had a car crash or something?

The nurse handed him a small square tablet.

"Pop this under your tongue, let it dissolve. Its glucose" she said, with Eric still unsure what was going on.

His lip was very numb, he thought, and the tablet fell out on first try.

"Hello Mr Strong" said a voice "you're back with us then" said the amused doctor "do you pass out often"?

Eric smiled back and proceeded to explain how his body liked to misbehave sometimes without consulting him first.

It was similar to when poisoning was around.

Many people use the excuse of eating something dodgy the day before to get off work, but when food poisoning kicks in…you can kiss your ass (not literally of course, especially during these extreme conditions) goodbye for a week.

Having eaten a warm corned beef sandwich on the National Express, Eric certainly enjoyed the pleasures of voiding his body, from both major orifices, at the same time for the first few days, amazed at how much could still be in there.

Though there are, obviously, other types of poisoning, one such... acid.

Eric had imbibed some LSD from a dodgy source, that had proved flat, so went to visit his sister, Tess whose old friend from their Oxford days was visiting.

A spread of vegetarian food lay on the table, mainly hot and spicy curries of various descriptions, tomato and onion salad, cheeses, bean dishes...an array of non-alkali sustenance.

By the time the meal was finished, glugging down a glass of orange juice, the negative effects of the bad lysergic was crawling its way through Erics body.

Excusing himself, he went upstairs to the bathroom to was wash the sweat away, only to reveal the shakes that wanted to come out to play.

Staggering to the top of the stairs, he fell into the spare bedroom and landed on the small mattress groaning.

The impact was sudden. The pain jolted through his entirety, which decided to convulse his limbs at random, no position alleviating the discomfort he was experiencing.

How long he had been there writhing in agony and hot and cold sweat he was not sure, but the doctor was attempting to take his pulse, with

Cassandra standing in the background.

He always did like the song "Fool on the Hill" by the Beatles, now he knew why.

COME OUT, COME OUT

He couldn't decide which to play.

"Hmm" Eric pondered, tapping his chin.

"Hmm, which to play" he thought, looking down at the two boxes.

"Flounders or Magnetic Fish"?

Sitting on his blue and red tiger pouffe he looked down before him trying to decide which he wanted to play.

"Have you decided yet" called over Cassandra from the small open plan kitchen.

"I can't decide. Which would you like to play"? asked her son.

"Oh, I haven't got time to play I'm afraid" she said, hearing a small sigh in return.

Eric concentrated, thinking of his choices, but also playing through a game of Flounders on his own…it didn't quite work. All that dice throwing and you really needed at least two people to make it exciting.

"I guess I'll play fishing" he half dejectedly said, hoping his manner might persuade his mum to join in.

"Okay, you carry on darling" she replied.

Eric started setting up the underwater scenery frame and dropped the coloured plastic fish into the square, all the while pondering which rod, he was going to use.

"Blue" he unquestionably agreed upon. It was always blue.

He led down, head resting on the floor so not to be able to see where his targets lay and dangled his rod, with magnet attached, for the littles fishies to click onto. He liked games, but did prefer to play with someone else rather than on his own.

His love for games was equalled for his love for practical jokes. Whoopee cushions, fake chewing gum and the fake nail through the finger were all good main stays, but enjoyed plastic flies, ping pong eyes and guillotines more. The more sophisticated the better. Jumping out from behind doors was a great routine, never failing, learning that timing was everything, but playing dead (unconscious) was also a fantastic ruse, but one that people didn't react so favourably towards.

He rarely was without some trick or two in his pocket (as long as it wasn't filled with rhubarb crumble) having an affection for chattering teeth (that got confiscated at a school church service) and googly eyes on springs (which were a turning point in his escapades).

Having moved to the expanses of the countryside and all the ooh-ahhs it had to offer, fuelled his once inhibited exploits.

As a trial, the local comprehensive was offering an O'Level in Photography, but it was soon highjacked by the new movement of punk influenced youth who instead of wanting to learn about the formalities and structure, decided to push the practical uses of being given a cine camera, now all common place.

They revelled filming pranks on unsuspecting victims, making short idiotic films and producing general mayhem with the patience of the headmaster being sorely tested.

Most had been reared on Candid Camera, a popular 60s hidden camera show, and doses of Milligan, The Goodies and Python and now, with the help of anarchy in their blood, it was their turn.

Eric enjoyed being one of the instigators of the plans, having had years of unbridled restraint, plans a many stored, and brought back memories of a little boy hiding in a cupboard waiting for the ultimate moment to jump out on his unsuspecting prey, sometimes wanting to stay hidden longer, but the need to go to the loo being increased by the suspense.

He realised his true talent in his mid-teens at Halloween.

The peaceful, unaware Dorset village had plenty of good hiding places to jump out of, but Eric decided a more reserved approach could be called for.

The village had a small population, so waiting behind shrub on the upper bank of their front garden, that overlooked the only road, he was going to have to be patient.

An elderly farmer, wellies clopping as he went, came walking down the road, off to his nightly session at the local.

Eric shook the shrub subtly and gave a low growl…trying not to laugh.

The farmer poised momentarily and looked.

Eric growled lowly again.

"Fuck off, you twat". Came the farmers answer as he strode off…Eric thought with a little quicker pace.

Not bad. Must try harder…as all his school reports read.

Silence and waiting resumed.

Payoff.

Down the small country road, out of the darkness, into the light of one of the three streetlights in the whole village, Eric spied Mrs Tate walking with her six-year-old daughter.

His heart kicked into gear immediately, with

that old familiar feeling of needing a wee. This was going to be a good one.

Scenarios of how to deal with this one flashed through his mind, like a shuffling machine, sorting for the best possible set of circumstances.

Before they got to close, he emitted a low growl and rustle, just to set scene, just faint enough for them to hear.

They stopped.

"Mummy, what's that noise"

"Probably, nothing dear" in a broad Dorset accent, listening to what sounded like soft, heavy breathing coming from somewhere.

They moved on with definite trepidation, mother scanning the dim darkness, daughter now firmly in hand.

Eric eased his breathing, reeling them in…

Wait……wait………

The mother and daughter were almost in line with his bush when Eric screamed a yell as loud as he could. A blood curdling mix of snarl and pain.

How high off the ground the ladies leapt he could only marvel at, but their scream echoed his as the fled off into the night.

He smiled, broadly. That was a good one. He thought triumphantly.

Not realising how his actions might be having

unwanted implications, he carried on the years coming up with new schemes, until decades later, the penny would drop.

Still at school, another idea grew and blossomed.

Their drama teacher, who shall be made nameless, not that we're using real names as it is, agreed upon an experiment of social reaction within his younger class of pupils.

The small group if Year 6's, 5 in total, would disguise themselves with padding, balaclavas and stockings (for over the head, we're not at public school now), and burst into the drama lesson and pretend to be bank robbers.

Armed with artificial guns and setting off some rook scarers before entering, the band of desperados burst in on the unsuspecting class, shouting orders to lie face down and tied up the teacher (giving him a gentle kicking for good measure), just, by good fortune, a police car with sirens blaring went past.

A couple of kids were immediately distraught, so were taken to the attached foyer, away from prying eyes, an explained what was really happening, with the responses of:

"Ah, we knew it was you all along" and such like.

The event lasted a full half hour until the final reveal, and was hailed as great success and more enjoyable than the usual type of lesson.

However.

The fan got rather splattered.

The following day, the teacher, who shall not be named, received innumerable complaints from concerned and annoyed parents, calling for apologies and resignation, something he skirted by the skin of his teeth. Apparently, some children had wet themselves with stress and others had a sleepless night.

Eric and his mates all thought it had been rather good.

The more routine japes would be driving around Bournemouth years later in the front seat of Bettys home-made car, disguised as a dummy looking like a werewolf, only to surprise people crossing at traffic lights or hiding under a tarpaulin in the little open topped car with hand puppets of Mickey Mouse and Donald Duck… doing things.

Another successful rouse only came into being on the pivotal success of getting a letter printed in the girl's magazine/comic Jackie.

Being a roadie left a lot of time on your hands. Normally sleeping in the back of the van on top of the sound equipment was one way of dealing with a couple of spare hours as the band partied with celebs, besides, someone had to look after the kit.

Eric only attended a couple of the after-gig doo's and frankly found them pretty tame and boring, mainly people pretending too much. Not the type of climate you want to be taking drugs in.

So, lying on a stack of speakers, trying to find the right position, his mind would bounce around new ideas.

An inkling came and the next day, having a communal smoke with his house sharer, the plan developed.

The lead singer, of the main band he worked for, had a brother (the drummer) and girlfriend.

They shared a house and that house was also the recording studio.

Girlfriend read Jackie.

When finished, drummer read Jackie.

Drummer LOVED problem page.

Drummer FANTASISED about teenage groupies.

So, with great dexterity a letter was penned to Cathy and Claire about two girls, Tracy and Sharon, who LOVED the drummer of a local band.

Amazingly the letter was printed and advice given. The girls should stop being so shy and go and tell the drummer how they feel.

As luck would have it, the band was playing in town the weekend of the published letter and our dear drummer man was...excited is an understatement.

"Now Eric, you understand," he said "if any girls come up to you and say they're Sharon or Tracy, you bring them to me. Understand".

"Der".

The band played a great gig and afterwards, when Eric was packing the gear away…

“No girls then? They didn’t show” as drum boy.

“What? Girls”? replied the nonchalant roadie “Oh, yeah, there were a couple of girls, but they said they were too embarrassed”.

“WHAT? Where are they? Why didn’t you tell me”? came the incredulous torrent.

“Sorry, I was busy”.

Eric found it really hard not to give the game away, but they were saving that for another day.

The googly eyes on springs were worn with a small plastic moustache in Maths class, much to the annoyance of the teacher, who, wearing glasses herself, took it as a slight, despite the insistence that Eric needed spectacles himself for long distances,

They were confiscated and secured in her small office, with the instructions that they were only to be returned at the end of term.

Upset by his loss, Eric consoled himself with the small brown mouse (not a real one) he kept in his pocket.

That evening, after prep (enforced homework) Gary, a boy from his maths class came rushing up to him.

“Hey Hunter (no kid at boarding school gets called by his first name), here’s your glasses” he said in a puff.

Surprised at receiving the gift so soon Gary added.

“Miss said to give them back to you” and dashed off, obviously in a hurry for something.

The following day, another Maths lesson and to show how stupid he could be was wearing his boingy eyes when teach walked in.

Visibly shaking the shout burst out

“Where did you get those glasses from”?

The pin was heard dropping.

“Go and explain yourself to the headmaster this instant”.

The squeak of the chair sounded embarrassed at breaking the atmosphere in the class. Now Eric was trembling too.

It was a long walk to the study and he took a seat by the closed door after knocking and hearing no response.

The door eventually creaked open with the instruction “IN”.

The Head seated himself behind his large oak desk as the 12-year-old Eric stood the other side. Hands behind back.

“Well, boy”? he really didn’t mince his words.

Eric briefly explained the events, omitting key information, like, names, but it certainly wasn’t him who had broken into the locked office and removed various items. Though he did wonder what else had been taken…he’d have to find out later…he was very interested.

“Well, boy, what are we going to do”? said the Head rising from his seat, picking up his swishing stick.

Eric knew full well what he was going to do. Regardless of guilt or innocence. 6 strikes later he was dismissed and glad he was wearing his trousers.

And by the way, he was made to apologise for his behaviour that Halloween.

THE JOURNEY

The knight knelt in the throne room awaiting the presence of his queen having completed his tasks that had been set before him. He was weary, bloodied and filled with demons from the deeds of past and the multitude of ventures he had performed for his highness, though gratitude not came from those tender hands he sought. He wished only to break the spell that she was under and free them both of the evil that lay within the protected caves, though anger and violence, as to care and patience, were no match for the witch's power. So, hoping to prove his worth, he carried the burdens that were put upon him, knowing not where the answer lay, for it was hidden deep.

All he sought was to be clean again. Fresh and hopeful. Unburdened of guilt and the weight of the armour he had to wear to protect himself from dragons and use as an excuse for the lack of the ladie's touch.

And so, he knelt, hoping that perhaps, this time, the curse had been lifted.

Descending the stairs, with muted dignity and

innocence of her crimes trailing behind her like a gown of broken gems, the fragility of the knight's bones splintered in his mind, cracking and braking, all barriers failing, as he lunged in a possessed frenzy at the imaginary creature that stood before him, wishing to extract vengeance for the multiple scars that lay upon him, even though many were from times of old.

Harm inflicted, the courtiers pulled him from his clasp and dragged the stunned man who lay inside his once shining chainmail to the waiting dungeons, leaving his love behind, more damaged and retreated than before, consoling herself and children of the wounds that lay unfathomable.

No light shone through the narrow slit of his cell, save the flickering of a burning torch, casting its eerie shadows, jumping too and hither, mockingly dancing on wall and floor, not realising that they were as trapped as he. Despair clutched at his very being, for as he had lifted his hands in anger that final time, it was as if he were striking at his own very soul, though another had been harmed, and fought in a tumbling spiral the eternal fight of good conquesting evil, leaving him void and clear, vanquishing his past conducts, though now endangering his future.

Coldness gripped his form, no escape could there be and the shouts and screams of fellow captors echoed round the chambers.

The queen sat on her throne, still shaken by her ordeal, servants tending to her wounds, while she could still not fathom why the reasons for her gallants actions had unfolded, confusion lay all around, and fear lay in behind, laughing at her frailty and ridiculing her every move, controlling her actions and thoughts, just as they had done so for countless years, ever since the spells had been cast.

She had been a fair maiden, happy in her own world of books where she hid from the rejection of parental love and care and the strict guidelines of conformity set out by the priests, who tried to force her into an unachievable icon, doomed from the onset, when nurturing was all that was required.

The dark cloud grew within, covering the nature of her conflict and becoming a force of its own, separating her selves from each other, causing disagreement and conflict that she desperately tried to flee from, only for the monster to pursue her at each turn, easily following the scent of decay.

The Lady fled from land to land, many lords attempting to take her hand, yet none succeeding in holding on for many a length of time, save the first, whose actions, cruelty and love combined, struck hard at the very heart of the maiden, and that the cut, inflicted with poison, failed to heal properly, leaving an open sore to be infected once and once again, nourishment for the creature within.

Time passed for all in the kingdom and the knight was exiled for his acts, so roamed he the lands, seeking out, instead of fair ladies to be saved, for which there had been many, and ventures to be had, seeking instead answers for his crimes and reasons for the manner in which he acted.

Over hill and over dale he searched, his path leading back to his family fold, though there he found no solace or rest, for his parents were now with age, mother succumbed by her own torments and father in the early clutches of madness.

Not able to contain his distress, he fled, determined to end the suffering afflicted on all, only to be halted by his father's speed.

"Son" he said "Where do you fly so fast and where do you go, so to as assail our love and care for you"?

"Father" saith the knight "I cannot stay in this world with the pain on all. I cannot bear this final task".

"My son, you can endure much. More than you know. Your life is not yours to take, it belongs to God above and he wants you to overcome your trials and tribulations, as did his son".

The simple words struck true to the knight and he spent many hours meditating and praying for guidance and forgiveness, which was answered by a storm of unparalleled animosity in the quietest moment of the night.

The days past as the flowers withered under the coldness of the season, as the path delivered him back again to the land he was once banished from.

The path lay clear to the castle cited through the cobbled streets, resting solely in the middle of the citadel, soldiers standing, turning their backs as he stepped up the stairs to centre court.

No longer wearing his dented armour, nor no longer needing its protection, he felt exposed though reassured without the bulky steel.

He knelt again before the throne and waited...

FRACTURES

Now Mum had died, Robert's dementia came evident for all to see, having been covered up by his wife, either not realised or acted upon, though excused, for at least a few years.

Cassandras habit over hoarding medication and hiding bills (both found in every draw and under every surface) became evident, as Tess took over the unwanted role of her mother, creating even more friction than before between father and daughter. Robert being an independent type (not able to make himself a cup of tea and sandwich, choosing instead whisky and wine and packet of fags) and Tess being the controlling type (though unable to limit her alcohol intake or have an organised house).

Resentments lay deep in Tess, the screaming torrent hindering her daily life, with memories of sexual inappropriateness instigated by her father and possibly mother, climaxing in the almost abuse of her own daughter committed by the figure who should have been the archetypal protector.

The duties of their father's care were split in the usual manner and style between the three siblings. Dickie taking control of the Power of Attorney, as he lived "too far away to be of practical use and was always busy with work", though never liked to dwell on the subject of illness and his ailing partner, remaining a private character at most times.

Tess elected herself as Roberts main daily carer, despite having three visits a day from an external service, even though she was advised against from professionals and family alike, but the handiness of a washing machine, extra money and a free supply of booze was too hard to refuse.

Eric was left with the bits in the middle. He would eventually be left with the weekly shop, general repairs and social visits, though living an hour drive away, with a low income and unreliable transport proved testing at times.

Tess resented both her brothers lack of involvement, which she took personally and often vented her frustration in an aggressive manner towards any male in the vicinity, innocent or not, one time calling Eric a "sexist twat", for not agreeing with a decision and refusing to talk to him for two weeks.

But they muddled on.

Roberts virtually constant chest infections were encouraged by his eating in bed and coughing, sending bits of food into his lungs, which he only had one and a half of, since losing some to cancer some years before.

The diabetes didn't help either, though it was a lot better than before, in fact, virtually non-existent, due to his huge increase in scotch, almost burning it out entirely, stunning the doctor into silence.

Robert was quite happy in his own way.

He decided he was going to buy a car, having had his confiscated by the police at the same time his licence was revoked, and visit all his old haunts and possibly a trip to South Africa. Unfortunately, he could seldom make it to the bathroom to urinate, let alone get out the front door. A 3-hour session in the bath was quite a norm. refusing to budge, waiting for the water to reheat.

When he first lost the car, a mobility scooter was a compromise. Not much of one, true, but he accepted that rather than a Zimmer frame and it gave him a bit of freedom…

Robert decided, "Shop or pub"? so off he went.

He hadn't bothered changing his trousers, "…pyjamas will do and besides, slippers are much more comfortable…" he thought as he weaved down the pavement on his scooter, bumping into the occasional car "…really must get this steering fixed…" almost toppling sideways on the edge of a kerb, only to be saved by some builders chatting, admiring their mornings work.

He paused briefly to cross the road and carried on regardless of the horns "...fucking drivers, why don't they look where they're going..." as he bumped up the other kerb by the local convenience store.

He stopped momentarily and drove in, clashing into the pile of neat baskets by the entrance "... only wanted one of those blasted things..."as he sped on down the narrow aisle and honking his horn. Fortunately, not many people were in the shop and luckily no other pensioner or slow on the uptake person, as he came to his first of two corners. He eyed it carefully, working out if he could take the double corner, effectively a U-turn, in one move, though instead, as his mind was working quick enough, ploughed into the ice-cream freezer with an almighty dong.

Shaken, not stirred (...have I told you dear reader of one of his earliest auditions?) he proceeded to back up, beeping as he went, still determined on a few extra bottles, went forward, backed up and so one for quite a few minutes, while shoppers and sales staff alike tried to assist, but were met with oblivious looks and utter determination.

Eventually, mission accomplished, Robert headed for the till, for that is where the real treasure lay and he could see that the girl had already selected his usual choices and was at this very moment bagging them up. He licked his lips and swallowed. Hopefully, he was thinking of the drink.

"That'll be £53.60, please" she said, smiling.

Robert looked at her for a moment, blanky, reaching out his hand.

He stopped then patted his dressing gown.

"Erm, I seem to have lost my wallet" he said.

"Oh, I see" she replied concerned.

"I'll take this now" he said "and I'll pay for it later" reaching out again for his prize.

"Sorry, you can't do that here" the young assistant said, looking a bit nervous and ringing her bell for assistance as the queue built.

"What do you mean "I can't do that here". I shop here all the time" emphasising the "here" with incredulity.

"Sorry" she said getting more nervous "but I can't let you just take your shopping without paying for it" (ring,ring,ring).

"You CAN. YOU just don't want to" he shouted wagging his finger.

"Hello Robert" said a voice, causing the scooter to go into reverse, running over somebody's toe. "... shouldn't stand so bloody close...".

Robert looked around and saw the store manager, she was a pleasant lady, he'd known her for years...he licked his lips again.

"Having problems"? she enquired.

"Seem to have lost my wallet. This (pointy,

pointy) girl, won't let me have my shopping".

Whether it was good luck or not, Tess came in through the doors and noticed the commotion, her dad and instantly considered whether it would be possible to vanish into thin air. Instead...

"Hello Dad" she said tiredly, trying to smile at everyone at the same time instead of just scream "can I help"?

Tess paid for a quarter of the shop, enough to keep him going for the afternoon, but he did say "I'll be back later, for the rest" leaving the girl hoping she had finished her shift by then.

Eric would have loved to be able to visit more often, that was one of his reasons for moving back into the area as it was, though work and money was an issue, Robert was...a man who...

...happily, travelled 110 mph on the motorways, he knew his limit. Liked to smoke when and where he wanted, setting off fire alarms in hospitals because he had decided to smoke in the ward's toilets, regardless of being told how dangerous it was by oxygen cylinders. Gladly stood up to anyone, particularly what he viewed as fascist police. Refused, point blank, to be told "you have to" always replying "I don't have to do anything". And the list goes on.

Nicotine became an encapsulated example of all things Robert. With the ban of pleasuring yourself in public, know what I mean (nudge,

nudge, wink, wink), with pubs, shops, taxis etc banning the exhalation of possible noxious fumes, don't worry about the factories that are predominantly responsible for the world's pollution and people's health or the production of heat and electricity that contributes to over 25% of greenhouse gas emissions, instead focus the public's attention on passive smoking and the dangers of the little white (or brown) stick.

Robert never liked big companies, preferring to deal with the more local concern, partly due to his time in marketing, so it didn't surprise anyone to his response to "You can't smoke in here".

Eric went around for the weekly shop event and sadly prepared himself for the possible conflict with his sister, breathing relaxing breaths as he exited the car, feeling the ground under his feet, letting tension slip from his body, seeing the beauty in the flowers (remembering a round, side plate sized plaque he had bought his mother when young. A picture of a smiling frog with the words "Don't worry, don't hurry and don't forget to smell the flowers"), smelling their scent and wishing he wasn't here.

Much as he loved all of his family, despite the fractures that had occurred, home life was difficult, money and time was always short, the car not happy and time with Tess, not matter how short, had to be handed with patient diplomacy, tact, and sympathy. Not the condescending or patronising type, that would be quickly picked up on, shooting yourself in the foot and getting nowhere, learning how to deal with things accordingly was about being true to the moment.

The front door was ajar, signalling that Tess was definitely here and the smell of disinfectant and the sound of the washing machine going were also signs of activity.

“Hi Dad” Eric shouted, respecting that it was his house after all, but knowing he’d probably still be asleep.

“Hello” he shouted again.

Tess appeared, glove on, arm of damp tea towels.

“You’re late” she said in an unharsh but enquiring tone.

“No, usual time” Eric replied.

“Are you doing anything useful today, or are you just shopping and going” Tess said, obviously feeling terse.

“I’m not sure, is there anything Dad needs doing”?

“I don’t know” she snapped “Why not take him out somewhere? He’d like to go out. Take him for a drive somewhere. Why not take him to the pub”? she finalised in exasperation.

Erics brain quickly worked through the ramifications of the brief tirade.

First, he'd have to check on his father, see if he was awake, fit enough to go or even wanted to go, let alone able to. It would take at least an hour, maybe two, to get him ready. He would want a bath and shave first, then a coffee, then another cigarette, which Eric would have to go and buy first, so may as well do the shop at the same time. Robert's cigarettes were cheaper at the supermarket and Eric had a limited budget for them, the booze and food...prioritised in that order.

That wasn't the end of the decision making or thought process.

Robert's mobility was an issue, the journey from bed to sitting room arm chair, via the bath, would be exhausting for him, a nap would be had. Then the car journey. Robert would refuse help getting in and out of the car. "I'm not feeble" he would exclaim, taking at least 10 minutes trying to get out of Erics low ride.

On one occasion, after he lost his driving licence, but not his car, he had fallen asleep behind the wheel, after parking in his drive, woke up, fell out of his car, then fell asleep again, on the ground, only to be found by a neighbour in the early hours, cold and sore.

And after all that. If all that was achieved. His father would want to smoke in the car, which Anne, sensitive to odours, disliked, but the worst would be the pub. Robert would go to the bar and have to be assisted in ordering drinks as he flirted with the barmaid, sometimes offering his bed, scaring the young girl into nervousness as the 87-year-old lit up.

You could hear the looks customers gave him.

"I'm sorry Sir" the bar staff would say shocked by this defiant action "you're not allowed to smoke in here".

"Not allowed? Who says I'm not allowed"? came the usual challenging response.

"It's the law" the landlord would intercede "Sorry, but you can't smoke in here".

"Can't"? would come the incredulous reply. "I can smoke anywhere I like" and so on, until defeat, being asked to leave or showed where he was allowed to smoke. Always a show.

All this flashed before Eric's eyes when his sibling made her suggestions rather than the usual greetings, signalling how the day would unfold if discretion and tact was not employed.

As it was, Robert was fast asleep, half eaten bowl of cornflakes balanced on his chest, flask of coffee and urine bottle by his side and a fresh ashtray by his lamp, not that he used it, preferring his mug, food plate or bowl instead.

Eric kissed his father's forehead and gently shook his shoulder.

"Hey Dad, its Eric" he said, loud enough to penetrate the deafness.

Tess came in.

“Honestly, he hasn’t eaten his cereal” she exclaimed.

Robert stirred and smiled at seeing his son, annoying Tess even more.

“Why didn’t you eat your cornflakes Dad”? she shouted.

“They’ll be okay, I like them soft” he said taking a spoonful.

Whilst munching he patted his son’s leg.

“Lovely to see you” he said as Tess huffed and left the room to carry on her constant cleaning.

“Hi Dad, Anne sends her love. How you feeling”? saying it to guide as to how his afternoon would plan out.

No response came. Robert was back in his safe imaginary land, eyes already flickering in dreams leaving Eric to hope that they were pleasant and peaceful ones, away from pain and solitude.

He rose and went into the kitchen to find Tess cooking herself some food and munching on a chunk of cheese, her mood seemed to have changed, though Eric wished he could help her untangle her worries and let her reclaim the life she lost long ago.

He talked about childhood memories, swimming in the basement of the Kensington hotel, the hot, steamy changing cubicles, the warm stamp of chlorine and the mangle that stood in the corner.

For a while it distracted Tess from her daily torments, but no thing lasts forever.

The shopping list was subtly compiled while in conversation, making especial care not to forget essentials and see, if budget allowed, a small bottle of whiskey might be purchased.

By the time Eric had returned from the unexpectedly arduous task of the supermarket, dodging the shufflers and mentally blind, Robert was still in bed, though now awake, just, at the insistence of his daughter.

Unloading the bags into the cupboards Tess enquired again.

“Are you going to take him out”?

“I don’t think he’s up to it today” Eric said earnestly.

“That’s typical of you isn’t it”? Tess said in a raised voice.

“You turn up once a week, don’t do anything, stay for an hour, then go”.

There was little point in dissecting her sentence. It was true he only came once a week, but he didn’t live just around the corner like she did, apart from other details, and besides, Tess didn’t want answers. Part of her needed justification of her actions and the access to her father’s bank account, of which she felt entitled to.

BEING BLACK

The Sixties, full of colours and patterns against the back drop of grey, the music as varied as the spectrum it blossomed from, giving birth to long tendrils that reached forward in space to a time that would forget its roots.

Large brimmed straw hats, kaftans, beads, joss sticks, funny feet, gonks, tassel waistcoats, groovy lava lamps, peace and love, splattered over the top of existing structures, trying to show how a world could be before the corporations took over.

Life was burgeoning everywhere. Television, fashion, politics, psychology, all expanding into the publics view, with many failing to connect with the fast changes, always lagging behind like the preoccupied child not looking at where it was going.

The speed of the alterations would only quicken, mankind being left in arrears, easily being outsmarted in the end.

The family would attend church each Sunday, until Dickie left for full time boarding, when

Robert carried on the task with his two youngest children, normally leaving Cassie to rest.

Eric didn't mind the routine, the church was attractive, old and set in a quiet leafy spot and he enjoyed some of the songs, but didn't like it when they changed the tune or sang a hymn he didn't recognise and would tap or jiggle along instead, surrounded by scornful eyes in the busy pews. He never questioned the way things were until one day.

He already had an awareness of world music, liking the Kwa Zulu sounds of his father's homeland, but never connected the dots.

Watching television, as he always did, being littered with old westerns, the native Americans tribal music, regardless of authenticity, tickled his tastebuds, but one day was shocked at a discovery.

He had seen the blues songs performed by toiling workers on plantations, sea shanties by old sea dogs, top hat and tails, but nothing compared to the energy of Gospel.

Turning on the small TV set, sitting under the stairs, the black and white images suddenly burst full of vibrancy and excitement, dancing, clapping, with a wall of sound backing the emotional singers spread "the word of the lord".

Why didn't they have this at his church, why wasn't he allowed to wobble, why were some people so…stiff?

The first of many questions about the hypocrisy of some of the congregation, ending with him walking out of midnight mass one Christmas Eve, not to return for decades.

Having a South African father was a good source of ammunition that was to be had in general conversation at school. As kids do, talk would turn to families, and having a foreigner among the ranks was a too good an opportunity to miss.

“We’re half Scottish, because my father comes from Scotland”. Says one child.

“Well, I’m a quarter Spanish, because my grandmother came from Madrid when she was younger”. Says another.

“Where’s Madrid then”? says a third.

“Don’t you know where Madrid is? Its in Spain” says the first.

“Erics dad is black. He’s from Africa” says the third.

They all look at Eric.

“Why don’t you look black”? asks the first boy.

“I am a bit,” said Eric examining his arm “See”.

To be met with a mixed response. It never got old.

His father was an unaware font used by his son as an aid of mischievousness.

Years later, when Eric was discovering how to be successful in conquests, he would casually mention to his latest partner (when an imminent visit to the family abode was on the agenda) that not to pay attention to his father. If they should feel movement against their leg (while sitting up to the table), it would be his dad and his lecherous behaviour. Half the fun was in the telling of the tale, the other half reserved for the look in their eyes when actually Eric himself brushed their legs.

ANNE

A nervous anticipation was building up in the young girl as she got out of the car, making her way to the main hospital entrance, once used to treat infectious diseases for the Wirral's workhouse poor. Now, a general infirmary, Anne and her father were going to the geriatric ward, as usual, located near the mortuary, housed on the outer edge of the building, to meet up with fellow church goers to sing to the elderly.

As usual her father was his strict, domineering self, issuing commands about behaviour "Sit still", "Don't fidget", "Stop humming" were just some of his favourites.

The pale and faded mustard yellow walls of the ward came into view as they met up with several of the more devout congregation outside the open doors of the ward, a familiar smell of disinfectant and urine-stained armchairs wafting out.

As they entered in, Anne's eyes took in the scene with discomfort and uncertain fear, having never seen, or unprepared, for a gathering of old, gaunt bodies and faces sitting and lying alone waiting for either the healing touch or the hand of death to release them from their temporary prison. One way or other, they would be leaving.

She noticed the nurses, being directed by matron, busying around in their duties, preparing for visiting time, with trays of pills, various sized pans and cardboard trays, curtains being pulled open and closed and hearing the murmurs of gentle reassurance or discomfort, with the senile jabbering of two patients at the back of the room.

The doctor completed his rounds and left with a silent wave to all, his white coat whishing with a gentle flourish past Annes face, the breeze making her blink and refocus her mind.

She noted that now, more patients were sitting in their armchairs next to their cots and beds, dressed for the occasion, some chewing aimlessly on their gums, staring blankly into space or eager, deep-set eyes searching out to see if perhaps today they might have a visitor.

As if on cue, a momentary silence signalled the beginning of visiting time and the expectant looks of seeing the loved ones resigned to sadness, knowing, foolhardily, that today would not be their day...maybe tomorrow.

The small group of Christians, who had been ignored until now, started singing, the sound instantly filling the room with a different atmosphere, distracting the patient's thought patterns, for many reviving old memories of younger days, where life was full of comings and goings and vibrant in unrealised love.

As the songs continued, Anne saw all these changes occurring, her young mind recognising that agedness was just a few flights of stairs away for her parents, and that all these bodies had lived full lives, just as she was about to.

WORD

Having relocated work, to one of England's smallest cities, aiding his escape from the clutches of the dark squalid depths of drug life in the seaside town, Eric found himself searching out new contacts to fuel his existent habit. Fortunately, though unrealised and unappreciated at the time, life was not being forthcoming and he was having to rely on old haunts to get his fix. Though he knew that all things must pass. Over the years he had heard enough hints and shouts of how he should be conducting himself or how there was a better way of living, though often had failed to listen to the call.

His biggest shortcoming was The Chase. Whether drugs, money, sex, everything came down to the chase. Stringing one partner along after another, being duplicitous (even quadlicitious at times) and rambunctious, burning the candle heavily at both ends, finding less and less satisfaction driving him further and further on.

In the back of his mind, he knew he had to change. He had to stop all his tomfoolery and create a better life. He knew what had to be done, but shedding his past, losing everything he had, that was the only way he knew how to move forward. Clear out the desk and start again, hopefully not cocking it up...this time.

Life doesn't give you a clean straight forward path, it wants you to learn and develop. Only by trial and error do we truly acquire new skills, the pains and sorrows can be the gum stuck to our shoes or blocks of stone to help us build, placing them in the right place on our journey.

Eric was seeking answers, help from the universe, as no person he knew seemed to be succeeding fantastically, so turned to a little book that had presented itself to him not long ago.

The Tao (pronounced dow, as in d ou(ch)) of Pooh, was a friendly introduction into Taoism explained using the characters of Winnie the Pooh, one of Erics favouritist stories from childhood. Having enjoyed the aspects of the uncarved block, the next logical step was to read the Tao Te (pronounced: day) Ching itself and understand The Way, as it is loosely put, and in turn, study the I (pronounced: Ee) Ching itself, an ancient book of divination, using hexagrams to answer moral dilemmas and decisions.

Ever since his early days, watching psychedelic

rock and pop, shaking his butt like Elvis, Scooby Doobiedoobiedoos, Biba and mogadon, he knew that all things can be answered, but like Douglas Adams pointed out, it's great to have the ultimate answer (42), but what's the ultimate question?

Questions have been asked for millennia, in every culture, from South American Shaman to Indian Fakirs, seeking guidance from departed ancestors or trying to reach Nirvana. The act of Zen and the peace of Buddha, all seeking answers from beyond for the understanding of life on earth.

Eric was no different. A life time of influences and experiences, from music and T.V to things that go bump in the night, from Zapata to Archimedes. He made connections to times gone by, having had a grandfather who showed him a map from the First World War, a mother who loved history, a father from another country and seeing men, disfigured from bombs and warfare, walking around old London town. This wasn't only his life.

Casting the coins, focusing on the dilemma and opening himself to the universe (normally while stoned), he built his hexagrams, searching for the answers he already knew, but lay slightly hidden behind the veil of blindness.

On consultation, sometimes the answers fitted, sometimes not, probably because the universe was trying to tell him something he wouldn't listen to.

Before his relocation, promotion and onset of divination, he would sit in quiet contemplation, trying to seek out his hidden demons and vanquish them, that's when he heard his voice. In the stillness. Meditating on life. Knowing he must change. It spoke to him.

He hadn't heard his voice for years, drowned out by his constant excess of work, sex, drugs, drink and music. The cacophony noises.

But now. It spoke.

"You must go west" it simply said.

"Logical" thought Eric, unsure of what he had heard, but knowing his parents lived west and were probably in need of help on the farm. Just his thoughts making themselves known, but next came the unexpected surprise.

"You will be with a curly haired female with two children and talk to a vicar who is not vicar".

Shocked by the sudden sentence of specific information, clearly encapsulated and precise, almost loud enough for anyone to hear if they had been presented, his mind spun.

As if answering his next question before he could say it (which was going to be "Anything else"?) came the statement "Where the trees are".

Then it was gone. He was left with four events and he had no clue as to what just happened. The last most cryptic yet simple of them all, but all puzzling and intriguing.

Time passed, but the seeds had been laid and bounced around, piquing his curiosity, feeling impelled already to try and help his parents, but the thoughts slowly drifted away, stored and almost forgotten until one day...

Leaving the office, located at the back of store, Eric floor walked, checking displays, promotions and tidiness, when his eyes fell upon a lady pushing a child in a buggy. Sleight and attractive features were topped with a mass of noticeable very light brown curly hair and he smiled a greeting as he passed, not because of what he remembered, besides she only had one kid, but because she was attractive and looked like she needed a smile.

Anne walked past, ignoring his salutations, and carried on her way.

Eric was somewhat surprised and intrigued, most customers were convivial, but perhaps this one was having an off day.

Again, time wound on, and he rarely saw her again, but his business reputation grew, eventually being offered managerial prospects with a large brewery company that held retail units opposite where he worked.

Accepting the challenge, to his surprise, he found that the young mum who ignored him worked there as well.

They chatted easily, Eric enjoying her confidence and forthrightness, amazed to find she had an older child that she had given birth to when she was just 17 as, he ignorantly thought, she didn't look like a mum of two.

Though not seeking involvement at the time, they inevitably and slowly grew closer, Anne joining him on deliveries and enjoying each-others company. Their paths became entwined and Eric was advised by Anne to think carefully on his next steps.

"Before we get into a relationship" she said "you need to consider what you're doing very carefully".

"How do you mean"? he answered.

"You're not just taking on me, but also my children". She said earnestly "You're going to have an instant family. It's a lot to take on".

Eric had already been thinking of this, but now was prompted to be more conscious, now it had been spoken aloud, so thought deeply on the implications, though few could imagine what would transpire and how it would affect the next ten years and then the next ten after. Dominoes would fall, knocking one into another, rippling across the years, touching all involved, passing the legacy onto the children, children's children, and possibly further. Eric would be filled with sorrow with how his kinfolk had been touched, wishing he could wipe their slates clean, amend his errors and give them the lives they deserved, rather than the influences of his faults and ineptitudes.

It would only be a few years later, from when they first met, that he would experience a simple, innocent touch that would mean more than anything he had experienced in his life.

He sat on the edge of their sofa, the sun coming through the sitting room window, their young son taking steps in his pale blue baby grow, clutching a small toy car. Eric was checking instructions for a bookcase that needed putting together, judging how much space was to be needed and which extra tools to get.

His son waddled up to him reached out his hand and rested it on his dad's knee to steady himself.

For the first time in Eric's life, someone showed how much they trusted him. This simple act, without word, meant so much to him.

He then realised what responsibility was really about. He had wasted so many years, time, tears and money...

MOVING HOUSE

The call rang out through the house.

"Anne, Vinnie, sitting room, now" the direct order came from their dad and nerves immediately kicked in, making the kids wonder who had done something wrong.

They had only just got back from their day at school, only just mid-term, leading up to the summer holidays, with the new school year not yet being thought of.

Settling into their usual seats the bombshell was dropped.

"Right kids, we're moving house. Not far, but you're both going to have to change schools as I can't be driving you to and from and having to pay for buses all the time".

"But I've just started my C.S.E's" said a shocked Anne, realising that it would also mean leaving her friends behind, just as she had started to feel less disliked for having a preacher for a father.

It had been a hard road to travel, kids could be really cruel.

"Ew, stay away from her" some would whisper

behind her back, "...her dads a vicar..." or "... look at the clothes on that..." and "...don't get too close..." thinking that they might catch religion. The parents didn't help. Noticeably pulling their children away from the innocent young girl who might poison their darling offspring, but who actually only wanted to laugh and run, be free from her bonds and feel the freshness of youth wash over her skin.

"It's happening and that's all there is too it" said her dad emphatically, already getting short tempered with her brief remonstration, signalling to her that a conversation, as usual, was not going to be had.

Ignoring the silent threat Anne pushed on.

"But what about my friends? I'll never see them again"? she said, raising her voice, but not too much, calculating how much to go so as not to trigger the full wrath, though for possibly the first time in her life, needing to find her voice and stand up for something that belonged to her, something she had worked at and something that had been out of her parent's control.

Within weeks, with only about thirty days of the summer term left, Anne found herself at a new house and a new school, an all-girls school. Resentment and anger, that stayed lurking, unresolved for decades, were her only friends in her new environment, the girls already having already well-established cliques, which were difficult for a total outsider to infiltrate. Anne again felt like an outsider looking in, after all she had been through, and instead of having sympathy and understanding from her parents, was instead met with rebuke and intolerance of her demonstrations and upset.

The thoughts continued to whirl, unchecked or appeased, within, trying to come to terms with the transition and understand why the move had occurred at all.

"It's not as if dad needed to move to be closer to work" Jubilee (the inner child, wanting only peace and love) cogitated to Storm (her outer child, who was slowly gaining power, controlled by whatever lay behind the dark cloud).

Her two brothers, a lot younger as they were, had taken the move in their stride. Vinnie was changing schools anyway and Frank was still scribbling on paper and learning how to use a toilet, both always getting preferential treatment and Anne getting the blame for their errors.

The church community had its advantages. Having a wide network of associates meant that holiday time could involve visiting far afield locations or outings organised for large groups to attend, which for Anne meant escaping the confines of the vice type grip and an opportunity to discover a small bit of freedom. To be able to listen to another child's radio or watch a communal television without being told that it was the devil's work.

At the end of her disastrous part-term, Ann's mother decided that they were going down to Somerset for a week, visiting a member of the church, a much-needed break for all after the turmoil of the move.

The four-hour drive felt long, but looking out of the car window, watching the scenery change from grey to green helped ignore the elbows and wiggles of her younger brothers on either side of her.

They arrived at the large red bricked house with a pointy porch and gravel drive, the tall windows looking easy on the eye, and instantly Anne felt relaxed and calm, ready for a break and be able to take a breath.

The week flew by, especially as there were two children, a girl and boy of similar age as Vinnie and herself, and having room to roam and her parents distracted with their work, Anne started to forget her worries, putting it all behind her, resigning to her new path and determining that she would make it work and not be defeated.

Unfortunately, time waits for no man (it's got a bus to catch), no sooner as Anne had got into the swing of things, it was time to go home...though it still wasn't, in her eyes.

They packed the car, said all their goodbyes and took their prospective seats for the return journey.

The silence of the drive was broken by Annes father.

"We've decided to move to Somerset" came the bombshell.

Anne couldn't believe what she had just heard. "WHAT"? she uttered.

"I've decided we're moving to Somerset, probably in October".

Anne was stunned. They had only just moved and hadn't even got used to that. But Somerset! That may as well be the other side of the world. It would mean leaving her Grandad behind, all her aunts, uncles and cousins (and there were a lot of them). It was nice coming here on holiday, but to live! She would be leaving everything she knew behind. Her mind reeled.

"I can't move. Not again. Not now." she implored "We've only just moved. I'm in my final year. I've got my exams" the torrent of reasons spilled out, begging her parents to let her stay and finish off her last year of school, she didn't want to start all over again.

"Please Dad, please let me stay" was answered each time, more and more abrupt than the last.

"No, you're coming with us, final".

And that was that. End of. Years of doing as she was told. Years of being pushed into a tighter and smaller mould, years of hearing "You can't watch this", "you can't watch that", "we know what you're doing", "God sees everything", "don't lie", the fear and punishment, never being able to learn for herself, make her own mistakes, hand-me-down clothes and broken promises.

At that moment...Anne hated her parents. This was one step beyond. She would never forgive her parents. To many the school move is normal transition, but for Anne it was the final insult to injury. The years of carefree suppression, the lack of care and respect, she felt like her identity was inconsequential, only there to do their bidding.

Why, she thought, the vortex pulling her into its clutches, why would any parent do that to their child. 3 schools in 6 months. The anger lay brooding deep inside, plotting and gnawing in the pit of her stomach.

They moved in the October half-term, school break, and the culture shock of the north-south divide was probably more difficult to cope with than the school itself.

Compared to Liverpool, Bath truly was a world apart.

Now she didn't fit in for other reasons. Classmates were of a different breed, had different habits and different attitudes compared to her early estate life style. Her hatred for the airs and graces, innocent they may have been, didn't sit right were her down to earth, no-nonsense approach. Even the lessons themselves seemed alien, led by teachers who spoke a different language and dressed a different style.

Storm became bored of all the stupid behaviour and decided, at times, not to turn up for lessons, preferring instead to sit in the toilets or cloakrooms, only to appear for lunchtime, then resume her disappearing act after registration.

Even this became tiresome, so Anne would wipe away her hours in the park or wander the shops, only visiting school for games or registration again, making sure she was around for home time. On occasion, after registration, she would go home, claiming to have a special study period and shut herself in her bedroom for the rest of the day. Her parents never queried and the school never questioned, Anne made sure of that.

Exams came and went with inevitable failure, due to lack of interest, except for the subjects she enjoyed and had genuine interest in. But the hurt of that year stayed and became pivotal in many decisions, impacting for years to come.

It would be almost thirty years for Annes father to acknowledge the harm he caused to her schooling, but the damage had been done.

Anne would often look back at what could have been, even at the age of 50, only then being able to start to address the long-lasting impact of, what she saw now as, an abusive childhood. The shadowy curtain starting decaying, revealing the truth of what occurred, leaving it up to her to heal.

BITCH

"Get that BITCH out of here" Cassandra shouted at her youngest son.

It was the first time she had met his new girlfriend, having been away in South Africa for a couple of weeks in the wake of Roberts mother's funeral and Eric had been looking after the farm, with Tess attempting to tend to house duties.

The bleach had helped to keep the toilets clean, but Eric could still smell the unmistakable tang of her bulimia, even though she was still in denial.

"I want her out of the house now" Cassandra ranted, even though the area had already been vacated.

Eric noticed that his mother was evidently going through another, for want of another word, breakdown. He thought that time away might have helped, change of scenery and all that.

Instead, quite the opposite was true, hopefully it would settle down and fade away without erupting into a too fierce a storm.

The horses in the neighbouring fields had

settled down, now that his mother had stopped throwing stones at them, but the dog that trotted happily, up and down the road on his daily jaunt, now steered clear of the gated drive, fearful of being attacked again by the crazy lady with the rake.

The sudden snap that could occur was as uncanny as the look in her eyes. The madness would take her, despite the incompetent psychologists giving her a clean bill of health, and her eyes would sparkle with malintent as her mouth twisted into a satisfied sneer, with words misinterpreting actual events.

As he grew, his early allegiances shifted from maternal to paternal, understanding more and more of his father's habits, sympathising for both his parents lives and how one supported the other in destruction and aid.

Life, nature, whatever you want to call it, like water, has its own path. Try as you might it will do what it does. Mankind is but a blip, lost in its importance, though many cultures found themselves on the right path, they were diverted by other humans to destruction, themselves seeking answers that already lay at their feet, just as man cannot smell his own bad breath, though his mouth is right under his nose.

The small shelter sat on the sea front, large crashing waves throwing up spray, signalling how the weather was further out into the deep blue. It was a favourite spot for Eric to park up his bike and sit, watching the lightning hit the water miles out, undisturbed by the natural madness, feeling that it was nothing compared to what he was used to, but found its ferocity and power comforting. It offered no spite, it was what it was, as all nature, if you bathe with crocodiles, you're gonna get bit.

Every time he witnessed the white forks of unbridled power, he would momentarily recall his seat, whether it was driving in a car, seeing it spark on the road in the empty distance, late at night, anticipated stillness holding its silence, or standing in a back door porch, feeling the air charge up for an imminent strike.

The natural world was the home that Eric always wanted, the desire for hermithood with the uncomplicatedness of the man-made disasters, dealt with such disregard to fellow humans and the ground on which they walked.

Driving, one day, in the depths of winter, with Anne in the front and the two youngest at school, the other two having already left home to seek their own paths, they noticed how the road condition was deteriorating.

Works hadn't been implemented for some time, and the snow, rain and ice, along with lorries and heavy tractors, were not helping the situation. But looking closer at the pattern of damage Eric noticed something quite clearly.

"If you look at the main damage of the road..." he pointed out to Anne "...its where the trees are...".

The words jumped out like a flag and he explained to his wife what the phrase meant to him and how he had been wondering for almost 15 years. But now he knew, maybe. Maybe, he was meant to be here. Maybe this was the place. He would have to wait and see, he had not received any messages since, in fact, not since:

"I'm sorry, I can't be your guardian angel anymore".

THE END

The knight still knelt, though his long hair of grey now shone in the light of the moon, that lay full in the sky, as bright as his once tarnished armour and as cold as the pain in his knee.

He had vowed to await his lady, knowing the ice that imprisoned her heart would one day melt, and on that day, she might be in need of his warmth that once shone brightly, though now was a flickering shadow of its former self.

This had been his greatest errant, his chivalric virtue tested to the utter most of any courtly love.

He had knelt as his lady had passed him by, at first ignoring his expostulations and pleadings, until her anger fired so, refused to even acknowledge his being, as if some unwanted piece of furniture there he stood.

The castle stood in quietness, it too waiting and watching, the dust settling on ageing ledges, that soon might crumple under the sadness that also landed on their sills.

Days and nights fell into months, then years, as

the knight watched the queen, still wracked by the spell that had been cast upon her innocent body, ignore his love for her.

Time passed, as her own children grew of age and left the safe confines of the castle's walls, each unknowingly carrying a small piece of the evil enchantment, laying dormant in the recess of their souls, hoping to be fed and nurtured so to blossom again, but as a different flower.

The knight pled with his love to hear his voice and words as they were, not as she imagined, not slighted by her childhood nightmares that sort to control her innermost thoughts and deeds, but free her to become the person she was.

The dragon twisted in her gut as it writhed against what it thought was a spell being cast, not wanting to leave the safety of its cave and lonely prison.

The haze that once gripped the queen faltered as she saw the beast yell in pain and anguish, startled she became.

"How can this be so" she softly uttered as the clearness shone its light in the darkness of her soul, protected all this time by tattered shrouds and webs of creatures long since passed.

The light grew stronger as she felt its warmth against the bleakness which beckoned her back, yet she fought the gnarled claws and rejoiced in the new found glory and all that it promised.

Too soon came the end of the moment, that brief

glimpse that she had espied, like an echo she could sense that feeling still, as if an eternal fire had been sparked and though dim and flickering as it was, just needed sustenance and tending to grow as it should.

Aghast at her findings, she stumbled slightly so and was caught in the arms of her waiting knight. They stood, both unsteady yet with renewed strength, just as the castle stood, knowing that change had become and in each-other's arms they kissed again for the first time and lived ha...

[PK1]